DARK INTENTIONS

J.A. OWENBY

Best Wishes,
J.A Owenby

DON'T MISS OUT

Enjoy giveaways, the inside scoop about J.A. Owenby, and never miss a new release again! Sign up today at https://www.authorjaowenby.com/newsletter

I hated people. Well, that was an exaggeration, but not by much. In general, I really didn't like the human race. Maybe I was jaded from bouncing around foster homes, or maybe I'd gained more than my share of life experiences, which allowed me to see others' flaws. Regardless, the circle of people I liked was minute.

A shrill screech traveled down the hallway of the rental house I shared with my best friends, Benji and Avery.

Benji rounded the corner at high speed. An expression of horror twisted his handsome features as he backed into the counter of our small kitchen, which was decorated in roosters. *Cocks.* The room had rooster border paper, rooster dish towels, and rooster potholders. The decor was all Benji's idea. My man adored cocks in every sense of the word.

His hand fluttered over his heart as he gasped and pointed down the hall from where he'd just hightailed it. "Tensley. Please, girl, make her stop." He ran his fingers through his spiked blond hair as his chest heaved visibly.

Benji was absolutely gorgeous. His lean frame was perfectly balanced with just the right amount of muscle to be sexy but not obscene, and he was one of the best swimmers on Norman University's team. His glacier-blue eyes could melt even the most callous person, and his abs rippled like a lake's water after someone had smoothly skipped a stone. But women did nothing for him, not even our beautiful roomie, Avery, who had attempted to seduce him the first time they had met. He'd shot her down in a New York second, leaving her to pick her self-esteem up off the floor. After I clued her in that no girl would be able to turn Benji on, we'd laughed and brushed the incident off. Last year, we had all moved in together. Finding good roomies was the key to college success, and I needed to make sure I completed my last two years with a strong GPA.

I tilted my head slightly and closed my chemistry book. The current situation should have proved intriguing and deserved my full attention. When Benji was horrified, he was typically interesting. Not to mention highly entertaining.

"Make her stop." His voice was strained as the color drained from his face.

I covered my mouth with my hand and attempted to hide the ornery grin that was pulling at the corners of my mouth. "Benji, what's wrong?"

I propped my elbows on the only space left on the white-tiled kitchen island. Avery had just returned from the grocery store half an hour ago, and due to my studies, I still hadn't unloaded the plastic bags that littered the otherwise clean and tidy area.

Benji swallowed visibly and pointed toward the hall. "She's naked," he finally managed to choke out.

No longer able to hide my reaction, I barked out a laugh. "Our nudist is streaking around the house again?" I scooted my barstool back and grabbed some of the groceries to unload. "Avery!" I called as I opened our fickle refrigerator. We never knew from one day to the next if it would work, but our landlord continued to fix it. He was probably hoping it would limp along for a few more years. "Could you please put some clothes on so I don't have to call 9-1-1? Benji is about to have a heart attack."

My focus cut to Benji, who had begun to regain his wits. "She just does it to get a rise out of you." I bit into a Granny Smith apple, which spewed juice in every direction. "Well, maybe not a rise." I giggled at my own joke and gently elbowed him in the side.

Disgust twisted Benji's face, and he wiped the apple juice off his cheek.

"Sorry," I said around a mouthful of apple.

Benji pushed off the counter, snatched up a grocery bag full of frozen meals, then shoved them in the freezer. "I just don't understand her need to run around butt-ass naked in front of me. Aren't there ... boundaries?" He grabbed the loaf of bread next and placed it in the bread box his mom had donated to our humble abode.

His parents had helped us out a lot. Most of the furniture, his bedroom suite, pots, pans, plates, and utensils had come from them. Avery's parents had also kicked in. Mine hadn't. They hadn't contributed a dime. My father had split when I was three, and I hadn't seen my mom since I was twelve. Eventually, I'd come to understand that I was on my own, and I had learned how to survive on the bumpy road called life. Foster kids didn't have families—they were just a number in the government's system and a paycheck to the adults that pretended to give a shit when the social worker showed up to evaluate the kids.

Benji wiggled his eyebrows at me. "Are you ready to get your head out of your books and have some fun tonight?"

"Oh, I wasn't under the impression I had a choice." I grinned at him while I placed the gallon of milk into the fridge. Then I opened the Seattle's Best coffee package and poured it into an airtight container. We never skimped on the dark roast. It was our life force.

Benji huffed and placed his hands on his hips, staring a hole through me. "Seriously, Ten, you should probably get ready."

I arched my eyebrow and shot him an amused look. "I *am* ready." I blew a loose strand of blond hair out of my face and tugged on my oversized *Big Bang Theory* T-shirt that hit my skinny jeans midthigh. Maybe my dress code wasn't always up to par with Benji and Avery's, but my clothes fit and were clean. That was all I needed.

"Aw, hell no." Benji wagged a finger at me. "You'll never get laid wearing that. Besides, how long has it been? You probably have dust bunnies in your vajayjay."

Although I wasn't a nun, I rarely slept around. It wasn't because I didn't have needs—I just hadn't found anyone I wanted to have consistent booty calls with. Plus, I wasn't interested in anything long-term. The word "commitment" wasn't even in my vocabulary.

"Avery!" Benji called. "We need to borrow some clothes from your closet. Are you wearing anything now?"

A moment of silence filled the house before Avery responded. "Yes! I'm dressed. Come on back."

I snickered. "She's probably only *half*-dressed."

Benji's nostrils flared. "I'm sending you in first. Boobs and twats don't bother you. You're my first line of defense."

Grabbing his hand, I led him out of the kitchen, down the hallway, and into Avery's room.

Half an hour later, my long hair was brushed and straightened, I had a light dusting of brown eyeshadow that made my blue eyes pop, and Avery had dabbed mascara on my thick lashes. I used to wonder if I looked like my dad, although Mom had been pretty at one time.

I shut those thoughts down and focused on Benji. He'd selected a deep V-neck teal top for me to wear. It showed off more cleavage than I was comfortable with, but he'd literally blocked me from Avery's closet before I could grab something else. Avery had tossed her Citizens jeans at me. For the most part, we were the same size, except I was a bit bustier than she was.

"You look hot as hell," Avery said, grabbing my breasts and squishing them together to plump up my boobs even more. She was continually touching me, fluffing my hair, adjusting various parts of me, and patting my butt. It never bothered me, though. She was like my sister, and from what I'd heard, sisters did stuff like that.

My focus traveled over Avery's flawless tan skin. A smattering of freckles covered her perky nose, and her dark-brown hair accentuated green eyes that were framed by illegally long eyelashes. Avery was stunning. Her boobs, hips, and ass were perfectly proportioned. She stood at five foot nine and was thin without being too skinny. No matter where she was, she turned the heads of both guys and girls. She tucked her red shirt into her designer jeans and slipped her feet into her black heels.

Benji motioned for us to hurry up. "Let's go! It's almost ten thirty. Thank God tomorrow is Saturday and we get to sleep in."

I located my purse and double-checked that my phone was in it. Minutes later, we all piled into the gray Lexus Coupe Benji's parents had bought him the year before. It was his baby, and he would ream anyone if they left trash in it. He flipped on the SiriusXM radio, and we sang at the top of our lungs to "Say Something" by Justin Timberlake and Chris Stapleton. Their harmony was insane, and I could listen to the song on repeat for hours.

As Benji located an open spot in the parking lot of the bar, I leaned forward from the back seat. "Wow, it's packed!"

Barney's was the most popular college hangout. It was overall safe and clean, and the service was excellent. They had a dance floor in the middle of the room as well, and on occasion, I was coaxed into joining my friends in a drunken display. It was one of the few places I was comfortable going to alone, but normally Avery or Benji was with me.

Benji rubbed his hands together. "It's the big track meet tomorrow. Well, I'm guessing that's why it's so packed. Several other teams are in Spokane, and I bet we'll find lots of hunky men inside." An impish smile eased across his face.

"Oh, that's right. Maybe we won't be going home alone tonight," Avery piped in, turning toward me. "Right?"

I rolled my eyes at their constant attempts to get me laid. "Um, no. My cobwebbed twat and I are just fine, but thanks for thinking of me."

We got out of the car and walked to the front door of the bar. When Benji opened the door for us, the music and noise nearly knocked me backward. Packed wasn't even the word for it. It was standing room only.

A large group of rowdy drunk guys shouldered their way through the crowd toward us, and I quickly moved as they barreled through the exit.

"A table!" Avery yelled over the thumping tunes, pointing at a spot near the bar.

I grabbed Benji's hand and pulled him behind me as I followed Avery.

After making it through the mass of people, Benji eased down into a chair. "Perfect."

Avery pointed at the bartender. "I'll order drinks!" Then she disappeared into the throng of students.

"This is insane!" I said. "This track meet must be something special."

Benji's blue eyes drifted over the room and stopped on a guy in a burgundy-and-white baseball hat. I nudged him and nodded to the hottie he'd spotted. The guy's closely trimmed beard accentuated his angular jaw, and a few dark curls peeked out from the rim of his cap.

"He's dreamy, Tensley!" Benji chewed on his bottom lip as he continued to assess the stranger.

Benji was right. The guy was tasty. His smile lit up his face, reaching his deep-brown eyes, and his muscular biceps flexed as he reached up and placed his hands behind his head.

Benji sighed, his shoulders sagging forward. "I'd love to take him home, but …"

"Wait, did you and Thomas make up?" I secretly hoped Benji was going to tell me he'd finally kicked the D-bag to the curb, but I'd never admitted that I hated how Thomas treated him.

"Yeah. I told him I'd give it another try. Well, I'll give him one last chance." Sadness flickered across his face. "He's cheated on me twice."

I reached across the small, circular table and squeezed his hand. "Honey, you don't have to put up with that bullshit. You're better than that."

Before he could comment, Avery showed up with a Sex on the Beach, Cape Cod, and a margarita. She placed them on the table in front of us, and I took a long pull of my vodka cranberry through the straw, then sank back into the seat.

"I'll get the next round," Benji said as Avery settled in.

She grabbed her chair and scooted over next to me. "Oh, so much better. I can see the eye candy from here." She winked at me as she sipped her margarita.

We fell into a comfortable silence as the music blared and a group of approximately twenty people danced. I loved people watching. When I was younger and had been placed in my first foster home at age twelve, I would walk to the neighborhood park, sit on the bench under a giant oak tree, and observe families. I would make up stories about them in my mind while they played or picnicked. It was easier than approaching some kid and asking them to play. I'd learned the hard way after I'd been laughed at because of my Goodwill clothes or ratty hair. I had been incredibly shy, and no one could make fun of me creating make-believe friends if they didn't know what I was thinking.

"Let's dance, bitches!" Benji hopped up and grabbed my hand.

"Now? I'm not drunk enough," I argued.

Avery pulled on my arm until I stood. "Yes, now."

I knew when to argue with them and when it was a moot point. I followed them through the slightly thinned-out crowd until Benji found a spot for us at the corner of the floor.

The heavy vibration of "The Devil You Know" by the X Ambassadors traveled through my body. My skin hummed with excitement as I allowed the music to consume every part of me.

Benji slipped an arm around my waist and gave me a bump with his butt. "Look up on stage!" He nodded in the direction where the band typically set up. But that night, the platform was nearly empty except a few drums the bar owner had left there … for me.

A slow grin spread across my face.

Avery danced around us, her hips swaying to the music as she tossed her hands up in the air and laughed.

"I definitely need more alcohol for that, sweet cheeks!" I yelled.

"I'll be right back." Benji kissed my cheek and disappeared into the crowd.

Avery grasped my hand and twirled me around. "Let's give the boys something to talk about." She winked at me, and I giggled. She closed the small gap between us, and our boobs brushed against each other. Her hands slid down my back and patted my ass. I wasn't gay, but if I were ever to experiment, it would be with Avery. She was my best friend, and if I ever grew curious, I would trust her. But I wasn't interested. It was fun to watch all the guys walk around with rock-hard dicks, constantly shifting in order to regain some kind of comfort, but that was all it was—us being silly. Normally, Avery would have her pick of hot men after we gave them a show anyway. Turning around, she nestled against me as she guided my hands over her stomach.

"You two, break it up already." Benji stood in front of me with two shots of rum and a mixed drink.

Avery continued to dance as he handed me the first one.

"Oh hell, are you going to …" Avery's voice trailed off as she watched me slam the drink.

I reached for the second. "Next."

"You're all set up." Benji took my empty glasses and handed me the rum and coke.

I took a few gulps and shook my head, releasing a soft hiss as the alcohol burned the back of my throat. "Woohoo!" I threw my arms up over my head and released a loud whoop. The drinks quickly numbed my brain enough to help me loosen up.

Avery cupped her hands around her mouth and hollered at the top of her lungs. "Get 'em, Tensley!"

Benji walked me up to the stage and winked at me as he took several steps back.

A snare drum was waiting for me. Four different colors of paint were in clear plastic condiment containers on a chair next to them. A white painter's mat lined the floor.

I scooped up the rain slicker and slipped it on over my clothes. Avery would kick my ass if I messed up her shirt. My heart hammered against my chest like it did every time I was in front of an audience.

Drawing in a deep breath, I picked up the purple paint and squeezed an ample amount on the drum. I followed it with blue, yellow, and green. I glanced over at the DJ and nodded. The beginning of "Start a War" by Klergy boomed through the speakers, vibrating the wooden stage beneath my feet.

I raised the drumsticks over my head and lowered them in beat with the music. The crowd turned toward me and quieted.

"Get it, babe!" Benji hollered.

I grinned at him as the magic flowed through me. With each strike of the drum, paint splattered in every direction. Bouncing on the tips of my toes to the rhythm, I slammed a drumstick in the middle of the painted membrane and bounced it into the air. Everyone in the bar cheered as I caught it and sank into my own world. The longer I played, the more the audience disappeared, and I was the only one in the room, communing with the music that pulsed through my veins.

Once the song finished, a hush settled over the crowd. I covered the top of the drum with purple paint and glanced over at my two favorite people in the world for encouragement. Avery and Benji beamed at me, and my heart filled with their love and support.

I tapped an intricate rhythm on the rim, bounced the sticks off the edge into the air, spun them around, and caught them. The audience went wild as paint sprayed over my poncho and face. My eyes closed momentarily while I entered into a five-minute routine, and my mind quieted. Music and my drums were the only things that helped me truly find peace inside myself. When I played the last lick, I let out a loud whoop. Thunderous applause finally pulled me back to reality. I flashed a grin at Benji and Avery while I removed my now multicolored slicker and wadded it into a ball. I dropped it on the mat and hopped off the stage.

"Damn, girl, you get better and better every time I hear you!" Avery gave me a big hug, ignoring the blue and yellow splotches on my face and hair.

"I need to go to the bathroom and wash up."

"Coming through!" Avery called. Everyone let us pass by without us having to elbow our way through them.

"Oh my God. I am terrified when I'm up there, but it's such a fucking rush!" I exclaimed, turning on the cold water. I grabbed a few paper towels and soaked them. "So much for any makeup remaining in place."

"Lemme get it." Avery held her hand out to me, and I gave her the wet mass that was my makeshift washcloth.

She tilted my chin up and dabbed lightly at my skin. "I think that performance calls for more drinks. On me." She smiled while she cleaned me up.

"Thanks. Since I'm broke until next payday, I'll take you up on it." I tilted my head so she could reach my neck.

A few minutes later, we exited the bathroom and made our way to the bar.

Avery rattled off our order, and I glanced over my shoulder, locating Benji chatting up a guy I hadn't seen before. My gaze returned to Matthew, the bartender, and I flashed him a shy smile.

"You're hot as hell up there," Matthew said while he made our drinks. His big brown eyes never left me as he poured a jigger and a half of vodka into a glass, then topped it with cranberry juice.

"Thanks." Heat rose in my cheeks. I rarely received compliments, much less about my appearance, and I immediately turned stone cold inside. I'd worked for so long not to be seen, so I never really knew how to take praise or what to say in return. Unfortunately, my first thought was to wonder what the person wanted from me—my body or a blow job. Dark memories of my last foster home ripped through me, leaving me trembling slightly.

"Yours is on the house. If you performed more often, I think it would definitely pull in a crowd. Plus, I'd pay you in alcohol." A huge grin split Matthew's face as he winked at me.

"I might take you up on that sometime." That wasn't the first time Matthew had flirted with me, but it was just harmless. He wasn't really interested.

Avery discreetly nudged me in the ribs, and I narrowed my eyes, shooting her a *knock it off* look before taking a drink of my Cape Cod.

"Thanks, Matthew. I appreciate it." I gave him a grateful smile and scanned the room to see where Benji was. A flicker of something familiar caught my eye, and I turned toward the end of the bar. Eyes the color of blue-gray stormy skies stared back at me. My breath hitched as a chill tingled down my spine. The drink slipped from my hands and crashed to the floor.

"Are you okay? You look like you've seen a ghost or some shit." Avery grabbed my arm and shook it slightly. "Hey, Tensley." Her other hand gently patted my cheek as she demanded my attention.

I dragged my focus away from the guy at the end of the bar and swallowed hard. *This can't be happening. How did he find me?* Bile rose in my throat, and I willed the foul taste down.

"I gotta go," I croaked. "Sorry I made a mess, Matthew."

Matthew nodded at me. "You don't look too good. Don't worry about it. We'll get it."

Before Avery could say anything else, my focus landed on the guy at the end of the bar again. I wanted to tell myself I was mistaken, that there was no way in fucking hell Layne Garrison was staring back at me. But I couldn't deny it.

2

G asping for fresh air, I bolted through the front door and into the parking lot. Tears pricked my eyes, and I angrily forced them back. I'd sworn off crying years ago. It was a sign of weakness and vulnerability. One thing I'd learned from bouncing around to different homes and families was to never let them see me hope or cry. *Hope I would fit in—cry when I didn't.*

"What in the world?" Avery asked, running through the parking lot after me. "Tensley, stop!" She pulled on my arm and whirled me around to face her. "Shit, you're pale. Are you sick?" Her eyes narrowed while she analyzed me.

"Yeah." I would go with that excuse. I'd had several shots close together, which would support my lie. "I needed some air before I puked all over Matthew. Sorry. I didn't mean to scare you." I held my breath, not knowing whether she would see through me. I hated not being honest with my best friend, but I didn't know how to even begin to process that Layne Garrison was in Spokane, Washington. *Fuck.*

A brisk wind kicked up and I wrapped my arms around

myself. It wasn't that cold yet, but October was right around the corner, and the temps would take a hard dip.

"Nope. Your reason isn't working. Try again." She tapped her finger against her chin while she studied me.

My shoulders sagged in defeat. Avery wasn't going to let it go.

"You were looking at some hot dude when you turned ghostly white on me. Even those cute freckles on your nose and cheeks paled. Something is definitely up with this guy, and I'm not sure I like it."

"Tensley?" Benji hurried toward us. "What's up? Why did you guys leave so fast?"

Shit. Apparently, my shock had sent off a beacon warning to my friends, casting me in the spotlight. But I didn't know how in the hell I would explain who Layne was.

I dabbed at the little beads of sweat that had formed over my brow, and my attention bounced between Avery and Benji.

"Spit it out already." Benji motioned for me to hurry up. Patience had never been his strong suit.

I closed my eyes. "He's someone I know from Arkansas. We went to high school together." I peered at them through one eye, afraid of the million questions they were sure to fire my way like rapid torpedoes.

"Oh, this sounds delish." Benji looped his arm through mine. "Why the mad dash, then? I mean, you know him. Why not wave and say hi?"

A group of loud guys barged through the door of the bar, their voices echoing through the parking lot. I peered over at them and my heart skidded to a stop. Layne had lagged behind his friends and was staring at me. He didn't look much different than he had a few years ago. He'd always kept his dark hair short, but long enough for him to comb his fingers through it. His shoulders had broadened since I'd seen him last, but he appeared to have topped out at a little more than six foot. Although I hated him with every fiber of my being, even I couldn't deny that he had a fabulous ass and muscular legs. But he knew it, which made me despise him even more.

Avery elbowed me in the side, her eyes narrowing slightly. "Are you going to talk to him?"

She was testing me. I hadn't been able to reroute her suspicions that something was off.

I shook my head. "No." Maybe if I ignored him, the demon spawn would disappear and go back to the hell he'd come from.

The bright-red neon lights of the open bar sign blinked, casting an eerie shadow over Layne's face. It was then that I noticed how exhausted and sad he looked. *Hollow.*

"Layne, dude, come on!" one of the guys called to him.

Layne shoved a hand into the front pocket of his jeans, stared at me another few seconds, then joined the group. A massive sigh of relief whooshed out of my lungs.

Benji looped an arm through mine and dragged me toward the car. "Girl, you got some 'splainin' to do."

"That's it? It's only midnight, and we're leaving?" Avery hurried behind us, her heels scuffing against the asphalt. I had no idea how she walked in those shoes, but she loved them. She had multiple pairs that worked with her jeans, and even more for her dresses. Avery's closet looked like a section out of Nordstrom's.

"Well we can't talk in there because it's too loud." Benji nodded toward the bar. "And I know this shit is going to be too good to miss a single word of, so it's off to grab a midnight bite and some coffee. Besides, I wasn't going to score tonight anyway."

He opened the car door for me, and I gratefully slipped into the back seat, tucking myself away from the world once again.

Avery hopped in the front, and in seconds, Benji started the car then pulled out of the parking lot.

Avery twisted in her seat and stared a hole straight into my soul. She'd always had the uncanny ability to do that, and it made me incredibly uncomfortable. There were some things not even my best friends knew about me, and I wasn't planning on sharing. "He's hot and you know him, so cough up the deets. If you don't want to talk to him, I will."

"No!" I covered my mouth with my hands in order to not say anything else.

Benji peered in the rearview mirror at me, and I went limp.

"He's not a good guy." Maybe that was enough information to calm their curiosity. It was bad enough he was there. I didn't want to dredge up bad memories too.

Avery's face was filled with intrigue. "Why?"

Fuck. Layne wasn't a part of my past I wanted to revisit or cough up details about. Yes, he was gorgeous, but underneath his hot exterior, I was sure he had horns and a forked tail.

"Give her a few minutes to think, and she can talk when we have some coffee in front of us. Besides, I don't want to miss anything." Benji flipped on his turn signal while we waited for a few cars to pass us in the opposite lane before turning into the Satellite Diner and Lounge.

As soon as he parked, I jumped out of the car and hurried toward the restaurant entrance. I stepped inside the warmth of the rustic diner and held the door open for Avery and Benji.

The soft glow of the lights illuminated the few faces that were scattered at tables across the room. A whiff of hamburgers lingered in the air, and for a moment, I was hungry. But then Layne's face appeared in my mind and my longing for food dissipated.

"Almost snow weather," Benji said as he draped his arm over my shoulder. We strolled through the restaurant and selected a cozy, private booth for four in the back corner. Avery and Benji sat across from me, and I sank into the hard, unforgiving leather seat as deeply as I could.

Holly, one of our regular waitresses, approached us, grinning broadly. "How are my favorite people tonight?"

"Hey, honey." Benji gave her a million-dollar smile and a

wink. Although Holly knew Benji wasn't into women, they flirted like they were going to go hook up in the bathroom. "Just the usual for us, please."

"Got it. Pot of coffee, cream, and pancakes for all." She didn't even scribble the order down on her little pad.

We were there at least once a week. It was cheap and something I could afford. My job at the college library covered living expenses and left me with a bit of side money, but not much. I'd made the cutoff for the work study applications by the skin of my teeth, so I wasn't going to flip off fate and look for something better right now. When Avery, Benji, and I had looked for a house to rent, I'd offered to take the smallest room in order to reduce my costs a bit. What I hadn't anticipated was the fight between them for the master, but Benji had finally won by offering to pay part of my rent as well. I wasn't sure why he'd played it that way, but it had gotten him what he wanted.

"All right, toots, fill us in on Mr. Smoody." Benji squirmed in his seat with anticipation while he waited for me to begin.

I looked at him and Avery, pondering how much I should tell them. Then it dawned on me what Benji had said. I frowned. "Smoody?"

"Smoking hot and moody. I saw him sitting at the end of the bar, staring at you like you were an edible. Girl, it was smoldering." He fanned himself, closing his eyes briefly.

Although Benji had an amazing ability to read people, he was wrong about Layne. Really wrong.

"Oh, I like that." Avery leaned her head on Benji's shoulder, but her attention never left me. "Enough stalling, Tensley. Spit it out like it's a bad, skunky beer that just hit your tongue."

I sat up ramrod straight in my seat. Maybe it was safe to tell them at least some of the story. "His name is Layne Garrison, and we attended high school together."

"You already said that," Avery said, drumming her fingers on the table impatiently.

"Mm-hmm. I got that part already. Keep going." Benji propped his elbows up and leaned forward, ready for more.

"In Arkansas … I-I just have no clue why in the world he's here, like, in Spokane." My forehead creased as I searched for a good reason, but my mind only came up with a big, fat blank.

"Okay, wait." Avery pressed her fingers to her temples. "I've had more to drink than I realized. Tonight, while we were at Barney's, you turned around, and Mr. Smoody was at the end of the bar, staring a hole in your head because he knew you from Arkansas?"

"Is he your kindred hillbilly folk?" Benji chimed in.

I rolled my eyes. "We're not hillbillies. Well, I take that back. Some are, but he wasn't, and neither was I."

Avery harrumphed and reached for the pot of coffee and cups Holly had just set down in front of us. She filled it, topped it off with creamer, and scooted it toward me. Then she began to pour her own coffee but hesitated, her green eyes landing on me. "Whoever he is, he meant something to you. I can't put my finger on it yet, but there were sparks between the two of you. I just don't know if they were good or bad."

"Bad, definitely bad." I focused on my steaming cup and took a sip. "Layne …" My heartrate spiked at the mention of his name. I'd sworn I would never speak it again once I left Arkansas, yet there I was a few years later, discussing *him*. "Layne bullied me in school. I have no clue why, but he hated me. He and his girlfriend, Chloe, made my life hell." There, I'd said it.

"Oh, hon." Benji reached across the table and took my hand in his. "What happened?"

"A lot. Too much to go into, but said torture included, but was not limited to, pulling my sweatpants down in front of the entire school during lunch, filling a paper bag with dog shit and putting it in my locker, and tapping my pubic bone with a glass bottle when I walked by. The last one doesn't sound like much, but somehow that son of a bitch knew right where to aim. It doubled me over every time."

"Jesus," Avery said. "This wasn't some silly high school nonsense, Tensley. That's brutal. Mean."

"That wasn't even the worst of it, but I can't ..." I held up my hands, waving any additional questions off.

Benji's eyes grew serious. "Do I need to rough him up?"

There was no doubt in my mind that Benji would be a good match for Layne, but there wasn't any need for anyone else to get hurt. "Thanks. I really appreciate it, but I'm sure the college campus is big enough to provide some separation."

"Well, you and I have three of our five classes together, so if I see the smoody shit anywhere around, I'll scream bloody murder. He won't fuck with you again," Avery insisted.

My chest warmed with affection for both Avery and Benji. For the first time in my life, I'd not only developed deep friendships, but I knew they would do anything in their power to protect me. What they didn't understand was that I had needed someone like them a long time ago, but now it was too late. Only one person could protect me—me.

"I appreciate you both."

We grew quiet, focusing on our coffee. Layne's smoky-blue eyes flashed in my mind again, and my anxiety crept up another notch. I hoped like hell he left me alone, but just in case, I needed a backup plan. Like pepper spray, a kick to the groin, or a strike of my hand to the soft tip of his nose. Although the thought should have provided me a bit of peace, it didn't. Every time Layne had cornered me at school, I'd frozen. His sneer and laughter flickered through my memory, and my leg began bouncing nervously beneath the table.

"Here ya go," Holly said as she set down our pancakes, breaking through my internal horror.

"Thanks." I grabbed my knife and fork. The smell of fresh pancakes tickled my nose, and I took a large whiff. I nearly groaned as I shoved a forkful into my mouth. "Never do I grow tired of fluffy buttermilk pancakes."

"Right?" Benji dabbed the corners of his mouth with his napkin, then began to cut another bite. "Why do you think he's here? I mean, seriously, Tensley, what's the likelihood that he'd leave Arkansas and land in the same place as you? That shit only happens in movies."

Dammit. I'd hoped they would let it go when our food arrived. I really didn't want to talk about it anymore.

"He was an all-star track athlete back home. Maybe he got a scholarship. I can guarantee you, his girlfriend, Chloe—if she still has her vile claws in him—is also here. She'd never let him move across the country without her." I squinted as the lights from a car entering the parking lot flashed through the window and into my eyes.

"As a teacher's assistant, I have access to student records," Avery offered. "I can get a little bit of information if you want it. At least you'll know where his classes are so you can steer clear."

I didn't like the idea of Avery checking into Layne, but it sounded like the best option to stay out of his way. Although I'd left Arkansas and my past behind, it never hurt to have some knowledge in order to protect myself.

"Deal. Let me know what you find out."

The bell on the door jingled, and I glanced in that direction. A lead ball plummeted to the pit of my stomach. "Son. Of. A. Bitch." My fork dropped out of my hand, bounced off the table, and clattered to the wooden floor.

Layne's intense stare fell on me for the second time that night as he walked straight toward our table.

3

If Layne hadn't already spotted me, I would have slithered right under the table with no shame. I'd developed a survival instinct that often urged me to run when danger was near. Since that wasn't an option for me at the moment, my body decided to turn on me instead. I sat on my hands in an attempt to control the tremble that fought to take me over.

Seconds before Layne reached me, one of his friends ran into the restaurant behind him. "Over here, man."

Layne paused, then turned in the other direction, but his gaze lingered on me for a few more seconds.

When he finally looked away, I blew out the breath I wasn't even aware I'd been holding. "Fuck." I scooted across the booth and stood. "I'll wait for you guys to finish in the car." I reached out to Benji, my palm up. "Can I please have the keys?"

He waved at Holly. "We'll get everything to go. You're not going out there alone."

"Fine. I'll be in the bathroom." Without another word, I scurried off like the little mouse I was. Tears blurred my vision as I slammed into a stall and dropped to my knees. My stomach churned, and I clutched the toilet seat, praying I wasn't going to toss up my evening.

"Tensley? I'm here with you," Avery said. "Do you need a damp paper towel?"

"Yeah." With one huge heave, the contents of my night landed noisily in the commode.

"Oh, hon." Avery entered the handicapped stall with me. "Here." She placed the wet hand towel on the back of my neck and smoothed my hair out of my face. "I'm sorry he was such a huge asshole. Would you like me to kick him in the nuts the next time I see him?"

I gagged again while I gripped the toilet for dear life.

"It's okay, hon. I'm right here."

"I'm sure it's the food mixed with the alcohol."

"Nice try." Avery wiped the perspiration off my forehead. "You're a terrible liar. Plus, you've drank Benji and me under the table numerous times without even a hangover."

Shit. Seeing Layne again had me so rattled, my lies weren't working.

"He can't hurt you anymore," Avery assured me.

"Yeah," I squeaked. Little did she know that Layne wasn't the worst of it, not even close. "I-I shouldn't let him get to me like that." But it wasn't just him. It was the onslaught of memories from my last year in high school, including the fat slob of a foster father who felt it was his right to crawl into my bed every night. The memory of his slimy touch slithered over my skin, and I leaned forward, heaving again.

Avery rested her hand on my back. "I'm here. It's okay."

My hair hung over my face, hiding the tear that had escaped down my cheek. My mom had never helped me like Avery was. I placed my arm on the toilet seat and propped my head against it.

Avery's phone vibrated, and she pulled it out of her navy Tory Burch bag. "Benji is warming up the car. He got our food to go. I'll just text him back that you're sick and we'll be out in a few."

I nodded, too weak to give a shit, but I didn't want to puke in his Lexus either. "Sorry," I muttered.

"Girl, please. I'm just sorry you went through hell. Whatever happened, I hope you can find some peace. I know how crappy it is when something in your past haunts you. No one should ever be able to fuck you up like that. You're one of the strongest people I know."

I wished she were right. I wasn't strong at all. I'd just lived a lot of life, and if I wanted to stay alive, I had to be smart about it. I had to slide under the radar and out of sight.

Taking a deep breath, I leaned back against the wall, and my stomach began to settle down. "Can you peek in the restaurant and see if Layne is around? If the coast is clear, I'll wash my face and we can make a run for it." I sounded like a coward. Maybe that was because I was a coward. My head hung in shame over the fact that some guy could shake me up to such a degree, but maybe it wasn't just him.

The creak of the bathroom door broke my thoughts, and I stood slowly, willing my stomach to stop rebelling.

"It's clear. I don't see him anywhere."

I hurried to the sink, washed my face, then joined Avery.

Avery looped her arm in mine and held my hand. "You've got this."

I kept my focus trained on the exit as we briskly walked through the restaurant. The chilly night air greeted me, and we made a beeline for Benji's Lexus.

"Victoria! Wait!"

A lump lodged itself in my throat, but I didn't turn around. Goosebumps peppered my skin at the sound of Layne's voice, but I kept going.

"Victoria?" Avery asked in a hushed tone. "Why in the hell is he calling you Victoria? Tensley, he must think you're someone else."

My only response was silence. Oh my fucking goodness, there

was a God. And for one brief second, He smiled down on me. Relief washed through me as we reached Benji's car, and I slid into the back seat. I lay down and let the soft leather cool my overheated cheek.

"Are you still sick to your stomach?" Avery asked.

"No," I managed.

"Girl, I love you tons, but no puking in this bitch," Benji warned. "If you gotta hurl, I'm happy to pull over and just slide you off the seat, out of the vehicle, and onto some grass."

Although I felt like shit, I laughed. Leave it to Benji to make a bad situation funny. He was serious, though. I'd seen him move double time to get someone out of the Lexus before they vomited.

Avery peeked around the front seat at me, her eyes sympathizing with my predicament. "Tensley, he thinks you're someone else, hon. It's all right."

I slowly released a pent-up breath and put both hands over my face in an attempt to still my spinning head, but it wasn't because of the alcohol. It had been a long time since I'd heard my real name. *Victoria Alison Benton.* Not even Benji and Avery knew me by that name. I'd left that girl behind when I moved to Spokane from Little Rock. When Layne had called out to me, my heart had pounded against my chest like an angry buffalo stampede. *What in the hell am I going to do?* I wondered if he was just visiting or if he was there to stay and make my life miserable.

AFTER I WAS PLACED in foster care, I'd quickly picked up a skill that still served me well—hiding. Fortunately, I had been a small kid at twelve and could squeeze into tight spaces. Before long, I'd learned to fold myself up in the back of a closet and cover up with shoes or dirty clothes.

Although I had privacy and my own room in the three-bedroom house I shared with Benji and Avery, when I was over-whelmed, I would curl into a fetal position and squish myself against the wall and into the corner of my queen bed.

Even though it was sparsely furnished with a secondhand, petite, light-green dresser and nightstand with chipped paint, the room was mine, and I preferred only a few things in my space.

I wished I could have told Avery and Benji everything, but I couldn't. Instead, the mental images had come rushing up from the center of my being and landed noisily in the toilet. Seeing Layne and hearing my real name roll off his tongue had jarred me back into a darkness that still had its claws hooked deep inside my soul.

A small cry slipped from my lips as I rocked myself and struggled to block out the memories.

A light knock sounded at my door, and I immediately stilled.

"Tensley." The hall light filtered through the crack as Benji peered into my room. "Babe?"

For whatever reason, Benji had referred to me as babe since we'd met. He wasn't bisexual, and there had never been anything between us but a deep friendship. Although he was probably the most intimate relationship I'd had, I had never told him about much of my past, only the need-to-know items, like the fact that I'd spent several years in foster care.

"Yeah?" My voice faltered, revealing the vulnerability that had swelled up inside my chest.

"Are you all right?" The door quietly clicked closed behind him, and he moved toward me in the semidarkness. He'd already changed into plaid pajama bottoms and no shirt. The moonlight peered through my window, illuminating his silhouette. He almost appeared angelic ... almost.

I uncurled my body and stretched my legs out in my bed. "Would you believe me if I told you I was?" Adjusting my sleep tank and shorts, I moved my oversized Minion pillow and patted the available space next to me.

"I don't think so." Benji crawled under the blanket while I remained on top. "I know you're super quiet about your past, but babe, what happened tonight?" He took my hand in his. "Talk to me."

I hesitated, and a long silence filled the room. "I'm not sure I can." I blinked back tears as I peered into my bestie's concerned eyes. If only he were straight. Benji would be *the* guy for me. Or maybe he was safe because I knew the intimacy between us could only go so far.

He plumped up the pillow on his side and got comfortable. "Did you move here from Arkansas for more reasons than just college?"

I internally cringed. "Yeah." He would definitely want to know more.

"Why? Like, do people in Arkansas even know where Washington state is?" He snickered at his own joke.

"Apparently a few of us do." I squeezed my eyes closed, hoping that I could wish the lousy situation away. "I have no idea why Layne is here, but I needed a fresh start. I mean, I've told you I was in foster homes until I graduated. After that, I was on my own, and all I knew was that I had to get out of there. I needed to be around people who hadn't formed an inaccurate opinion of me. I no longer wanted to be *that* kid, the foster kid who smelled and showed up to school in the same set of clothes all week, with tangled hair."

"Ten, I didn't realize it was that bad."

"It was worse." My heart sped into overdrive. Layne showing up had left me no choice but to share more. I couldn't risk Benji thinking I'd lied to him. "I moved to get a fresh start and changed my name. I don't think I can talk about it tonight, though. Maybe someday, but it's not far enough behind me."

Benji's brows puckered while he studied me. It was obvious

he was storing a million questions, and I could tell it was going to be too much for him to wait.

"Please, not right now."

"Are you Victoria?" His question floated on a whisper and traveled straight to my heart.

A silent tear streamed down my cheek, and I brushed it away. "I was."

A deep understanding flickered across Benji's expression. Although I hadn't gone into any detail, Benji realized at that moment that my past was so much more than I'd ever shared with him.

"Come here." He patted his shoulder, and I immediately slipped under the covers and laid my head against him. His arm wrapped protectively around me, and I knew I might have a chance to sleep that night because my best friend cared enough to ensure I felt safe. "If I were straight . . ."

I smiled. "I know. Me too."

He placed a gentle kiss on the top of my head. There was no doubt in my mind that Benji loved me, and I loved him. If he weren't gay, though, I would never feel safe enough to be that close to him, physically or emotionally. But I believed it went both ways.

"Thomas is performing at the standup club tomorrow, and you're going with me, so be ready by nine," he said.

Ugh. I had to pretend I liked Thomas when I truly despised him. I looked up at Benji, my heart softening when I saw the worry in his expression. I just wasn't sure if it was about Thomas or something else. "Why do you want me to go?"

"First, you need a good laugh, and some of those guys are fucking hilarious. Second, I don't want to sit in the audience alone. And third, because I said so." He flashed an infectious grin at me.

There was no way I could turn him down. "All right. For you, I'll go." I stifled a yawn and cozied under the blankets, moving my head off Benji's shoulder and nestling it into the pillow.

Benji held my hand tightly and inhaled, his chest rising before he spoke again. "When you're ready, Tensley, I'm here for you. Your secrets will always be safe with me."

4

Unwanted memories plagued my dreams even though I slept next to Benji all night. Layne and Chloe's faces were everywhere I turned: the high school gym, locker room, and hallways. There was no escaping them or their minions. I rubbed my eyes, willing the thoughts away, but I couldn't shake the daunting feeling that nagged at me. *Why is Layne in Spokane? What does he want from me?*

Sighing softly, I patted the bed next to me. But Benji was gone, which was typical. I wondered if Avery knew how many nights we spent together. It wouldn't bother her, but she never said a word.

For whatever reason, I was as comforting to Benji as he was to me. The first night we'd shared a bed, we were drunk off our rockers and passed out in his room. Since then, if we had an issue sleeping or wanted to talk, we just spent the night together. Somehow, it was more intimate than if we were having sex, maybe because I knew he didn't expect anything from me. Just being me was good enough for him.

Since it was nearly noon on Saturday, I figured it was time to drag my lazy ass out of bed even though I didn't want to. I would have been happy if I could curl up with a good book all day and be alone, but I had chores to do, including laundry, if I wanted to go out with Benji that night.

I wandered down the hall, rubbing the sleep out of my eyes and entered the kitchen.

"Hey, sexy," Avery said through a mouthful of sandwich. "How are you feeling this morning ... afternoon?"

"Fine." I wasn't awake enough to converse beyond one-syllable words yet.

"There's coffee left in the pot if you want it."

I nodded and reached for a mug, filled it, then sank onto the barstool next to her at the island. "I'm not sure why I got up." I took a sip of coffee. "Oh, yes ... I have to do laundry. For some reason, I don't think my pajamas are appropriate attire for the comedy club tonight."

Avery smiled at me. "I'm glad you're getting out of the house again. You spend way too much time in your bedroom alone. If you were in your room, getting laid, that would be acceptable, but not all the hours you're holed up alone." She scrunched up her nose at me like it was the most distasteful thing she'd ever heard.

"Well, I like it. Plus I rarely had a moment to myself for years. Now I do. It's just that simple." I'd never told Avery how grotesquely accurate that statement was. Although it had appeared to the social worker that we'd had our own bedrooms, we hadn't. Five of us slept together in a room that was no bigger than ten by ten. Mama Joy would toss down sleeping bags for us on a filthy carpeted floor and tell us to deal with it. Then she would shut the door so she didn't have to see or hear us. By eight o'clock most nights, the house would be full of her and Papa George's friends. They would drink and holler all night even though we had to go to school the next day while the adults slept. The rooms supposedly meant for us had been used for people to screw and pass out in. I still felt disgusted by it all.

"Are you doing anything fun tonight?" I asked, slamming the window closed on the ugly memories.

Avery's face lit up. "I'm seeing Justin."

I took a drink of my coffee and raised my eyebrow at her. "You like this guy, huh?"

"Yeah. A lot." She crunched on a barbecue potato chip then took a sip of her milk.

"Ew, barbecue and milk? That's nasty."

Avery giggled. "No, it's not. Anyway, he's taking me to meet his parents tonight."

"What? That's huge! Why didn't you tell me sooner?"

"I would have, but he just mentioned it this morning while you were still asleep. I didn't think you'd appreciate me waking you up for the news. I mean, if it were a proposal, then hell yeah, I'd have jumped up and down on your bed, screaming like a giddy teenager."

"Are you guys going out to eat or to his parent's place? Fill me in, girlfriend." I leaned forward in my chair, eager to hear about her life. Justin and Avery had dated for about four months, so this was a big deal. I listened attentively while she updated me on the upcoming evening and filled me in on how she and Justin were doing. Although I wasn't the best person to judge the situation, since I'd never had a boyfriend before, it seemed as though the relationship was growing pretty serious.

A familiar pang of longing swelled inside my chest. The more Avery talked about her and Justin, the more I wanted that kind of relationship. I was a junior in college and had never had a date. I'd never experienced the feeling of belonging next to someone and waking up in bliss every morning. I realized the feeling didn't last forever, but I would cherish even one day of it. I would cling to the memory of someone wanting to be with me and bask in the moments in which I felt good enough and worthy to be loved, valued, and worshipped. I mentally slapped myself in the face for allowing my thoughts to wander down a road in fantasy island.

Avery snapped her fingers in front of me. "Tensley? Where did you go?"

"Sorry," I mumbled. "I'm still waking up."

"Are you really okay? This entire conversation, we've managed to dance around what happened last night. I know it did a number on you." A frown line creased her forehead as she examined me.

I suppressed my sarcastic laugh. She had no idea how not okay I really was, and if I could help it, she never would know.

"Yup." I sipped my coffee. "I think the alcohol complicated the situation. I mean, so what if Layne is here? However, the more I think about it ..." I drummed my fingers against the countertop of the island. "It would help if you could check to see if there is a schedule for him. At least I would know whether or not he is a student or just visiting. If he is, the campus is plenty big enough for me to avoid him. I just need to know where he is so I can avoid him."

"I'll take care of it on Monday. Consider it done."

"Thanks. I really appreciate it. But ..."

Avery tilted her head, waiting for me to weigh in.

My palms suddenly grew clammy, and I rubbed them on my flannel pajama bottoms. "Avery, I can't explain everything to you. I promise I will in time, but apparently I need to get a little bit ahead of the situation."

She folded her hands in her lap, her gaze unwavering.

I inhaled a shaky breath. "I'm Victoria. My birth name was Victoria Alison Benton. When I left Arkansas, I needed to leave that girl behind, the one who had been used and tossed away. In order for me to be true to myself and start a new life, I became Tensley Alison Bennett."

"Holy shit."

A pregnant pause filled the air, and it was my turn to wait for a response. The silence was killing me, so I continued. "I'm sorry I withheld that from you, but I never expected to run into anyone from my past here."

Avery nodded, pulling her bottom lip between her teeth. "I've always known there's more to you than you allow me to see, and that's okay. I think we all have a piece of us we protect at all costs. I'm just trying to wrap my mind around the idea that life could be so devastating, you didn't even want to keep your name. That shit was so bad, you needed to separate yourself by distance *and* change your name in order to feel safe. I think my heart just broke, and at the same time, I have even more respect for you. And now all I want to do is protect you from whatever is going on. Ten, you're not just my best friend, you're my family, my sister."

I inwardly heaved a major sigh of relief. "You're not pissed at me?" Between Benji and Avery, it was Avery I'd been the most concerned about.

"I'm disappointed, but maybe I would have done the exact same thing. And the bottom line? It's not about what I think right now. It's about what is going to make you happy. So whatever is haunting you, please know I'm here, day or night, to help in any way I can. It's what sisters do for each other."

Relief flooded me as though someone had just opened the dam. I hopped off my barstool and wrapped my arms around her.

"I love you." I laid my head on her shoulder and counted my blessings.

"Right back atcha."

"YOU LOOK HOT TONIGHT," Benji said, beaming at me from the driver's seat. "Did Avery help dress you?" He snickered at his slight dig.

I smoothed my plum-colored blouse and tucked a stray hair

behind my ear. I'd paired the top with boyfriend jeans and black boots. "I realize you think I can't doll up all on my own, but I'll have you know"—I directed my hand from my face down my body—"this was all me." I winked at him and laughed as he pulled into the comedy club parking lot.

"Shit. Do you see any available spaces? I can't believe it's this packed." He leaned forward in his seat, scouring the area for a vacant spot.

"No. I wonder if it's so busy due to the track meet coming up?"

"Yeah. I have no clue, but this is completely unacceptable." He blew out a sigh, and his attention cut toward me. "Are you okay walking a little bit? We can see if there's any availability near the back of the building. People park in the alley all the time."

"We've parked there before. Go for it." One thing I didn't mind was walking. When I was younger, I would walk for miles in the middle of the night if I couldn't sleep. There was something about it I found soothing. Maybe it was the fact that I could get one over on whatever foster parents I was with for the week, or maybe I was most comfortable when the darkness concealed me.

Once Benji parked, he hurried out of the car and around to my side. He looked terrific, but Benji never had a bad day when it came to his looks. His clothing style leaned toward metro, and he adored loud colors. That night, he'd opted for a bright-red button-down tucked into his designer jeans, which were rolled up at his ankles.

"Ma'am," he said, opening the door and extending his hand to me.

"Ah, you're so sweet." I put my fingers in his and stood, grinning. Maybe it was silly, but Benji was the only guy who made me feel special. Valuable.

He locked up, turned, and held out his arm to me. I looped mine through his and we hurried toward the club.

Every time I saw the redbrick building, it reminded me of home. I was astonished by the lack of brick homes in Spokane, but they rarely had a tornado there. I grew up in tornado alley, so not only did people need a solid home, but most houses included a basement.

Benji pulled me through the entrance, then he came to an abrupt halt. "Shit," he muttered. "Thomas is already performing."

I bounced on my tiptoes and attempted to peek over him, but there were too many people for me to see the stage clearly. "What? I thought he wasn't on until later."

"So did I." Benji's eyes darted around the crowded room then grabbed my hand and pulled me toward the farthest wall. There was standing space only.

I gave Benji's hand a reassuring squeeze. "Thomas has a bright spotlight on him, so he probably can't see people very well in the audience. Maybe he doesn't realize you're late."

I leaned against the wall, and my thoughts fell on Thomas as he continued to entertain the room. His hair was teased into a long afro, and although I didn't care much for him, Thomas was handsome. His short-sleeved yellow shirt showcased his well-sculpted arms, but I had no clue why he thought burgundy skinny jeans worked well with such a bright-colored top. *But what do I know?* I relied on my roomies to dress me most of the time.

The crowd roared with laughter, breaking my thoughts. I peeked at Benji, who was mindlessly fiddling with a hangnail on his thumb. He was stressed, and my heart ached for him. I wasn't sure why Benji couldn't walk away from Thomas after the guy had cheated on him, but there was some kind of unhealthy pull in their relationship. I never talked to Benji about it because I was in no way qualified to give dating advice.

The room thundered with loud applause as Thomas bowed to the audience, his eyes landing on us in the back. The announcer jumped on the stage and began to introduce the next comic.

Thomas hopped off the platform and made his way over to us. "You made it," he said to Benji, practically ignoring my existence. He leaned over and gave Benji a quick peck on the mouth. "Hello, Tensley."

My lips pursed together with a curt greeting. "Thomas." I offered him the best fake smile I could. "You were great tonight." And that was all it took, a stroke to the male ego, for his walls to melt faster than butter in a hot cast-iron skillet. I stopped myself before I made a gagging sound.

"Yeah?" Thomas asked, taking Benji's hand in his and threading their fingers together. "I think it went over well. I wrote all new jokes this week."

"You brought the house down," Benji said. "I'm so proud of you."

"Too bad you missed the first half." Thomas's eyes narrowed slightly while he pinned Benji with his unforgiving gaze.

I cringed slightly at Thomas's steely tone. "It was my fault." It wasn't, but I didn't want an argument to start.

"It won't happen again. Promise." Benji's expression pleaded with his piece-of-shit boyfriend while fury boiled in the pit of my stomach.

After all the years of pretending to feel differently than I'd portrayed, something inside me snapped for the first time. I grabbed Thomas's arm and whirled him around toward me. I didn't miss the horrified expression on my best friend's face, but it was too late. My anger was accelerating full speed ahead.

Jabbing my pointer finger into Thomas's chest, I unloaded on him. "You listen to me, you entitled asshole. Benji loves you, and you've done nothing but treat him like shit. You cheated on him —not once, but *twice*—then have the audacity to get pissed because he's late? Who do you think you are? He's the most loyal person you'll ever find, so I highly recommend you get your shit together before he tells you to fuck off. He's too damned good for you."

A gasp escaped Benji as his hands flew over his mouth. Dammit, I'd fucked up. I never spoke to people like that, but something inside me had broken, and I wasn't sure it would ever be fixed. Maybe I'd finally crossed the threshold on my bullshit-and-disrespect meter.

"I'm sorry, Benji. You deserve someone who treats you better." Shit, I sure did pick a great time to share with Benji how I really felt.

Thomas's deep-brown eyes flashed with anger, but he didn't say a word to me. I wasn't sure if it was because he was shocked or if he thought better of it in public.

"Benji, I'll be outside waiting for you." I whirled around on my heel and elbowed my way through the throng of people and out the front door. *Shit, shit, shit.* I had inserted myself where I didn't belong, and an alien creature had taken over my mouth. One thing I was skilled at was keeping my trap shut and hiding.

I barked out a laugh and leaned against the building near the entrance. Allowing the cool night air to calm my anger, I recalled the last time I'd lost my shit and stood up to someone. Chloe Sullivan's sneer and giggle rang through my mind as I recalled one of the many times she'd targeted me during lunch our senior year.

She'd purposefully run into me in the cafeteria, her shoulder smacking mine. My milk teetered off my tray and landed with a loud splat on the tile floor and my food followed. Milk exploded in every direction, soaking my worn tennis shoes. I'd just loaded my tray with as much food as the cafeteria workers had allowed me to. Not only was it my meal for the day, but I tried to save the apple or orange for the younger foster kids wherever I was staying. Now it was scattered across the surrounding area, and the only place it would go to was the trash.

Chloe's words taunted me. *I never saw you there. Guess you're just see-through.*

Every pair of eyes in the cafeteria was trained on us. My

temper had traveled from zero to sixty when my plastic tray had clattered to the floor. Chloe's cackle rang throughout the room. She obviously thought it was funny, but I couldn't get any more food for the day. Then I grew some balls and approached my nemesis. I was sick and tired of being targeted by her and Layne. Fuck them. Someone needed to put them in their place, and I had officially volunteered.

As we stood toe to toe, a mixture of hate and disgust twisted Chloe's grin into a sneer. Her jaw clenched while I leaned near her until my face was only inches away from hers. I insisted she buy me another lunch, and of course, she declined. Chloe's brown eyes narrowed as she grabbed a handful of my hair and yanked. A yelp escaped me before I could stop it. I reached up, attempting to pry her cat claws away from me.

A deep voice from behind me yelled her name. My gaze cut sideways. Great, my second tormentor, Layne, was approaching us. He casually strolled over to her while he assessed the situation. Layne reached for Chloe's hand and coaxed her into letting me go. She whined as Layne assured her they would deal with me later.

But before I had walked away, I'd made it clear to both of them that the situation wasn't over by a long shot.

The comedy club door burst open, pulling me away from the haunting high school incident. A tipsy group of guys stumbled across the parking lot while they slapped each other on the backs, hooting and hollering about a party later that night. A girl's name was tossed back and forth between them, along with more catcalls. I secretly hoped whoever she was had some mace. From the way they were discussing her intimately, I could tell they were assholes.

I shook my head in disgust while my thoughts returned to Chloe and Layne. This wasn't the first time I'd wondered if things would have gone differently had I just walked away, if I hadn't lost my shit and told Chloe it wasn't over. And I'd been right. It hadn't been over, not by a long shot.

A chill traveled down my spine, and I rubbed my arms, warding off the continued thoughts of my bullies. The front door burst open again, and Benji tentatively stepped outside into the dark parking lot.

"Benji!" I moved out of the safe shadow of the building. "I'm so sorry."

His faced morphed into relief when he saw me. He pulled me to him and wrapped me up in a warm hug. "I wasn't sure where you went," he whispered against my hair.

"Just out here. I was afraid I'd say something else. I don't know what came over me." I broke our hug and stepped back, glancing up at him. Pain and anger flickered across his face, and I traced his cheek with my fingertips. "Are you okay?"

"Yeah, but we're done. I'm done. Thomas doesn't deserve me. I can't really explain it, but watching you … Listening to you stand up for me brought some clarity. I mean, here we are in public, and he's chastising me like I'm a child. Mmm, no. It was like a bolt of lightning that traveled through me, and I saw the situation differently. I saw Thomas differently."

"Yes!" I yelped and performed a happy dance in the parking lot.

"I'm a free man!" he shouted into the star-filled sky.

"Oh, maybe you'll run into that guy from the bar last night." I wiggled my eyebrows at him, giggling. "Ya know, the hottie with the ball cap?"

Benji's shoulders sagged, and he draped his arm over my shoulder. "Thank you for sticking up for me." He began to walk slowly toward the car. "I should have stood up to him myself, but dammit, he's got a magic stick like no other."

I snickered. Benji and I didn't discuss his sex life in great depth, but he'd shared a few times how well-endowed or not a partner was. We rounded the corner of the building in silence while my heart swelled with pride. I knew Benji had struggled to stand up to Thomas, but he'd finally done it. That called for a celebration.

"It's still early. Do you want to go clubbing?" Benji twirled a strand of my hair around his finger. "Maybe we can find us both a plaything after all."

"Ha. No, thanks. But ya know, dancing sounds like fun—only if you allow me to buy you a few shots, though."

A wide grin played across his lips. "Deal."

"Are you sure you're okay about Thomas?" I asked.

Before he could answer, a clammy hand slipped around me, covered my mouth, and ripped me away from Benji.

5

My eyes widened in terror while a dark-haired, sturdy guy grabbed Benji's arms and pinned them behind his back. A shorter blond approached him and immediately swung his fist into Benji's gut, doubling him over.

I squirmed against the body that confined me, but the man was too strong. Tears stung my eyes as Benji's cries rang through the alley. My heart pounded wildly against my ribs as I lifted both my legs off the ground and threw my weight forward, sending myself and my captor to the ground. I rolled over and attempted to scramble across the asphalt, but he was too quick and he crawled on top of me. Then he flipped me over on my back and immobilized my wrists over my head.

"Aren't you a hot little piece of ass?" He palmed my breast through my shirt and ground his hips against me. His knee forcefully parted my legs as a scream ripped from my throat. In seconds, he had my jeans undone and his cold fingers against my lower abdomen.

The pain of sharp pebbles cut into the back of my hands and brought some clarity to my muddled brain.

"You stupid fuck." I picked my head up off the ground and

spit in his face. Most of it landed in his eyes. *Thank God I have good aim.* My cousins had taught me to hock a hell of a loogie when we were young, but I never figured I would need it as a weapon. Maybe Arkansas had served a small purpose in my life after all.

"Bitch," he growled, wiping off my saliva with his shirt.

I bucked my hips off the ground, sending him sideways and onto the unforgiving asphalt. My eyes landed on Benji, and bile swam up to my throat. Benji's eye was quickly swelling shut, and blood poured from what I assumed was a broken nose.

"Benji!" Dammit, someone had to be nearby. "Help!" My desperate cry was only met with strong fingers wrapping around my ankle and tugging me toward the asshole who wanted in my pants. He slammed his hand over my mouth and rolled me over to my back again.

I chastised myself for cutting my nails short. I would have loved to claw the fucker's eyes out. Squirming, I fought with everything inside me, but the guy still managed to get my pants down past my hips. My nostrils flared with red-hot anger, and I stilled. I mentally surveyed as much about him as I could. I would hunt him down the rest of his life if he raped me. *Reddish brown hair, broad shoulders, five o'clock stubble on his round face. Brown T-shirt, black jeans, crooked front teeth.*

The sound of his zipper rang in my ears, and I attempted to bite the hand that held my mouth closed. A loud thud caught my attention, and the bastard was pulled off me, his arms flailing as he landed ass first on the ground.

I scrambled to my feet as another guy slammed his fist into the asshole's face. Not wasting any time, I adjusted and buttoned my jeans, then hurried toward Benji, who was curled into a ball and lying motionless. I jumped on the back of the blond-haired assailant who was kicking Benji over and over in the ribs. I pulled his hair and attempted to claw his face with my short nails, forcing him to stop assaulting my best friend. The dark-haired guy whirled around and pinned me with a hateful glare, but I kept going.

Before I realized what was happening, the dark-headed asshole dropped to the ground. He held on to his side and whined like the little bitch he really was as a booted foot made contact with his gut. He rolled away and scrambled to stand. His fist balled up and he swung wide, clipping the jaw of whoever had joined us. I couldn't see who my hero was, but if we got out of this alive, he would forever have my gratitude.

Losing my balance, I hopped off the back of number one and stumbled backward. He turned toward me, and for the first time, I saw his face. I'd done some damage, and blood was trickling into his right eye. But I hadn't done enough.

In one fell swoop, the guy jerked me into a standing position by my blouse, ripping the thin material open and sending the buttons pinging off the ground. "You'll pay for that, bitch. You and your faggot friend shouldn't be out in public."

Sucking in a quick breath, I kicked full force, and my foot connected with his groin. A loud crack split the night, then number one released me and sank to the ground. His eyes widened as he covered his crotch with both hands, and his mouth gaped open like a fish out of water.

I scanned the area for additional attackers, but the only man facing me was Layne Garrison. A groan filled my ears, and I tore my gaze away from Layne. Terror coursed through me and split me wide open as I hurried to Benji, followed closely by Layne.

"I'll call 9-1-1. Don't touch him," he ordered.

I couldn't miss the soft lilt of Layne's southern accent. God knew I'd worked to lose mine, but it had taken some work.

"Benji." I took his hand in mine, ignoring Layne's orders. "Benji." A messy lump of emotion clogged my throat. He was barely conscious. "Hang on. The ambulance is on the way."

"Tensley," he whispered, his voice cracking. "Okay?"

I nodded. "I'm fine."

Layne continued the conversation with the operator and provided our location. I silently thanked the heavens someone had shown up to help. Sirens split through the otherwise quiet night. I peered over my shoulder to ensure the three men that had attacked us were still on the ground.

"Are the police coming?" I asked, my gaze connecting with Layne's smoky-blue eyes.

"Yeah, along with the ambulance." He quickly tugged off his jacket and tossed it around my shoulders.

I glared at him. Granted he'd just saved us, but I didn't want or need anything else from him.

"Your shirt." He pointed to my open blouse, and it was only then that I noticed my lilac push-up bra and cleavage were on full display.

My cheeks flamed red as I let go of Benji's hand, slid my arms into the sleeves of the jacket, and zipped it. When my attention landed on Layne again, he'd turned away to allow me a moment to cover myself. That wasn't the Layne I knew, but it didn't matter. Benji was my number one priority.

A low moan escaped Benji again, and I sat next to him, willing my tears away. He was a mess. Blood had pooled on the ground near his head, and I whispered a prayer that the ambulance would hurry.

"Victoria."

My head snapped up. "That's not my name."

Layne's brows knitted in confusion, but the police and para-medics arrived at that moment, halting any conversation between us.

I stood on the sidelines, helplessly watching the horrifying situation unfold. The next several minutes were a flurry as the EMTs loaded Benji onto a stretcher and into the back of the ambulance. Although I realized I'd been banged up during the fight, I declined medical care. The last thing I wanted were more strangers' hands touching me.

Layne was on the other side of the alley, speaking with the police. His body was rigid, and he folded his arms across his chest then dropped them to his sides again. He looked nervous.

After the police finished with him, they approached me. I told them everything I could recall, but I was eager to get to the hospital with Benji. I had to call his parents and Avery as well. A nagging thought continued to pull at the edge of my mind, and I realized I needed to tell the cops.

"I'm pretty sure this was a hate crime," I said to Officer Palmer.

He folded his arms over his belly and arched a brow. "What makes you think so?"

"Because he said that the faggot and I shouldn't be out in public. They beat Benji within an inch of his life. *Two* guys were on him. I only had one to deal with."

"We'll look into it further. Thanks to that young man"—the officer pointed to Layne—"your friend might have a chance to make it."

I nodded. Although I hated Layne, he'd shown up at the right time. There was no way I could dispute it. Plus, he could have walked away and left Benji and me for dead. But he hadn't. My heart suggested he'd changed, but my mind refused to acknowledge the possibility.

"If you think of anything else, give me a call." Officer Palmer handed me a business card and said goodnight.

Layne shoved his hands in his jeans pockets and slowly walked toward me. A conflicted look painted his expression, and an abundance of different emotions flickered in his eyes. I understood. It was the first time in three years we were face-to-face again.

"Are you all right?" he asked. His voice was low as his eyes traveled up and down my body.

"Yeah." I rubbed my arms, not wanting to say the next part. I swallowed hard and glanced toward the police, who were in the process of leaving the scene. "Thank you." I pointed at his dark-blue shirt. "It's torn." There, I'd done something polite even though it went against every fiber of my being. "I have to get to the hospital."

"Wait, let me take you." Layne's expression softened, and I thought I saw a glimmer of compassion.

"Ha!" I barked before I realized it. "Listen, Layne, nothing has changed. I don't know why you're here, nor do I give two fucks, but let's get something straight. I hate you. I hate what you did to me." My eyes narrowed while my angry gaze raked over him. "Leave me alone." With that, I whirled on my heel, leaving him standing by himself, and headed toward Benji's car. Then it dawned on me that I didn't have keys to Benji's Lexus. I would have to call an Uber, which would take at least twenty minutes to show up. I would be left alone in the dark again. My body trembled at the thought.

"Victoria, or whatever your name is, please let me take you to the hospital," Layne said from behind me.

My shoulders stiffened as I weighed my options. The quickest way to Benji was to go with the gorgeous asshole behind me who had made my life a living hell. My heart hammered against my chest as I turned around to face him. Through all the commotion of the night, it was the first time I'd really looked at him. His thick brown hair, smoky-blue eyes, broad shoulders, and lean, muscular frame would make any normal girl want to devour him. But not me. Not ever.

"Tensley," I huffed, folding my arms over my chest defiantly. "I don't have keys to Benji's car, so I can't drive. I need a ride, but I can call an Uber."

"Tensley?" A frown furrowed his brow. "Why? What was wrong with Victoria?"

I held my hand up, halting any additional questions.

"Please let me take you. Otherwise you'll be waiting even

longer ... in the dark and by yourself. I would worry about your safety at this point," Layne said gently.

He'd obviously thought it through like I had.

"I need to call Benji's parents," I conceded, pulling my phone out of my back pocket. "Dammit!" My screen was cracked, and my phone showed no life at all.

"You can use mine on the way to the hospital." Layne nodded toward a newer Camry parked up the street. "Let's go. Maybe we can get there before he goes into surgery." He hurried to the car.

"What?" I two-stepped to catch up with him. "You think he needs an operation?"

"Most likely." He clicked a button on the key fob he'd produced from his pocket, and the red glow of the taillights broke through the darkness. "I'm not certain, but he didn't look good, Vic—Tensley."

There was no denying that Benji had been brutally beaten. Layne opened the passenger door for me, and I settled into the black leather seat as he hurried to the driver's side.

He started the car. "Are you cold?"

I hadn't noticed before he'd asked, but I was. "A little." Once I gathered my wits, I turned to Layne. "What in the hell were you doing tonight anyway? Like, why were you there? Are you following me?" With all the commotion, the thought had just dawned on me, and I wanted an answer.

"I was having dinner with my uncle next door. I was almost to my car when I heard you scream. I ran over as fast as I could."

"Oh." I probably should have said more, but I'd just accused him of stalking me. "Why are you here in Spokane?"

"I live with my uncle, and I'm attending college." He turned the heat on high. "It won't take long to warm up. Here's my phone." He handed me the newest iPhone, then pulled onto the street.

I dialed Benji's parents' number without hesitation. His mom, Marilyn, picked up on the third ring.

"Hello?" I didn't miss the apprehension in her voice. It was after ten on a Saturday evening, a little late for phone calls.

"Hi, Marilyn. It's Tensley."

"Tensley? Honey, are you okay? What's going on?"

My gaze traveled to my boots, and a feeling of dread spread through me. What if Benji wasn't going to be okay?

"It's Benji. He's been hurt. He and I were attacked when we left the comedy club. I'm on my way to Sacred Heart now with a … friend, but they took Benji by ambulance."

A cry filled the phone line, then I heard rustling.

"Hello, Tensley?" Michael, Benji's father, asked.

"Yes, sir."

"He's still alive? He's going to be okay?" His words were thick with concern, and fear weaved through me. I didn't know. I wasn't sure what to tell him.

"Put it on speaker," Layne urged as he turned onto Division. "I can help."

"Sir?" I asked. "Layne is driving me to Benji now. Actually, he … he saved our lives. He might be able to answer some of your questions better than I can. I'm still shaken."

Pushing the mute icon, I turned toward Layne. "You listen to me, Layne Garrison. These are good people, wonderful human beings, and the only family I have. Don't fuck with them, or you'll regret it."

"Promise," he said.

I unmuted the phone, put it on speaker, and Layne began to talk.

"Sir, I'm Layne. I'm no doctor, but I can tell you that your son was severely beaten. His nose appeared broken, his left eye was swollen shut, and he had a large gash on his forehead. When I reached him, one of the men was kicking him in the ribs. I suspect there's some damage there, and they will want to make sure he doesn't have internal bleeding. I think that's the biggest concern, but I'm not completely certain."

"Dear God." Michael muffled the phone and muttered something unintelligible to Marilyn. "We're on our way."

"I'm so sorry," I whispered, struggling to breathe above the panic running riot inside me.

"We'll understand more when we get there. Benji is tough, and his injuries might not be serious," Michael assured me, but it did nothing to calm my nerves.

I hung up the phone and handed it to Layne.

"I have questions," he said, taking it from me and setting it in his seat between his legs.

"No." I turned to stare out the window. I didn't care if he had saved Benji and me or not—he didn't deserve any answers. Facing him again, I narrowed my eyes suspiciously. "What? What are you doing here?" I snapped. "Does the universe hate me so much that it sent you to torment me again?"

A heavy silence hung in the air. "It's a long story." He spun a silver ring on his middle finger as he took a deep breath and focused his attention on the road.

Maybe it was a long story, but my stomach stirred with something I hadn't experienced toward him before: compassion. Layne sounded … broken. Defeated. With a little work, I finally convinced myself that my moment of sympathy toward him was due to the highly emotional evening I was having. Nothing more, nothing less. And I needed answers. I wanted to know why he was there and why he'd treated me like crap in high school.

Most importantly, I wanted to know why I should trust him. The only reason my brain could grasp was that Layne owed Benji and me nothing, yet he'd stepped in to defend us, to save us. That said something. I just wasn't sure what yet.

"We're almost there," he said as he guided the car up a steep hill to the emergency entrance.

Layne parked, and I hopped out and bolted toward the sliding glass doors before he turned the engine off.

Hurrying to the front desk, I glanced around for Benji's

parents, but I didn't see them yet. "Benji Parker. He was just brought here by ambulance."

"Hi, hon. Are you a relative?" a middle-aged nurse asked.

"I'm his sister. I was with him when we were attacked." Sometimes I was amazed at how quickly I could lie, but I knew they wouldn't share anything if we weren't related. My fingers drummed nervously on the desk while I waited for her to provide an update.

"He arrived about twenty minutes ago and was rushed into surgery." Her large doe eyes filled with compassion. "I'll see what I can do about an update for you soon, but it might be a while."

My shoulders sagged. That wasn't good, but I had no idea how bad it really was. Until we had additional information, my mind was left to its own devices, which meant it would taunt me with the worst possible scenarios. I turned around slowly, made my way to the waiting room, and sank into a blue chair as far away from the other three people in the room as possible. I wouldn't call it a love seat necessarily, but two people could sit in it together. Surprisingly, the ER wasn't too busy, which was fine with me. The fewer shrieking little kids or crying adults I had to deal with, the better.

Suddenly, I was overwhelmed with exhaustion, and my entire body ached from defending myself. I closed my eyes briefly as the events of the evening rushed over me like a tidal wave. The seat next to me gave way, and I peered through one eye to see who had sat down.

"You're still here?" I asked, aggravated. "Why?"

Layne combed his fingers through his hair and pinned me with an intense gaze. "What did they say about Benji?"

"He's in surgery. I don't know anything else." I leaned back in my chair and willed Layne Garrison to disappear.

"I'm sorry," Layne said in a low tone. His jaw muscles clenched for a moment before he spoke again. "I'm sorry for how I treated you in high school, I'm sorry I didn't reach you sooner tonight, and I'm sorry about Benji. I wish I could have done more." His eyes met mine then drifted to the floor.

Who is this guy in front of me? There was no way of knowing if he'd changed for real or if he was blowing sunshine up my ass. *Can someone like him even change?* I shook my head and clung to my anger, refusing to consider the possibility that he was different. He didn't deserve a second chance.

"Tensley?" Marilyn hurried toward me, her heels clicking on the tile floor. Her eyes were puffy and red-rimmed. Typically, there wasn't a hair out of place on her head and she was impeccably dressed, but not tonight. She'd haphazardly put herself together after hearing the news about her son. She'd pulled her shoulder-length dark hair into a messy bun, and her face was free of makeup. But what killed me the most was the pain etched into her beautiful features. I silently cursed the gods for allowing the Parker family to be hurt like this.

I stood and allowed Marilyn to pull me in for a big hug. Benji's parents had treated me as their own, and I couldn't ask for better.

Shit, in all the excitement, I'd forgotten to call Avery. I would have to borrow Marilyn's phone. The less conversation I had with Layne, the better.

"Michael," I said, pushing up on my tiptoes and embracing Benji's dad. Dark circles shadowed his weary eyes, but he appeared strong. I knew him well enough to know that he would want to be Marilyn's rock and not allow his emotions to show, at least not yet. No loving father could keep his feelings tucked away for long.

He hugged me, then held me at arm's length and assessed me. It hadn't occurred to me that I probably looked like a complete mess.

"Are you hurt?" Marilyn asked, concern in her expression as she gave me the once-over.

"I'm shaken and bruised, but that's all. Some Advil would be awesome, though." I didn't feel the need to see a doctor, but I'd taken some hits on the asphalt, and it wouldn't surprise me to find bruises on my back and legs. I self-consciously rubbed my cut-and-scratched hands.

Layne stood next to me and extended his hand to Benji's parents. "I'm Layne. I showed up on the scene and did what I could to help tonight. Hopefully it was enough."

Marilyn flung her arms around his neck and broke down sobbing on his shoulder. Layne did his best to comfort her, but I didn't miss the awkwardness of the situation. Marilyn finally backed away and rummaged around in her purse for a tissue.

"I'm so sorry," she whispered, her eyes swollen. "The nurse at the desk said Benji was in surgery."

Layne and I sat back down while Michael and Marilyn settled into seats across from us.

"How do you know Benji?" Michael asked Layne.

"I don't, actually." Layne rubbed his chin, and I wondered if he was trying to select his next words carefully. "I'm friends with Tensley."

I mentally kicked him in the shin. Hard. *Friends? Not ever.* But I knew my manners, and there was no way I was going to call him out while we waited to see how bad off Benji was. At least he got my name right.

"Marilyn, can I borrow your phone?" I asked. "I need to call Avery. Mine was broken during the ... the attack."

Once again, Marilyn performed a deep dive into her purse. "Of course, hon." She gave me her iPhone and held her tissue tightly in her trembling hand.

"I'll be right back." Without even a glance at Layne, I hurried toward the exit and into the fresh night air. I rounded the corner of the hospital building and planted the palm of my hand against the cold brick. My breaths came in short bursts as the events of the evening plagued me. I'd been seconds away from being raped in an alley while Benji ... A small cry slipped from between my lips, and agony coursed through me. *What if his injuries are so severe that we lose him?* I sucked in a quick breath, attempting to keep myself together. I spotted a few cement benches and flower beds with remnants of summertime roses. The walkway circled around an area cordoned off by a row of well-trimmed bushes.

"Avery," I whispered, focusing on the phone and reminding myself of why I was outside. My hands shook as I tapped out her number. The call went immediately to voice mail. *Dammit.* I hated to leave a message about Benji, but I had no other choice.

"Are you all right?" Layne asked, rounding the corner. "I mean, really okay? I understand you wouldn't want to worry Benji's parents, but you were attacked tonight."

My head snapped up at the sound of his voice, and although I willed it not to, my chin trembled. I'd sworn a long time ago that Layne would never see me as weak, but there I was—a mess and vulnerable. I shoved Marilyn's phone into my back pocket, folded my arms over my chest, and leaned wearily against the wall. I didn't have the strength to lie, not even to Layne.

"No. I don't think so. I'm not … I hurt, but I …"

"I got these for you." Layne held his hand out, and I greedily snatched the three Advil tablets from it. He produced a small bottle of water next, and I downed the pills. "Michael promised he'd come to get us if there was any news on Benji. Why don't we sit down on the bench?"

My body and exhaustion were beginning to turn on me, and I hesitated briefly before I staggered over to the stone seat. I took another drink of water, and the plastic bottle crinkled loudly in my grip. "Why are you being nice to me?"

"I have a lot to explain, but the important thing is that it wasn't me, Tensley. I had no idea what happened until the next morning when I saw you. I realize the timing is shit, but it's been three years, and I might not have another chance to tell you the truth. I need to make this right." Sincerity flashed in his eyes.

My anger simmered below the surface while I chewed on his

words. *Is he for real?* "That shit doesn't fly with me. Chloe never made a move without you." Thick tension filled the space between us. "I'm too tired to have this conversation, and my only concern is my best friend, Benji. So maybe we can deal with it another time."

Layne nodded. "Can I sit next to you?"

I scooted over without a word. He'd saved Benji and me tonight, so the least I could do was let him sit down. Fear swirled inside me, causing my chest to ache. Benji had to be all right.

"What did you tell the police?" I asked, not looking at him.

"From what I saw, two men were beating Benji, and the other guy was attempting to rape you. You put up one hell of a fight, by the way." He attempted a smile, but apparently the night's situation was weighing heavily on him as well.

"I've had a lot of practice."

6

Layne's brows knitted together in confusion.

"A lot of foster families come with horny, drunk men. Not all of them, but the majority of the ones I was in. They felt as though they were granted access to my bed when the system placed me in their homes."

"Jesus. Did you tell anyone?" Layne's shoulders squared. I'd rattled him.

I laughed quietly then repositioned my body on the bench so I could look at him. "No one cared. If I reported it, I would have been perceived as the troublemaker. I would have been placed into another home, maybe worse than the one I was in."

"That's not okay, Tensley. That's never okay." He shook his head in disgust. "And you had to deal with shit at school too. You probably never felt safe." Regret danced across his face. "I'm so sorry for everything that happened."

I snapped, my temper rolling to a boil like a volcano ready to erupt. "Why would *you* apologize? I thought you weren't behind it?"

"I wasn't. I had no clue. But the moment I saw you at school that morning, I knew who was responsible."

I jumped off the bench and paced back and forth in the small space. "Why didn't you stop it from happening? And if it weren't for you, Chloe wouldn't have found me!" My voice echoed through the area, but I didn't care. I finally had an audience with Layne, and I wasn't going to hold back.

"I know." Guilt clung to his words. "I did tell her I saw you sneaking out of the janitor's closet. After you left, I opened the door and saw a sleeping bag and your backpack. I realized you'd been living at the school, and I told Chloe."

I squeezed the water bottle, crunching it in my fist. "Okay, fine. I guess we're having this conversation after all. So let's do this, Layne. Right fucking now. You say you didn't have anything to do with it, but you just stated you ratted out the only safe place I had to live. So tell me, goddammit. Stop bullshitting me and tell me the truth." I marched up to him and bent over until my face was so close to his that our noses nearly touched. Then I straightened and tapped my boot against the cement. "I'm all ears, so spit it out." I was seething. Could he really not understand that he'd caused the epic show? Chloe had hated me for no other reason than breathing the same air she did. She'd put mean girls to shame, and once she'd had access to me, she took advantage of it. My skin crawled as the memories assaulted me.

Layne stood and shoved his hands in his front pockets. "Why were you living in the janitor's closet? And for how long?" His voice was haunted, and I wondered what was behind it.

"My last foster dad was a disgusting pig. He had crawled into my bed for the last time. I was finished. The school was the only safe place I could think of to hide but not call attention to myself. If I attended classes, there was no reason the teachers would think there was anything wrong. Plus my foster parents would continue to receive a check. They wouldn't report me missing or they'd risk losing the money. I found the old janitor's closet our senior year, so I knew I had an option. I showered in the girls' locker room and robbed the vending machine at night. I was doing well until …" My eyes narrowed, shooting venomous darts at him.

His shoulders slumped. "I had no idea."

"Of course you didn't. Your life was perfect. You never wondered if you were going to eat that day or if you were able to wear clean clothes. Layne Garrison was the school's track and swim star. The girls loved you, and the teachers and parents thought you could do no wrong. You even dated the most popular girl in school. Why would it have even crossed your mind that another human being was going through hell?" I whirled on my heel and rubbed my temples, my pulse kicking into overdrive. Placing my hands on my hips, I faced him again. "Do you want to know what your girlfriend and her cronies did to me? What you instigated when you gave away my hiding place?"

Layne's jaw tensed, but he showed some guts and nodded.

"We were only days away from graduation, and I stupidly thought I was going to make it without any major issues. The first thing that I had planned … I was going to change my name and leave Arkansas. All I wanted was to fit in and be accepted, and the only way I knew how to do it was to start over. Cut my past off like a cancerous skin growth."

"That's why you came to Washington?"

"Yeah, and I gave myself a different name. No one knows me by Victoria. When I left Little Rock, I left her behind." I took another drink of water. My throat was tight at the thought of speaking the horror out loud. "It was after seven that night, and I was headed to the shower in the girls' locker room. When I rounded the corner, Chloe was waiting for me. She wasn't surprised to see me, and I immediately knew in my heart you'd betrayed me. Before I could take off in the opposite direction, a foul-smelling cloth covered my nose. I don't remember anything after that. Only when … I woke up." I squeezed my eyes closed, unwilling to allow the tears to fall in front of him.

"When I parked the car that morning and saw you, it horrified me. I'd never witnessed anything like it. And how a human being could do something like that to another ..." His jaw clenched. "The teachers were already with you, and I hurried into the school building to find Chloe. When I did, she was with a group of girls, laughing about what they'd done. I grabbed her arm and reamed her right in front of her shitty friends. I told her how disgusted I was, then I broke up with her," he admitted, shoving his hands in his pockets.

My brows shot up, and shock traveled through my entire being. "You broke up with her?"

"Yeah. I couldn't associate with anyone so coldhearted and ruthless." He scrubbed his face with his hands and exhaled a heavy breath. "Our relationship was over before she did that to you; I just didn't want to deal with her dramatics until after graduation."

I rubbed my arms, realizing I was still wearing his jacket. "I didn't even know the extent of what she'd done until they removed me from the flagpole." My voice almost sounded foreign to my own ears. Hearing Layne finally speak about what had happened ... It was almost as if I were reliving it all over again. But I needed to know the truth.

Pinching the bridge of my nose in order to hold on to any semblance of sanity, I inhaled slowly, filling my lungs with the fresh evening air. "I woke up hours before anyone found me. I can't explain to you the terror that consumed me when I was unable to move. My heart was pounding so hard that I thought it would betray me. It would have been a blessing if it had." My voice shook as I recalled the trauma. "As you saw, my mouth was taped closed, and I was duct-taped to the flagpole that stood at the entrance to our high school. It was then that I realized Chloe hadn't acted alone. There was no way one girl could have held me up and ran the tape around me."

"Tensley." Layne's gentle tone did little to calm my nerves. He placed a hand on my shoulder, but I shrugged it off.

"When the teachers broke me free, I was too weak to stand, but it didn't escape me that I was completely naked." A hard, clipped laugh rushed out of me. "I stood naked in front of two male teachers. Thank God they'd cleared out the rest of the students. They covered me with a blanket as the cops showed up. Mrs. Glendale walked me to the locker room, and when I passed the mirror ..." I lost the battle, and tears streamed down my face. "They'd chopped off my hair, and all that was left was short, jagged pieces jutting out of my head. Bitch was painted in red across my forehead." I angrily swiped at the tears that fell. "They stripped me of my clothes, hair, and dignity, Layne. The entire school saw me! I fucking hate you for telling her where I was hiding." Spittle flew out of my mouth, and I sank to my knees as my sobs wrecked me.

A strong arm encompassed me as Layne sat next to me on the ground.

"They got away with it too. A cousin of one of the girls was an attorney, and all they had to do was community service. What the fuck kind of sentence was that?" I continued to cry into my hands, furious with myself for showing my vulnerability to him, but it was the first time I'd spoken about the incident since it happened.

"I had no idea. Please, you have to believe me. I know you had a tough time at home, but you and I had classes together. Hell, we were study partners in tenth-grade biology. I realize we weren't friends, but I never wanted you to get hurt. When I mentioned to Chloe that I thought you were living in the janitor's closet, it wasn't because I was trying to be mean. I was concerned, and I asked her because I wanted to know if her dad could help you find a better place to live. I was worried."

My cries settled down, and I pulled away from him. "What?" That was the opposite of what I'd expected to hear.

He leaned his head back and stared up at the star-filled sky. "I never meant to cause problems for you. I actually tried to help. No one lives at school, hiding, unless it's super shitty at home."

I sat up, surveying him. He seemed sincere, but there was no way to know if he was lying to me.

Layne's arm slipped away, and I leaned against the cement bench, even though my back screamed in protest. Maybe I was more banged up than I thought.

"I realize you have no reason to forgive me, but I'd like to try to make it up to you. Let me help while Benji is recovering. Give me a chance, Tensley." His blue eyes pleaded with me, but somewhere deep inside my soul, I had a feeling I wasn't the only person he was trying to make amends with.

Unable to answer him right away, I mentally reviewed what had just occurred between us. Had I been blaming him when he hadn't had anything to do with what had happened? *Maybe. Maybe not.* Or maybe something had changed him. If I understood anything, it was leaving my past behind and creating something better, or at least new.

"You're on probation." I looked at him, gauging his reaction to my comment, but it didn't seem to faze him. "Benji is my best friend, Layne. You have no idea how much I love him or what I would do for him. What happened to him tonight was a hate crime, and I hope those motherfuckers go down, but I might need a ride to the hospital some ... or someone to talk to about shit. Since you were there and witnessed it—"

"Anything you need," he interrupted.

My pulse did a double take, and my walls crumbled a little while he stared at me. How had everything changed in an evening? With one brutal beating and a near rape, my world as I knew it had turned on its axis.

"We should go back in and see if there's any update, not to mention you're shivering." Layne stood, then held out his hand to me.

I placed mine in his and allowed him to help me stand. "I hurt," I admitted.

"I know. You put up a hell of a fight tonight. Would you let a doctor look at you?"

Placing my fingers over the sharp pain in my side, I nodded. Layne continued to hold my hand as he guided me back into the emergency room and directly to the front desk.

"Excuse me, she needs to be seen. She was in the same attack as Benji Parker," Layne said, keeping his focus on me.

"Of course," the nurse said. "Just fill out this information and have a seat in the waiting area. We will tend to—"

"Tensley!" Layne scrambled to catch me as I teetered.

Black dots blurred my vision as I sank to my knees and crumbled to the floor, grabbing Layne's arm.

"Hang on. They're coming," Layne whispered.

I moaned as I was lifted onto a gurney.

Marilyn and Michael appeared next to me, concern flickering across their faces. "Oh, honey. You're hurt, and I didn't realize it. It's going to be okay," Marilyn assured me as she clasped my hand. "We're right here with you while they take you for an ultrasound."

Bright lights burned my eyes as I was hurried in for an test.

"We'll be here waiting," Michael promised.

A sudden sharp pain speared my lower right side. I gritted my teeth, bound and determined not to scream. I moved my head and peered behind me to find Marilyn, Michael, and Layne standing at the end of the hall, watching me with worry etched deeply into their expressions.

I WAS LOOPY AS HELL. A silly smile eased across my face when my wobbly focus landed on Marilyn. "How's Benji?" I croaked, my throat raw and parched from the anesthesia.

"Hang on." Marilyn moved over but continued to hold my hand.

"How's my patient feeling? I'm Lily, and I'm here to take care of you tonight." A young nurse dressed in hot-pink scrubs approached my bed. "Are you nauseous, hon?"

I started to shake my head, then thought better of it. Surgery had left me woozy.

She smoothed a loose curl away from her face and smiled. "Do you remember why you're here?"

"The doctor said I had appendicitis," I replied.

"Yup. It ruptured this evening. I suspect your attack pushed it over the edge."

I didn't respond. Instead, I worked on pushing back the wave of nausea.

"Uh-oh." Lily snatched up a little bag and shoved it in my face seconds before I vomited.

"Shit." I grabbed my right side as pain erupted. "Shit."

"Let me take that for you." The nurse took the used barf bag and tossed it in the biohazard container.

I grimaced as my eyes landed on Layne. *He stayed?* Leaning into the pillow, I wiped my mouth with the back of my hand. "Benji?"

"He's out of surgery," Marilyn said, stepping up to the side of my bed and patting my arm. Her fingers were freezing cold. "Michael is with him in ICU."

"ICU?" My forehead creased in confusion. Apparently the anesthesia had hit me harder than I thought.

"He had internal bleeding and, well, we're waiting to talk to the doctors. They're monitoring him closely. The next twenty-four hours are critical." Tears silently slipped down Marilyn's cheeks as she spoke.

"No. No. No." I tossed the covers off me and attempted to sit up. "I need to see him."

The nurse gently pressed my shoulder, forcing me back in

bed. "Nope. No, ma'am. You're to rest right now." I was too weak to fight her.

"I'm going to join Michael now that you're awake, but Layne offered to stay with you. I'll send word the second anything changes," Marilyn promised.

"What about the men they arrested? Have they been charged?" I asked.

"They're investigating what happened, but we don't know what charges they'll face yet." Marilyn's expression fell. "Apparently they were in the comedy club and saw Benji and Thomas together."

"That's so messed up." I took a deep breath before I asked the next question. "Are they waiting to see if Benji lives or not?" I snapped my eyes closed, trying to block out the nightmare. I couldn't lose Benji. Marilyn and Michael couldn't lose their son due to something as awful as a stupid hate crime. Faggot was such a hateful word, and it shouldn't be used to describe anyone, especially Benji. He was a beautiful man with a heart and soul that people loved. He was a human being who had as much right to live in this world as anyone else.

I shook my head, guilt overwhelming me. "I should have told him no when he said he'd park in the alley. It wasn't far from the parking lot, and I didn't think it was a big deal. I'm sorry, Marilyn. If I'd only said no." My shoulders shook with my sobs, and I swore a blue streak while I grabbed my side.

She sat down gently on the edge of my bed and allowed me to cry. Her own tears flowed freely. "In no way did you make those men hurt you and Benji. This isn't your fault. It's not Benji's either."

"He's going to make it. Dammit, he's strong and hardheaded. He'll fly those bastards the finger and get out of his bed tomorrow." I willed all my energy and strength to Benji. He would need it to recover. My injuries were superficial compared to what he'd already gone through, not to mention what waited for him ahead.

I would be walking within a few hours, but Benji might still be in ICU ... or worse.

"I agree. He's going to be all right." Marilyn fished a tissue out of her purse and dabbed her eyes. "I hate to leave you, but I need to check on Benji." She leaned over and hugged me.

Avery darted into my room at that moment. "What the hell happened?"

"A lot," Layne said from the corner of the room. He'd remained silent until that point.

"What are *you* doing here? I know why Tensley is here." Her eyes narrowed, and her clenched fists landed on her hips. "But you have some explaining to do."

Layne stood, exhaustion flickering in his face. "I'll tell you everything I know."

"Avery, you and Tensley are in good hands. He saved them both. Give him a chance." Marilyn patted Avery's arm, then left the room.

"You saved her?" Disbelief colored Avery's words.

"Yeah." I motioned to a chair. "You might want to sit down for this one."

She pulled a seat toward my bed, the legs noisily scraping the floor, and sat next to me. Gripping my hand in hers, she glared at Layne. "I'm all ears."

I almost felt sorry for Layne ... almost.

7

I had no idea what time I'd finally drifted off to sleep. With the pain medication, I'd probably crashed out before Avery and Layne.

The bright Spokane sunshine penetrated the windows in my hospital room. I rolled my head on my pillow to face the opposite direction and spotted the activity around the nurses' station. It was then that I saw Layne slouched in his chair, his hand propping up his head, sound asleep. I raised my arm to rub my eyes, but it wouldn't move. Squinting against the light, I noticed Avery. She'd leaned over my bed, placed her head on a small available spot on the mattress, and had fallen asleep holding my hand. Suddenly overwhelmed with emotion, I looked away. I welcomed that moment with no one else awake. Things had moved so fast the night before, I'd not been able to process it all very well.

"Hey," a deep, gruff voice said quietly. "How are you feeling?" Layne stood and stretched, making a twisted and hilarious face. "Man, that felt good." He flashed me a sleepy smile.

Although he'd slept in a hospital chair, he looked yummy. I recalled the first thing ... no, the second thing I'd noticed about him, next to his eyes: his lips. They were full, soft, and kissable. Shit, the pain meds were really fucking with me.

"Didn't anyone miss you last night?" I finally asked.

"Nope. I called my uncle when I realized I wouldn't be home."

"*That's* who you're staying with?" It wasn't any of my business, but we were trying to move forward.

"Yeah. Last year, he told me to apply to the university and said I could live with him. You weren't the only one looking for a fresh start." He smoothed his hair back, then stifled a yawn.

"Good God almighty," Avery said, slowly lifting her head off my bed.

"Your neck hurt?" I asked, imagining the pain she was in.

"Yeah, but it's nowhere near what you're feeling." Avery wiped a smidge of drool from the corner of her mouth.

"Mmm, it's not bad right now, but it's probably because of the pills they gave me." I giggled a little, but I had no clue why. "Was there any update on Benji after I fell asleep?" My gaze bounced between Layne and Avery. I didn't want anyone sugarcoating shit because I'd had surgery. I was fine.

"Marilyn stopped by to let us know there hadn't been any real changes, but he made it through the night." Layne took my hand and gave it a gentle squeeze. "That's great news, Ten."

Deliberately ignoring the little spark from his touch, I stared at our hands. It was the first time I noticed how red and bruised his knuckles were from fighting our attackers.

"It's excellent news," Avery added. "I'm going to find some coffee downstairs. Can I grab you one, Layne? I mean, do you drink coffee? Normally, I know these things before I spend the night with a guy, but I wasn't expecting you to be here."

Boom! The Avery slam. Even though we'd gone through hell and Layne had stuck by me, Avery wouldn't easily forget how scared I'd been the first evening I saw him. I would still have been terrified of him if Benji and I hadn't been attacked. It was crazy how a crisis brought people together. Plus I suspected Layne was telling me the truth and hadn't been involved in my flagpole incident. I nearly scoffed out loud. Incident definitely wasn't the right word for it.

Layne pulled out his wallet and handed her a ten and a five. "If there's a Starbucks or Dutch Brother's in the food court, I'd love a pumpkin spice latte. A venti." He held his hands apart to emphasize the large size.

She smirked at him but took the money.

"I want one!" I cried, hoping she would have a little pity on me and buy me at least a small one.

"You're probably going to have Jell-O for breakfast," Layne said, grinning. "Or maybe even some broth on the side. Yummy hospital food."

Avery snickered, then left the room.

Layne sat down in the chair that Avery had occupied earlier. "Does she know everything? With us?"

"How could she? I just found out last night. I did tell them about high school, and they saw how much you upset me when I spotted you at the bar."

My words were sharper than I'd intended, and I silently apologized to him. Saying sorry wasn't my strong suit, and it was definitely something I would have to work on with him.

Layne nodded in understanding, his focus never leaving my face.

"Why are you still here? There's nothing keeping you at the hospital." My heart pitter-pattered against my rib cage while I waited for his response.

"You are. Benji is." His eyes bore into mine, and silence descended over us.

"Are you really not the douche I thought you were in high school?" I scratched an imaginary itch on my forehead, preparing for his answer.

A chuckle rumbled through his chest. "I was. I mean, as I explained last night, I had nothing to do with what happened to you, but I still hurt you. I can't imagine how painful it was when I tapped you with the empty glass juice bottles."

I cringed. "What the fuck was that? Like, dude, if you crack a girl on the pubic bone, it's excruciating."

He swallowed hard. "I'm not excusing my behavior at all. I was a stupid, hormonal sophomore. I ..." His voice trailed off.

I leveled my gaze at him. "What?"

A small smile pulled at his mouth. "I had a crush on you."

Startled by his confession, I jerked back, pulling at my surgery site. "Fuck." I gripped the bed railing, my knuckles turning white, while I waited for the pain to subside. Leaning back into my pillow, I rubbed my forehead with the palm of my hand. "I don't think I heard you correctly." My hands dropped to my side, and I turned my head toward him, studying his expression for any sign he was joking.

"It was before Chloe moved to our school. You still smiled. Your hair had grown out over the summer, and it was beautiful. All I wanted to do was touch it, feel it in my fingers. And guys do stupid shit when they're crushing hard."

Thank God he hadn't seen my ratty hair a few years earlier, or he would never say that again. "You pulled my sweats down in front of the entire school! I was absolutely mortified, but at least my T-shirt covered my ass."

"Sorry. I don't know what else to say." A flush dusted his cheeks. "The only way I can convince you I'm not that guy anymore is for you to spend some time with me."

My face heated at the thought. I'd never been social, much less with a guy. Except for Benji.

"I need to explain one more thing. I did something that I still regret to this day." Sadness flickered in his eyes. "I'm not positive, but during a party our junior year, someone mentioned I'd been interested in you ... in front of Chloe." His shoulders slumped. "I might have been the reason she hated you so much. I'm so sorry."

My mouth gaped open. Not only had he been interested in

me, but he'd shared it with some of his friends. A slow-burning fury stirred to life inside me. Chloe was a fucking bitch. Who in her right mind targeted another girl because her boyfriend had been interested in the girl over a year prior? Was she that insecure, or was she the epitome of a cruel person with no conscience?

"I'm not sure how to respond to that right now, but regardless, you didn't force her to put me on the flagpole." My fingers clenched into balls with my words. I needed to process everything. Logically, I realized Layne wasn't behind the brutality, but my heart still hurt and the memories still haunted me.

Avery entered my room, eyeing me to see if I was okay. "Good grief, they were busy downstairs, but lucky for us, they had a Starbucks." Then she handed a large cup to Layne. Inwardly, I gave a sigh of relief that she was back.

Layne stood, allowing Avery to have her chair back, but I didn't miss the regret in his eyes.

Butterflies ran amok in my chest. What was happening? He'd admitted he'd been an ass, had a crush on me in high school, and wanted to spend time with me. My thoughts spun in a million different directions while I watched him sink into his seat.

"Hi, hon," Marilyn said, entering the room. "How are you feeling? I just talked to the doctor, and you get to go home today."

"That's great!" Avery said.

The fear and sadness on Marilyn's face spoke volumes. There was more.

"What is it?" I pulled myself up in the bed, ignoring the pain in my side, and braced myself for what I was about to hear.

Marilyn covered her mouth with her hand. "He's awake, but …" A tear slipped down her cheek. "Benji is paralyzed. He will never walk again."

8

The world halted abruptly, and time no longer seemed to move forward. I reeled from Marilyn's words, and the weight of the implication crashed down on me full force. I grabbed my pillow, covered my face, and released an agonizing cry. Those fuckers would pay. I prayed they would walk free because I would hunt them down and take from them what they had taken from my best friend.

I scooted down in my bed the best I could, refusing to look at anyone while I came undone. Benji deserved better. He had his whole life ahead of him. He was vibrant and full of dreams.

"I'm going to step back out for a bit, but Avery, please call me before she leaves." Marilyn's heels announced her exit, but I didn't move.

The nurse, Lily, entered the room next. "Hi, hon. It's time for your medication."

I held my hand out, refusing to look at her. The pill hit my palm and I gladly popped it. I hoped like hell it would stop all my pain, including the emotional torture, but I knew better.

"The doctor will be in soon to go over your care at home."

Lily patted my shoulder, then her thick-soled shoes squeaked on the floor as she left my room.

"I'm going to run to the house and bring you back some clean clothes," Avery said gently. "Layne said your blouse was ripped." She kissed the top of my head before she left.

I ignored the scrape of the chair as someone sat in it again. Warm fingers covered mine and I swallowed hard, fighting to contain myself from another outburst.

"We don't need to talk, Ten. I just want you to know I'm here if you need me," Layne whispered.

Before I realized it, I gently squeezed his hand. Maybe it was the grief, or maybe I was in shock, but suddenly, having Layne there wasn't so bad.

A FEW HOURS LATER, the doctor visited and provided me with follow-up and wound-care instructions. I would be back to my normal self in a few weeks, physically anyway. After everything Benji had gone through, I would never be the same again. Logically, I knew Benji could have said no about parking in the alley, but I still warred against the guilt inside me. I should have at least given him a good argument.

After Avery returned, she helped me dress in clean clothes while Layne waited outside for me.

"Good thing you've seen my tits before," I muttered while she helped me into my bra. It was crazy how my movement was limited and painful.

"And great tits, might I add." She flashed me a sad smile. "Layne asked me if he could drive you to the house. How do you feel about that?"

I gave a half-shrug. "It's all right."

Avery slipped my shirt over my head and gently pulled it down over my incision. Next, she helped me into my jeans. "I'm glad you're coming home. It will be really empty without Benji." She tugged on her bottom lip with her teeth and tears welled in her eyes.

"I want to see him before I go, but I'm not sure they'll let me since he's in ICU."

A firm rap sounded at the door.

"Come in," I said.

"Hi, Tensley." Marilyn approached and sat on the side of the bed next to me. Layne followed her silently and leaned against the wall, folding his arms over his chest. "Avery and Layne have promised me they'll take good care of you over the next few weeks."

My focus bounced between Layne and Avery. When had they discussed that, and why hadn't I been included? Avery, I understood, but I was surprised Layne was planning on sticking around.

"I don't think you should be alone. This is going to be very difficult for you when you realize Benji isn't coming back to the house with you and Avery."

Shit. It hadn't dawned on me that he wouldn't be sleeping in his bed ... or mine. He would most likely never live with us again. My heart dropped like a lead ball into my stomach at the thought. *How in the world am I going to actually make it without him?* He always made me laugh, kept the night terrors at bay, and was the only reason I had a social life. *Stop. Don't be a brat. This isn't about me—it's about Benji.*

I squared my shoulders and faced Marilyn. "What can I do to help?" It was time for me to grow a pair and give everything I could to my best friend, who had breathed life into me after one of the darkest times I'd ever experienced. Even now, Chloe and her goons haunted me.

A smile pulled at Marilyn's lips. Dark circles were beneath her eyes, and her slumped posture confirmed the level of exhaustion she was battling. "He can't have visitors yet, but he's in and out of consciousness. I suspect he will need to see you after the doctor …" Marilyn's voice trailed off, and she covered her mouth with her hand, inhaling a shaky breath. "When the doctors tell him that he will be confined to a wheelchair for the rest of his life."

I wrapped my arms around her, and we clung to each other in silence.

"Anything he wants. I'll be there every step of the way." I cringed at my choice of verbiage. There would no longer be steps for Benji.

"Don't regret your word choice. We can't tiptoe around his condition. He's strong, and he wouldn't want us to treat him any differently."

I agreed. She was right, and I loved Benji for his strong will. When he was ready, he would meet his new life head-on.

"Do you still have my phone?" Marilyn asked.

"Yeah. It's right there." I nodded toward the little table next to the bed.

"Keep it. I'm going to pick you up another one in a few days. Why don't you give me the broken one, and I'll see if they can possibly pull any pictures and numbers from it. I'll have Michael's on me, so you call or text as often as you want. I'll keep you updated."

"Thank you. It will help to know I can keep in touch. I was a bit worried since my phone broke. Avery, would you please hand me my bag with my old clothes?"

Avery scooped up the bag and brought it to me. My stomach lurched when I remembered my clothes had been taken by the police while I was in surgery. There would be DNA evidence to help convict.

Marilyn stood and I handed her my phone. She bent down, kissed me on top of the head, and smoothed my hair. "I always wanted a daughter." She tilted my chin up with her finger. "The night Benji brought you home to meet us, I knew my prayers had been answered, just in a different way than I'd expected."

Tears clouded my eyes. "You're the first real family I've ever had. I love you too."

"Get some rest." Marilyn turned without another word and left the room.

Clearing my throat, I glanced at Layne and Avery.

"Are you ready?" Layne asked, pushing off the wall. "The nurse is outside with a wheelchair."

"Yeah."

Avery shot me a look, and I nodded. I hadn't changed my mind about Layne giving me a ride to the house.

"I'll be right behind you," Avery said, her words carrying a warning to Layne.

Layne didn't miss a beat as he let the staff know we were ready to leave.

Minutes later, I was greeted by the chilled autumn air. I tipped my nose up, inhaling deeply. It was a welcome change from the stench of illness in the hospital.

Layne pulled the Camry around, and the nurse assisted me into the passenger's seat. Avery's white Nissan beeped from behind us.

"Let's get you home," Layne said, pulling out of the pickup line.

We rode in silence for the first half of the drive, which was fine with me. The trek from the hospital to the car had worn me out.

"I have to get back to my uncle's, but can I stop by tomorrow?" Layne asked, his thumb tapping against the steering wheel.

If I didn't know better, I would think he was nervous. Holding back my giggle, I nodded. "Sure, but only if you show up with Kentucky Fried Chicken. Crispy." I grinned wearily at him. "I'm starving."

"Ten, you can eat. Do you want me to stop by now?"

My face must have lit up like a Christmas tree. "You don't

mind? I'd love a three-piece with two breasts, mashed potatoes, and a biscuit—oh, don't forget the honey—and a Dr Pepper."

A huge grin eased across his face. "So you know how to eat. You're not one of those girls who picks at her food? I bought Chloe a steak dinner one time, spent a hundred dollars, and she ate three bites and refused to take it home. I was so pissed, *I* took it home." His expression immediately fell with the mention of her name. "Sorry. I'm just happy you eat like a normal person."

I was too worn out to give him shit about bringing up Chloe's name. It would most likely happen again. "I never knew how many meals a day I was going to have. Let's just say during the school year, I could count on one most of the time. It stuck with me. I still never miss an opportunity to eat." My mind flickered back to the memory of Chloe knocking my tray out of my hands. Layne had stepped in, breaking up a soon-to-be fight. I hadn't realized it at the time, but he had been taking up for me. My eyes cut to him as he pulled into KFC. "Thank you."

A frown line creased his forehead while he moved up to the order speaker. "For what?"

"The day Chloe knocked my food and tray out of my hands then grabbed my hair, you stopped her from doing anything else. I didn't realize it then, but you actually took my side."

Layne shrugged. "It wasn't enough." He turned his head and focused on the menu options. After he ordered for both of us, we waited in line.

"My purse is in the bag. Just grab some cash for my food. I can't quite reach it without pulling at my stitches."

"I've got it." Layne lifted his ass cheek off the seat and produced his wallet from his back pocket.

"No. I don't want you paying for my food. Really."

"I didn't ask what you wanted." He smirked and pulled forward. "Oh, before I forget, give me Marilyn's phone."

"Wow, I say thank you, and all of a sudden you're seriously bossy." I wrinkled my nose in distaste.

Layne responded with a big laugh and held out his hand.

I huffed and gave him the phone. Then I leaned forward, watching him. "What are you doing?"

"Here's my number. Call or text day or night."

My eyes narrowed at him suspiciously. Although we had bonded a little bit over the attack, I wasn't some weepy, vulnerable girl he could sweet-talk just to get into my pants. If he thought that, he had another think coming.

"Tensley." His voice was low, and I nearly shivered from the goosebumps that pebbled my skin. "You're going to need rides to get to school and to go see Benji. I'm sure Avery has a full schedule, so I'd like to help. Plus, the nights ..." His words trailed off. "The nights are the hardest."

Holy shit. He sounded as though he were speaking from experience, which made me wonder what he wasn't telling me.

He moved forward to the window, paid for the items, and handed the food to me. I held the bag open and took a deep whiff, secretly letting him off the hook from dishing details about his difficult evenings.

I licked my lips in anticipation. "Yummy. Fried goodness."

A broad smile pulled at the corners of his mouth. "Now that I know food makes you smile, which is breathtaking by the way, I'll never show up at your door empty-handed."

I stared at him, dumbfounded. No one had ever called my smile breathtaking.

"Thanks," I mumbled, trying to hide the red flush creeping up my neck and face.

Layne flipped on the radio, and the soft bass of "Bad for You" by Billy Raffoul filled the car.

"Love him!" I nearly squealed. "And his hair." I wiggled my eyebrows, attempting to bring some humor to the ride home. God knew we all needed to laugh. Usually, making everyone laugh was Benji's job, but I'd officially been passed the baton. I could cry at night when I was alone, but when others were around, I vowed I would make Benji proud.

Layne's chuckle filled the car, and my heart lightened for a moment. I sang while he drove, beating my fingers on the dashboard and pretending I was playing my drums.

"The first time I saw you in Washington was at the bar. I was shocked when you stepped up and performed. It was amazing. The paint flew in every direction, and you were covered. I've never seen anything like it. I wanted to talk to you then, but I chickened out. I knew you thought I'd helped Chloe."

A lump formed in my throat. I hoped she wouldn't be in our conversations often. Just the mention of her name brought flashbacks with it. Although I'd not sought therapy, I'd officially been diagnosed with PTSD by my doctor in Spokane. I had been familiar with the term, but people weren't kidding. PTSD could sneak up on someone without any warning, and within seconds, they were no longer in reality. The memories would get so vivid, it was as if I were living the nightmare all over again.

"Is Chloe in Arkansas?" My insides quivered as I waited for an answer that I desperately needed to know. At the same time, I was terrified to hear.

Layne glanced out the side window and cleared his throat. "You don't have to worry about her anymore. I promise."

I nodded, chewing on my lip. Deep in thought, I processed everything he'd said and done since the night of the attack.

"I believe you." I stared at him, taking in all the shit that had happened in the last twenty-four hours. Maybe it was because of the pain pills or the fact that my body had gone through surgery, but something had shifted inside me. That didn't mean I trusted Layne a hundred percent, but I was willing to get to know him. Besides, I'd finally realized I'd had it wrong. Yeah, he'd done some mean shit to me in high school, but even Layne had admitted it wasn't the right way to treat someone, and he'd been a stupid, hormonal guy. Now if he popped my pubic bone with a glass bottle, his face would meet my fist. I almost chuckled at the thought. But when he'd told me he'd broken up with Chloe over what she'd done, I realized I hadn't had all the facts.

"What you've done for Benji and me ... I believe you. I think you're a decent human. And ... I forgive you." My voice barely hovered above a whisper. I cleared my throat as he pulled into the driveway behind Avery. She'd passed us on Division, which worked since Layne could follow her.

Layne turned off the car, released his seat belt, and faced me. My breath stuttered. Maybe he thought I'd said something else. His intense gaze swept over me. "You have no idea what that means to me." With that, he hopped out and hurried to my side to open the door. He extended both hands toward me. When I placed mine in his, electricity zinged through my body, and like a dumbass, I gasped.

A frown furrowed his brow. "You okay?"

"Yup. I just got shocked," I lied. Well, it was close to the truth. But holy shit, I'd never experienced anything like it. It felt as if I were ready to melt right out of my panties with a simple touch.

Layne gently helped me out of the car, and I leaned against him while I found my footing. My focus traveled up his chest and neck, then lingered on his mouth before our eyes locked.

He held me steady while my pulse spiked from his close proximity. Layne pulled me in for a gentle hug. "Thank you, Ten. Sometimes forgiveness is only a whisper of a wish and never a reality."

A light, woodsy scent engaged my senses, and I swayed slightly. I wondered if it was his cologne or bodywash from the day before.

"Sorry. The medicine makes me dizzy." It was the best excuse I had.

"I've got you." His deep and husky voice elicited a new tingling sensation throughout my body.

"Layne?" Avery pointed at him, then to her eyes. "I'm

watching you." She cocked her eyebrow to emphasize her words. "Can you manage to get her inside? If so, I'll unlock the door."

Layne's hold on me loosened. "Is she always like this?" he asked.

"Mm, yes, but you're getting an extra dose because she knows you terrorized me in high school."

Layne's lips pursed. "Got it. At least I understand why." The next thing I knew, he'd scooped me up into his arms, crouched down, grabbed the bag of food from my car seat, and hauled me into the house.

Good God. Southern charm wasn't dead, and I was about to swoon right there. He placed me on the couch, and his attention drifted over me. "I didn't hurt you, did I? I didn't want to take any chances of you falling and popping your stitches."

I stared at him stupidly, unable to articulate any words for at least twenty seconds. "I'm good," I croaked. My stomach growled in protest. "The kitchen is that way." I pointed him in the right direction, knowing full well Avery was in there, and I imagined she was waiting for him. She'd been sharpening her claws since she'd first seen him in my hospital room.

Carefully, I scooted down to the end of the couch and listened. I would give anything to hear the conversation, but I couldn't even catch one word. Avery was fierce if she thought someone was messing with me. If she even suspected he wasn't for real, she would remove his balls and hand them to him before he realized what was happening. I covered my mouth, hiding my snicker. Benji and Avery were definitely the best friends in the world.

9

Nearly five weeks had passed since the attack, and the beginning of November arrived along with the rain. I'd had multiple phone conversations with Benji, but he wouldn't let me visit him at home yet. I begged and pleaded, but he held his ground. My heart snapped in two every time we hung up. A blanket of depression settled over me every night, but instead of fighting it, I allowed it to consume me. I grieved hard. And in the morning, Benji was my reason for getting up and moving forward every day.

He had given me permission to use his room and sleep in his bed. I held my Minion pillow against me, wishing it were him instead. We'd shared a bed all the time anyway, so it wasn't a big deal for me to sleep in his room, but I'd wanted to make sure it was okay with him first. It was a small piece of comfort, and I would hold on to it for as long as I could.

Layne had visited several times and had chauffeured me around over the last month. I'd seen him every day for at least a few hours. Our conversations had bounced from the attack to high school and college. When he'd asked about my parents, I'd redirected the conversation. He'd taken the hint and hadn't brought them up again.

Avery had lightened up on him a little bit, too, but I knew she was watching him. So was I. But every time I took a step back, I only saw kindness and compassion from him, and in my heart, I believed he was doing everything he could to make things right between us. More importantly, he held true to his word and never showed up at my door without food for Avery and me. Even though it seemed my heart was healing from our high school days, I was fully aware I wasn't the only demon in Layne's past. Flickers of grief and regret danced across his face when he thought no one was looking. But I was, and I suspected that whatever he was running from cut him to his very core.

I woke up to a soft pattering against my window. One of the few things I missed in Arkansas was the ongoing days of rain. Although it rained in Spokane, it was usually only for a few hours. If I could, I would run outside and listen for the thunder, inhale the aroma of the fresh water, and allow myself to get lost in the moment while the grass and flowers soaked up every drop. It energized me.

"Hey," Avery said, knocking on Benji's door. "How ya feeling?"

"Fine." I turned away from the window and smiled. "I'm cleared for duty, ma'am. Doc said I'm good to go." I saluted her and smirked. I grabbed my new phone off the bed and tucked it in the back pocket of my jeans. Marilyn had dropped it off last week, and I was surprised at how happy I was to have it. I'd excused myself and deleted all the calls and texts I'd had with Benji and Layne before I returned her phone. There wasn't anything inappropriate, but it made me feel better.

Avery leaned against the doorframe, watching me. "Plans tonight with Layne?"

"Nope. He's helping his uncle with whatever, and I need to spend some time at the library, catching up on classwork. What about you?"

Avery chewed on her thumbnail. Uh-oh. Something was up.

"I know it's only been a few weeks, but I was wondering how you'd feel if Justin moved in and shared the expenses."

She might as well have slapped me. "What's the rush?" My tone was clipped, and she knew she'd approached the topic too fast. "Marilyn and Michael have offered to pay our rent through the school year so we could focus on work and studies."

"I want him here," she replied softly. "I love him, and we want to live together. No matter how much I wish I could turn back time, Benji isn't coming back, hon. If we can get a new roomie, then it relieves Benji's parents of the financial responsibility too. I mean, I know they have a lot of money, but I want to do the right thing for everyone. It sucks, and I'm sorry."

Her words churned in my stomach like curdled milk. "I'm fucking well aware of that, but it doesn't mean we have to rent out his room within a matter of weeks like he doesn't mean anything to us!"

She crossed her arms over her chest. "That's not what I meant. You've got to move on. He's not coming back."

Move on? Move on from the night my best friend lost his life as he'd always known it?

I stormed past her, anger pouring out of me. She needed to stay the fuck away. I snatched up my backpack near the front door, hefted it up onto my shoulder, and marched outside with no damned coat. I whirled around, burst back into the living room, and grabbed the necessary items to help me fend off the winter air and rain. Then I hoofed it to school, swearing under my breath the entire way, but the best thing for me at the moment was a long walk to help me calm down.

THE DAY CREPT by slower than … hell, I didn't even know what. My anger had continued to simmer over Avery's suggestion that

Justin move in. I assumed they would want Benji's room, and possibly mine to store his belongings in. That would force me into the second largest one, and my rent would increase. Even though I had some time to save, I couldn't afford the additional cost.

I glanced at my iPhone and saw that it was almost five. The sun had descended an hour ago. I reluctantly closed my English lit book, ran my hands through my hair, and groaned quietly. There was no way I could hide from Avery for long. My stomach growled in agreement.

I slipped my coat on, then stuffed my belongings in my backpack. I used it for a few bicep curls then tossed it over one shoulder. My strength was back to normal after my surgery. Depending on other people had sucked. It wasn't my thing. I'd taken care of myself for years.

I descended the stairs of the library and meandered through the main floor. A feeling of dread tugged at me. I didn't want to talk to Avery about the roommate situation yet. I needed some time. I needed to be able to see Benji before I gave up his room. At the moment, it seemed that was all I had left of him to hold on to.

I pushed on the front door and stepped outside into the darkness. *Shit.* A chill crept up my spine as I recalled the attack. I hadn't been out at night alone since then. My mind immediately relived the feel of the man's hand clamped over my mouth. I squeezed my eyes closed, then swallowed the fear down. I'd never been afraid of the dark before, and I would be damned if I was going to lose something else I loved. I'd cherished the night hours since I was old enough to slip out the window without being detected.

I identified the streetlights along the sidewalk and turned toward home. I glanced over my shoulder at the library, which grew smaller and smaller. With each step, my anxiety continued to climb. I needed to call an Uber. There was no way I would make it to the house in such a state. I hustled back to a large oak tree near a light and took cover. The rain had started again, and I hurried to order my ride. A flash of lightning illuminated the sky, blinding me temporarily, and a downpour followed it. *Shit.* I would be soaked in no time. I swore and glanced at my phone. I had another five minutes before my ride showed up.

A loud wail broke through the sound of the pouring rain, and I froze. *What the hell?* Another less intense flash of lightning lit up the sky, allowing me to see a hundred yards in front of me. My eyes popped open. Someone was standing there in the pouring rain. *Are they hurt?* Fuck it. I slipped my arms through the straps of my backpack and hauled ass in the person's direction. An agonizing cry filled my ears as I grew closer.

"Hey, hey," I said, approaching from the side. My sneakers squished through puddles of water with every step. I dropped my heavy backpack, allowing it to fall to the saturated ground. Squinting through the rain, I was finally able to identify a man with a bottle in his hand. He'd sunk to his knees, opened his arms, and the most broken and painful cries ripped from his throat. His agony speared me.

"Sir?" I asked, approaching cautiously, but he didn't acknowledge me. Another wail rang into the night, and as I walked in front of him, my heart splintered. I'd never been touched by such raw and deep emotion, and it was shaking me to the depths of my being.

The man crumpled in on himself, sobbing. I had to do something. He needed help. I reached out and tapped his shoulder then jumped back. His head snapped up. Streams of water poured down his cheeks, and his eyes were full of anguish as they landed on me. My brain recognized Layne, but he wasn't himself. Not even close. This wasn't the man who I'd spent so much time with over the last few weeks.

"You're here." His voice was ragged from his cries.

I spotted my chance. "I'm here. Take my hand." I held it out to him, shivering from his emotional overload.

Layne dropped the bottle placed a palm on the ground, and staggered to an upright standing position. "You're here." He swept his drenched hair off his forehead and pinned me with the most intense gaze I'd ever seen. I wasn't sure if I should be afraid, but it was apparent he needed someone.

In two long strides, he closed the gap between us. His breath didn't reek as much as I'd anticipated, which made me think he was drinking vodka.

"I'm so glad you're here." His hand gently caressed my cheek while the other one slipped around my waist, and he pulled me flush against him. To my surprise, the length of him pressed through his jeans and into my stomach.

The heat of his body seared me, and I fought the desire he'd just ignited inside me. No way could something physical happen between us, not like this.

"You're so beautiful," he said, utterly oblivious to the pouring rain and thunder.

A little whimper escaped me when his hot mouth brushed the corner of mine.

"Please don't leave. I need you," he whispered, his breath tickling the sensitive place on my neck.

"Layne." I tried to break the spell he had me under, but it wasn't working.

"Shhh," he groaned at the base of his throat before his lips crashed down on mine.

All logic rushed out of my brain as his mouth took mine. My knees wobbled as he cupped my cheeks, and his kiss intensified, lighting my soul on fire. Layne had just rocked my world, but he had no idea.

His lips parted, and every fiber of my body melted as his tongue caressed mine. Layne pulled away and leaned his forehead against mine. My breaths came in short gasps while we stood clinging to each other in the pouring rain.

"I'm so sorry." He kissed me again, and every wall inside me crumbled. This man had undone me with one kiss.

Layne stepped away and dropped his hands to his sides. Then he ripped my heart out and stomped on it with his next words. "Chloe, please forgive me."

10

I'd never experienced anger so fierce that I bordered on the edge of blacking out. But at the moment, I was clinging to any shred of sanity I could. *Chloe?* He was so drunk, he thought I was Chloe? He'd kissed me like that, thinking I was that hateful bitch?

"Fuck you!" I screamed. Fuck him for making me feel. Fuck him for making me want him. Fuck him for making me think he was a good guy.

Headlights appeared in the parking lot, and a horn honked. My Uber was there. Shit, I'd almost forgotten. I grabbed my backpack off the soggy lawn and glared at Layne. "Stay away from me, Layne Garrison!"

"No, wait. I never meant to lose Nicole. She was so small, so tiny."

My anger screeched to a halt. *Who the hell is Nicole?* I stared at him, wondering if his secrets were about to spill out of him like a geyser.

"What happened to Nicole, Layne?" I took a step toward him, ignoring the blare of the car horn in the parking lot behind me.

He shook his head, then grabbed clumps of his hair with both hands and tugged as if it would relieve some of the pressure that was building inside him.

I uncurled his fingers, took his hand, and held it between mine. "What did you not mean to do? It's okay. You can tell me."

"Chloe, I'm so sorry." He squeezed his eyes closed as though he could snap out of the pain.

My teeth ground together with the mention of Chloe's name, but I forced myself to stay focused. He was flipping back and forth between the past and the present. The alcohol had done a major number on his head, and he was shit-faced, but something was torturing him. I wanted to know what it was so I could throw it in his face when he was sober. I wanted to hurt him as much as he'd just hurt me.

A cry muffled his next words. "When the tornado siren went off, I thought you were next to me. Since I had Nicole, I ran across the yard toward the house. She was so tiny, and I was terrified I'd smother her if I held her too close to my chest." Layne sank to his knees, and his eyes pleaded with me for relief from the inner torment.

I knelt with him. "Why was she so little?" I asked, a lump growing in my throat.

"She had just turned three months old, and Chloe brought her over in a new pink dress. She was so beautiful, so small. I never knew I could love someone so much until I held her for the first time. When her tiny fingers grasped mine. ..."

Please don't say it. Jesus, please don't say the words I think you're going to.

"I hesitated before going into the house, and when I glanced behind me, you were gone. At the time, I wasn't sure if you'd found a closer hiding place or if ... The tornado was picking up shit left and right. Cars, lawn chairs, people. My only thought was keeping Nicole safe. She had her entire life ahead of her, and she was my daughter. I would protect her with everything I had."

Tears mixed with the rain that streamed down my face.

"I made it into the house, but when the roof was torn off"—Layne doubled over, clutching his stomach and sobbing—"she was ripped away from me. I lost my baby girl."

His words stabbed me in the heart. I jerked him forward, flung my arms around his neck, and pulled him to me. Our sobs were muffled against the thunder as we cried together. No way would I ever throw that in his face. *His baby.* Chloe was dead too. I didn't understand how horrible shit like that could happen. An intense ache filled my chest while I tried to imagine what Layne was going through. My life had been nearly destroyed because my parents hadn't wanted me, and Layne's had been shattered because all he wanted was his daughter.

After another minute, Layne's body relaxed.

I pulled away and placed my hands on the sides of his face. "Let's get you home." I kissed his forehead and stood.

Once he was on his feet, I draped his arm around my shoulders, picked up my backpack again, and headed toward the impatient Uber driver.

After some careful persuasion, I coerced Layne into the back seat with me. At least he'd stopped calling me Chloe.

"What's your address?" the driver asked as his dark eyes met mine in the rearview mirror.

"Vilonia. Vilonia, Arkansas." Layne's words were slurred, and I suspected he would pass out soon.

Then his words hit me. *Shit. It was* that *tornado?* It had leveled the town, taking fifteen people with it. I had no idea he'd been involved or that Chloe had lost her life.

"Where to?" the driver asked, tapping the dashboard forcefully. He was irritated, and I didn't blame him. We were soaking wet in his back seat and had made him wait.

I gave him my address while Layne laid his head on my shoulder. It looked like I would have company that night after all, just not in the way I'd expected.

Chewing my bottom lip, I could almost feel Layne's mouth on

mine. My body tingled, but then I remembered it wasn't me he was kissing. It was *her*.

I took a deep breath. I was relieved that Chloe could no longer hurt me. *Does that make me a horrible person?* What she did to me was evil. People didn't come back from evil. But maybe she'd changed after she had a baby. *Layne's baby.*

The Uber driver made it to my house in record time. I tossed a five-dollar bill onto the front passenger's seat for an extra tip and thanked him for waiting.

Somehow, I managed to haul Layne into the house and then to my bedroom.

He moaned as I flopped him onto my bed. My dark-green comforter bunched underneath him, and I was grateful he hadn't landed on my Minion pillow. It would have gotten soaked. His jeans were stuck to his thighs, but it felt wrong to remove them. After pulling off his shoes and socks, I stood at the footboard and stared at him. Even in his drunken state, he was beautiful. His shirt was plastered to his washboard abs and muscular biceps. His full lips gaped open slightly, and a soft snore filled the room. I slapped my hands over my face and chastised myself. The guy was much worse off than I'd thought, which meant he was off-limits.

The memory of his dick pressed against me sent blissful shivers through me. I'd had sex plenty of times but never because I loved someone, never because I wanted to connect on a deep level and give a guy everything I had to offer. A lump formed in my throat. The last few weeks with Layne had been good. Different. He had continuously put me first, and I didn't know how to manage that. In the back of my mind, I kept wondering what he wanted from me. At the same time, I wanted to backpedal from our new friendship like a crazed motherfucker. But I was pulled to him like he was a strong magnet, and I was unable to fight it.

"Fuck," I muttered. "Layne, I at least need to get your shirt off you." I walked to the edge of my bed and attempted to pull him up to a seated position, but he was passed out cold. His upper body refused to cooperate with me. He was too heavy for me to lift on my own. I rolled my eyes. *Dammit.* I needed help.

I stepped into the hallway and knocked on Avery's bedroom door. It cracked open slightly, and one eye peeked out at me. "What?" she asked, her tone leaning toward the unfriendly side.

"I need your help. Layne is in my bedroom."

That did it. She opened the door and stood there, gawking at me as if I'd grown fish scales all over my body.

"What? Did you—"

I held up my hands, halting the rapid questions. "He's passed out drunk." I shook my head, attempting to collect the right words, but they were escaping my overloaded brain. "I'll fill you in later, but I need to get him out of his wet clothes."

Avery darted around me and to my bedroom door. "Ugh, I sorta hate you because your room is so impeccably spotless. But good God, he's delicious."

"Avery!" I chided. "He ... Just help me." I brushed past her and to the foot of my bed. "I don't know what to do about his jeans. I mean, what if we're able to tug them off, and he doesn't wear underwear? Then he's just flashed us, and it's something else to be humiliated about tomorrow."

Avery nearly fell over giggling. I placed my hands on my hips and faced her. "What the hell is so funny? If someone took my pants off ... Well, flashing my twat to the world isn't my idea of fun. I'm trying to be helpful but respectful."

"He could catch pneumonia and also ruin your bed mattress. Off with those wet clothes. Like, seriously, Ten. I know you two are deep diving into each other, but we're talking about his health right now."

I covered my eyes and took a slow, steady breath. "Let's do it."

There was absolutely nothing funny about getting a drunk guy out of his clothes, but Avery and I broke into a fit of giggles every time his shirt got stuck. Layne ended up in some awkward positions, but I kept reminding myself that he could get sick. I didn't want that for him. He'd gone through enough shit.

Avery stood at the foot of the bed, eyeing a shirtless Layne. "Are you ready?"

"Yeah. I guess so."

"What if he has, like, the tiniest peen we've ever seen? On the plus side, at least you know to look elsewhere to get laid." Avery lifted an eyebrow at me like her advice was the best thing ever.

"Averrrreeee." The girl just didn't know when to quit. I stared at Layne, who was still passed out cold. I suspected he'd downed the fifth of vodka and would be out until sometime tomorrow. *Fuck.* Well, this was it. I was about to find out Layne's intimate choices: free balling or not.

Avery grabbed one pant leg, and I grabbed the other.

"One. Two. Three." I tugged with all my might while Avery grunted as we worked to free his leg of the wet fabric.

I released his jeans, which we'd only managed to pull down a couple of inches. "Shit. Like, his pubes are right there, and in no way has he given us permission to look. This is wrong."

Avery held on to his clothes as she frowned at me. "How are you going to feel if he gets pneumonia and you could have stopped it? It's all for the highest good."

"What? Are you speaking hippie mojo now?" I shook my head, my eyes returning to the happy trail and dark hair that hovered above the waistband of Layne's jeans. *Keep it together, girl.* And I tried, but all of his glory was about to be exposed. The funny thing was that I had never given a rat's ass about some guy's junk before. But not only had I begun to forgive Layne ... Fuck, I couldn't even begin to finish the thought.

Avery's expression flashed with mischievousness. "I'll give you a crisp one-hundred-dollar bill if you pull his pants off."

"Umm, hello. Hell yeah!" I grabbed the hem of his pants and yanked with all my might. With my eyes closed.

"Good God Almighty," Avery whispered. "If I hear you screaming his name, I'll know why."

I cracked one eye open. "Shit." Although I'd felt him through his jeans, I wasn't prepared for what I was seeing. He was huge. "No wonder Chloe stayed with him," I mumbled under my breath.

"What? Who's Chloe? Girl, you've got some explaining to do." She gathered his wet clothes and winked at me. "I'd go for it." Then she left the room.

I gawked for a few seconds longer, then hurried to cover him up. Guilt washed over me. I hoped he would understand I was trying to help him when he woke up naked in my bed. At the same time, there was no way in hell I would forget what I'd seen.

My phone buzzed in my pocket, pulling me back to reality. I smiled as I tapped the green answer button. "O.M.G., you'll never believe whose cock I just saw right now," I blurted.

Benji's laugh sent me into a fit of giggles.

"I wish you were here," I said. A slow ache spread through my chest. If Benji were home with me, none of this would have happened, and I wouldn't feel like a total perv for stripping Layne.

"Please tell me all about the cock, girl."

"Are you sure? There's a lot of baggage with this big dick."

Benji's laugh traveled through the phone, and my heart overflowed with so much love, I thought it would burst. I missed him so badly, but hearing him happy, even for a moment, meant everything to me.

"Who is this peen attached to, babe?"

Although his tone was joking, I heard the undercurrent. If I listened carefully, I could hear the truth he was sharing with me. Benji was pretending to be all right, but he wasn't. And neither was I.

"Come home," I whispered into the phone, sinking onto the edge of my bed, no longer aware of Layne.

"I'll be better soon, Ten. Don't give up on me."

"I'm so sorry. I should have stopped you from parking in the alley." My hand flew over my mouth in order to muffle my cry. That wouldn't help him any.

Benji blew out a big breath. "No, goddammit. You're my best friend. I don't need apologies. I need you to help me live again."

My lips pursed. Benji should be there with me, helping me manage the Layne situation.

"I have someone in my bed," I admitted, smiling. "But it's not what you think."

"Are you shitting me?" Benji gave a playful huff. "I leave the house for a few weeks, and *then* you bring a guy home?"

"I found him near the library." I chewed my lip as I replayed the scene in my mind.

"What? Are you picking up homeless guys?"

I stifled my laugh. "It's Layne."

Silence filled the line. "Ten, what's going on? Talk to me."

I could almost visualize Benji's expression growing serious. If he were there, he would be in his bed, patting the space next to him. I would curl up under the blankets, prop my head up on my elbow, and spill my guts.

"I was leaving the library, and the storm was bad. It was dark, and I started freaking out a little about the walk home alone."

"Stop. Tensley, promise me you'll never walk at night alone. Promise." His tone was demanding, almost harsh.

"I called an Uber," I replied softly. I peeked at Layne, then stood. I should get a trash can and some towels in case he got sick. Slipping out of my room, I made my way to the bathroom and grabbed what I needed.

"Thank you. I didn't mean to jump your shit like that."

"I know. It's fine. Anyway, I heard someone. It wasn't a yell or a scream—it was almost like … It was the most gut-wrenching, brokenhearted cry I'd ever heard. When I realized someone was standing in the middle of the lawn with no cover, I thought something was wrong, so I ran over to help."

"Alone?" Benji's tone bordered on bewilderment.

"It was Layne." I slipped inside my bedroom again and closed the door behind me. After tossing the towels on the floor, I placed the trash can next to Layne. He hadn't changed positions yet, but his chest moved, so I knew he was breathing. I sank into the chair next to my window as a flash of lightning filled the sky. It was going to be a long night, but I didn't want to leave Layne alone in case he puked while he was passed out.

"He was so shit-faced, he thought I was Chloe, his ex-girl-friend. Then other times, he knew it was me." No way would I tell Benji about the kiss. It might have been for Chloe, but it didn't mean I couldn't secretly savor every breathtaking moment of Layne's mouth on mine. "There was a bad tornado a few years ago back home in Arkansas. From what he said tonight, Chloe died ... and so did his daughter." I squeezed my eyes shut, hearing Layne's gut-wrenching cries echo in my mind.

"Holy shit," Benji responded quietly.

"I know. I need to Google it to see if he was getting his facts straight, but it's what he said." Eyeing Layne while he was sleep-ing, I put Benji on speaker, and turned the volume down.

"Beat you to it. And yeah, Nicole was his three-month-old daughter, the news article says. Layne was the only one to survive out of the three of them. That fucking sucks. I thought a wheel-chair sucked, but I can't imagine someone you love in your arms one second then gone the next."

We sat in silence for a minute, processing the confirmation. Although Layne was drunker than hell, the facts were so deeply embedded in his mind, he couldn't screw them up even if he tried.

"What am I going to tell him when he wakes up naked in my bed?" I chewed my thumbnail, mentally debating what to say. The moment Avery and I had agreed we needed to dry his clothes, I understood I was risking Layne being super pissed about it.

"The truth. You tell him the truth."

I nodded as though Benji could see me through the phone. "Do you think I should tell him what he shared with me?"

"Yeah, but maybe don't give him every detail. Just tell him you know. Maybe he'll be relieved. I mean, from what you've told me, you two have been spending a lot of time together lately."

"It's been good," I blurted.

Benji's soft chuckle filled the phone line. "Is there a possibility it could get better?"

I released a slow sigh. "I don't know. When he admitted he'd had a crush on me, I wondered what it would have been like, but it couldn't have ever happened. The dynamics of high school, Chloe … Layne was popular and came from money, and I lived in an old janitor's closet."

"What?" Benji nearly shrieked at me. "You never told me about the janitor's closet, Tensley. Dear Jesus. It was that bad at the foster home?"

My hands visibly shook. "Worse."

"I'm not such an ass that I need full details, but please bring me up to speed where Layne is concerned."

I hesitated, my gaze drifting to the gorgeous man in my bed. "I'm going to give you the CliffsNotes version."

"That will work. Just don't leave anything important out." I could hear the smile in Benji's voice. He always injected humor when shit got intense.

With a deep breath, I gathered up the courage to tell him about the foster dad, moving into the closet, and how Layne had found me. Before I realized it, the flagpole situation and Layne breaking up with Chloe came rushing out of my mouth. I hadn't intended to share that with him or with anyone else. But now that Benji knew, I never wanted to discuss it again.

"Dammit." I hesitated, and silence filled the line. "I shouldn't have told you all of that. I'm so sorry. I'm being selfish. You're healing from the attack and have so much to deal with, Benji. I'm sorry."

"Wow, Ten. I-I," he stuttered.

"You don't have to say anything. It's fine."

"No. No, it's not anywhere close to fine. That was … Chloe is … was. Oh my God, I can't even talk right now. No wonder you never brought it up."

"How would I? Hi, I'm Tensley, previously Victoria. I moved from Arkansas to Washington because I was stripped and duct-taped to a flagpole by a crazy bitch who thought her boyfriend liked me. Oh, and did I mention I used to wear my hair really short? It was called the flagpole butch cut."

"All this makes sense now, including why you were terrified of Layne the first night you saw him. But from what you just explained, he didn't have anything to do with what happened. It was all Chloe. Do I have that right?"

"Yeah. At first, I didn't believe him, but the more time we've spent together, he continues to show up as a really good person."

"Keep making him work for it, Ten. I mean from what Avery has told me, he's seriously into you."

Heat crept up my neck and cheeks. I'd never had a guy to discuss before, and I was dipping my toes into new territory. "I'm not sure who's more broken, him or me. I don't think it's a good idea to fall for him, Benji."

"Girl, please. I can hear it in your voice—you already have. Now you know he's a *package* deal." Benji laughed at his play on words. "Seriously, though. Be honest with him and see what happens. If he gets pissed you washed his clothes and dried them, then he's an asshole, and you need to move on."

I knew Benji had a point, but I wasn't sure I could move on, at least not after that kiss. My entire body tingled with the thought of it. His soft lips and demanding tongue had nearly taken my knees out from under me. I'd never been kissed like that in my twenty-one years.

"The reason I called," Benji said, interrupting my hormonally induced thoughts, "is because I was hoping you might want to come over tomorrow."

There were no better words he could have said to me. My heart jumped at the thought of seeing him. "Hell yeah. What time?"

"Well, Mom and Dad leave around one in the afternoon, and they would feel better if you were here with me, so what about twelve-thirty? They should be back by eight, so we can eat, talk, and watch movies."

"That sounds like the best day ever, Benji."

"If you're a good little girl, I'll even give you a ride in my wheelchair."

Even though I couldn't see him, I imagined he was waggling his eyebrows at me. Before I could catch myself, I barked out a laugh. "Oh my God, I've missed you."

"I've missed you too, babe. Take care of that hunk of a man in your bed tonight, then you can fill me in on all the juicy details when you come over."

"I can't wait to see you." A low moan pulled my attention back to the broken and beautiful guy under my covers. "I gotta go, but I'll see you tomorrow."

"Can't wait," Benji said, then disconnected the call.

Quietly, I stood from my chair and waited to see if Layne was going to wake up or be sick. Even though I'd taken care of a lot of younger foster kids, this situation was completely different. Layne was grown ... and naked ... with a huge dick.

Layne flung his arm over his forehead, and another moan escaped his full, soft lips. "Tensley."

"I'm right here," I replied quietly, but Layne didn't respond.

Sitting softly on the edge of my bed, I watched the movement of his chest. More emotions than I'd had in a long time pulled me in a million directions. The last few weeks with Layne had stirred something deep inside me I'd never experienced before. Sometimes I wondered if he had also felt it, like when his eyes darkened or when his gaze landed on my mouth. My breath would hitch in my throat, and longing would swirl low in my belly. Other times, Layne's hand would rest gently on the small of my back when we were walking in the grocery store or the hallway at college. It was almost as though—

I slammed my eyes shut, willing myself back to reality. The truth of the matter was that Layne was shattered, possibly beyond repair. Two broken people didn't make a whole.

Layne's arm moved to his side, and I brushed a strand of hair off his forehead. As the new information had unfolded in front of me, I'd realized that Layne had nothing to do with Chloe's crazy behavior in high school, but he was still trying to help me heal.

"How is he?" Avery asked quietly, poking her head in through the cracked door.

"Sleeping." I stood and crossed the room to her. "I have no idea how long he'll be out." I tossed a look over my shoulder at him.

Avery tucked a hair behind her ear and leaned against the wall. "Have you eaten anything? I ordered some pizza."

"That sounds good. I'll just leave the door open so I can listen for him. I don't want him puking in my bed."

Avery's nose scrunched up. "No shit. Let's keep our fingers crossed that all he has is a massive headache."

Following Avery to the kitchen, I debated whether to tell her why Layne was so drunk. A part of me felt as though I would be betraying his confidence, but I'd already told Benji. Plus, Layne hadn't even told *me* about it. He'd thought he was talking to Chloe. At the same time, the articles were in the newspapers, videos were online, pictures of Chloe, Nicole, and Layne were plastered all over the internet. It wasn't private knowledge.

Avery grabbed some plates and dished up the pizza. She slid a plate to me with a few pieces of pepperoni pizza on it. "Here ya go."

"Thank you." I bit off the end and chewed, savoring the delicious bite. I definitely loved food.

"How did you end up bringing him home?" Avery took a nibble off her cheese-filled crust, waiting for me to swallow so I could respond.

I put my food down and grabbed a napkin from the holder on the counter. "I was outside the library when I heard someone cry out. It was pouring rain, so I thought they were in trouble. It was Layne." I paused for a moment, recalling the anguish in his expression as the water streamed down his face. "In a nutshell, he lost his three-month-old daughter and her mother in a tornado a few years ago."

"Fuck. Ten, that's horrible. And he just told you all of this?"

I swallowed visibly. "Not exactly. He thought I was ... he thought I was Chloe. He asked me to forgive him for losing Nicole." I purposely omitted the kiss. I wasn't sure Layne would even remember it, and I sure as hell wasn't interested in asking him. As far as I could tell, he'd kissed *her*.

"Do you want my advice on handling this?" Avery asked, taking another bite, then wiping the corner of her mouth with a rooster-imprinted paper towel. *Benji and his cocks.* I inwardly smiled.

"Of course." I wasn't sure if I wanted her input or not, but she had a lot more life experience with guys than I did, so it was worth a shot.

"I've had blackout drinking nights too. Do him a favor and tell him everything if he asks. If you don't, it will come back and bite you in the ass. Plus, he's into you, so don't betray his trust. He's super cautious with you right now, so just be open with him even if he gets upset."

I inhaled deeply and rubbed my temples. It was only a few minutes after ten in the evening, but I was exhausted. All I wanted to do was crawl into bed and wish the night had never happened, but I couldn't. I would have to grab a pillow and blanket and sleep in the chair or on the floor. No way could I curl up next to Layne while he was naked, and I didn't feel comfortable leaving him on his own for any length of time.

"Are you going to be okay? It's a lot to handle." Avery searched me for any telltale sign that I couldn't manage the situation with Layne. Although I was nervous, these were by no means the worst circumstances I'd ever been in. I was more concerned about Layne than my own feelings.

Avery skillfully changed the topic, and she updated me on the progress with Justin. We'd agreed to hold off on anyone else moving in for a few months. I needed time to adjust to the changes of not having Benji around, and no matter what anyone said, I wasn't convinced that Benji and I couldn't be roomies again. People in wheelchairs led a full life, and I wasn't shutting the door on my best friend's growth. Once I'd explained that to Avery, she was on board. *Thank God.*

"Tensley?" Layne asked from the kitchen doorway, a deep frown furrowing his brows. He had pulled a floral blanket off my bed and wrapped it around his waist. "Why am I naked and at your house?"

11

"I've gotta get going. You kids don't do anything I wouldn't." Avery flashed me a big grin as she hopped off the barstool. "I'm off to meet Justin."

"Have a good time." I was sure she would have a lot more fun than I was about to have.

"Later, Layne." Avery scooted past him, her smile growing broader while her eyes greedily drank him in.

"Are you all right?" I asked, staring at the half-naked man in my kitchen. "You probably need some Advil, huh? There's some pizza as well."

"I'll pass on the food for now, but my head is pounding." Layne ambled over to the barstool and sank onto it, holding the blanket in place.

I hurried to grab the medicine for him. Honestly, I was stunned that he was awake. It had only been five hours, but maybe his system metabolized alcohol quickly.

"Thank you." Layne held his hand out, downed the pills, and took a big swig of the water that I handed to him. He cleared his throat and his eyes slowly found mine.

"Do you remember what happened?" I asked, sitting across the island from him. My pulse spiked at the realization that I was about to tell him everything, even about the kiss.

"Some. I don't recall how I got here." His attention fell to the blanket wrapped around him. "Or where my clothes are."

I mentally swore as my cheeks flushed. "They're in the dryer. You were soaked, and I was worried that you might catch pneumonia."

He nodded. "What did I say to you? You're acting funny."

"I am? No. It… shit. You told me about Nicole and Chloe." There, I'd said it.

We stared at each other, neither of us daring to speak first. Heated tension filled the small room, and I wondered if I'd done the right thing. Maybe I should have walked away when I'd found him in the rain, but that wasn't acceptable, and my conscience would never have allowed me to leave him there.

"I'm sorry," he finally said. "Sometimes it's too much for me to handle, and I drink. Storms … When there's a storm, it fucks me up pretty badly." His shoulders slumped while his gaze traveled far away for a moment.

"It would me too. I'm so sorry, Layne. I realize nothing I say will make it better, but if you ever need to talk, I'm here." I folded my hands in my lap, attempting to calm my anxiety. "You kissed me," I blurted.

Layne's facial expression never faltered as the words spilled out of my mouth.

"Then you called me Chloe."

From the way Layne's face cringed, I would have thought I'd just kicked him in the nuts. He ran his hands through his hair, grief flickering in his eyes. "I'm sorry for calling you Chloe. There's no way I would have kissed you, thinking you were her. I was obviously out of my head with grief and alcohol. After we broke up, the only contact I had with her was as the mother of my baby. I never kissed her. It's a messed-up time for me, Tensley, but I know who you are. I feel like an ass. That had to have hurt you. But I don't regret the kiss. The only thing I regret is that I don't remember it."

"What?" I shook my head in confusion. Layne's familiar musky scent swirled around me, making me light-headed. "What do you mean you don't regret the kiss? I ... you weren't ... It was like you were here with me one minute, then back in Arkansas the next."

"Shit. I don't know what to say. I'm sorry you found out that way, Ten. I guess I should have told you. I just—it's not a dinner or date topic. Plus, I'm trying to deal with a new dynamic. I'm fucked up, but at the same time, I can't stop thinking about you. After I lost Nicole and Chloe, I swore I'd never love anyone again, or even ask a girl out. Just mindless sex when I needed it. But there you were that night at the bar. You took my breath away during your drum performance. Every part of me came back to life. Over the last month, we've spent so much time together, my uncle wanted to know if I'd moved out."

My heart stopped beating. Was the conversation moving in the direction I thought it was, or would it take a sharp turn and send my emotions reeling backward?

"Well, we have been together a lot since Benji's attack," I offered, allowing him an opportunity to rephrase his words.

"We have, and I've loved every minute of it. But maybe this isn't the time. You've just learned how messed up I really am." His chest moved with his deep breath while he glanced out the kitchen window behind him.

"Don't. Don't shut me out. We both have a shitty past." Although I didn't want to push him to finish, I needed to know where we were going, or if there was a *we* at all. *But more importantly, what do I want?*

The timer on the dryer buzzed loudly. "I'll get your clothes so you can get dressed." I slipped off my barstool and opened the hallway closet doors. "They're nice and warm." My heart sank a little as I returned Layne's shirt and jeans to him. He'd been about to say something important. "The bathroom is next to my bedroom, where you were sleeping."

Layne nodded, and his hand grazed mine while he collected his clothes. He walked out of the kitchen.

My palm immediately smacked my forehead. Had Layne been serious about not regretting the kiss, or was he still drunk? I absentmindedly put the remaining pizza in the fridge and turned toward the dishes in the sink. I turned on the water and began to rinse the bowls and plates, then loaded them into the dishwasher.

Dammit, my mind was running rampant. I needed an explanation, but I wasn't sure I would get it tonight. It was a shame I couldn't mind-meld like Spock.

"Thanks for drying my clothes," Layne said, returning to the kitchen a few minutes later, fully dressed.

"You're welcome. I hope you're not mad that I removed them. I just didn't want you to get sick. And honestly, I thought you'd be passed out all night."

He slid onto the barstool again. "You'd think."

I dried my hands off on a rooster towel and faced him. "Is the devastation from the tornado the reason why you're in Spokane?" I asked, not beating around the bush.

"Yeah. My parents figured it would be good to move me to a new environment. Everywhere I looked, I saw Nicole and Chloe. I couldn't heal. I won't ever be able to fully let Nicole go, but at least here I can have a chance at a life again."

I fought the urge to throw my arms around him and tell him it would be okay. I couldn't promise him that, though.

A wistful expression flickered across his face. "I'm really sorry you had to deal with all of that tonight. I'm sure you have better things to do."

I didn't, but I would never admit that learning what was behind the moments of agony that materialized in his eyes had pushed me over the edge. I finally understood what was haunting him. And I was finding myself overwhelmed with my feelings for him. The harder I fought it, the faster they pulled me under.

"These last several weeks have meant a lot to me, Ten. *You* mean a lot to me. It's the first time in three years I thought I might be able to be happy again, to move on."

Shit. With me?

"I'm just putting it on the table because you know everything now." He stood, closed the gap between us, and gently rubbed my arms. Goosebumps peppered my flesh. "I'm falling for you. Hard. This is my heart, Tensley. It's fragile and a bit fucked up, but you're in my head every second of the day. I count the minutes until I see your smile again or hear your voice. Every moment we're together, I fight not to kiss you. Hopefully I didn't screw my chances up tonight. It wasn't on my radar for you to find me sloppy drunk and learn about my past. I'd planned on telling you at some point, but you're still healing physically. Not to mention, your heart is hurting for your best friend."

I blinked rapidly, trying to digest everything he'd said. I honest-to-God didn't know what to say now that it was all out in the open. It was one thing to dream about being with a guy, but something totally different when he was standing close to you, spilling his guts. At least I didn't have to guess any longer. I was clear on his feelings. *But am I clear on mine?* I'd never dated anyone. The only time I'd had sex was to get something I needed … or when I was raped. Attempting a normal relationship hadn't been anywhere on my radar.

Layne's thumb gently stroked my cheek. "Did I say too much?"

"No," I croaked, my voice betraying my wobbly nerves.

His eyes dropped to my mouth, his tongue darting across his bottom lip. "Did I ruin any chance with you?"

Oh God. I wanted that tongue on my body. I wanted to kiss those beautiful lips, and my hormones were kicking into overdrive, cheering me on. I was a goner, and I knew it, but I was terrified at the same time. "No. I understand. I just don't want you to blame yourself for Nicole and Chloe. It wasn't your fault, Layne." Tears pricked the backs of my eyes.

"Can I kiss you? I need one that I can remember. I need something good to hold on to after all the hell."

I nodded, unable to form words. Layne tilted my chin up with his finger, and my legs trembled with anticipation. This was different than him kissing me earlier. He wasn't drunk, and he knew who I was.

"I've thought about this so many times." His lips grazed the corner of my mouth, and a small whimper escaped me. "You're so beautiful." He closed the gap between us, leaning his hips into mine as he pinned me against the kitchen counter. He feathered kisses on the sensitive spot of my neck. His lips brushed across mine, and a soft moan slipped from his throat.

I threaded my fingers through the belt loops on his jeans. I needed something to hold onto or my hands would roam all over him. He would be out of his clothes in no time.

His mouth parted slightly, and his tongue caressed mine. Desire flamed through me as he deepened our kiss.

Breaking away from him, I took his hand. "Let's go," I whispered, guiding him out of the kitchen and down the hall to my bedroom. I shut and locked the door behind us in case Avery came home.

Layne wrapped his arm around my waist and pulled me to him. His mouth crashed down on mine, and my body turned to Jell-O. *Jesus, can he kiss.* No one had ever reduced me to a hormonal puddle like he was at that moment.

I backed him up to my bed and gave him a little push, then smiled as he toppled backward onto my mattress. I straddled him while his hands cupped my ass cheeks. In the back of my mind, I wondered if I would have been willing to sleep with him if I hadn't seen him naked a few hours ago. But who cared? All I wanted was him inside me. For the first time, I wanted to have sex, to make someone feel good, to share an intimate experience on a different level because I cared about him.

Layne rolled over, flipping me onto my back. He sat on his heels and his gaze raked over me. My core throbbed with need. Any logical reasoning for not sleeping with him had flown out the window the minute he'd kissed me in the kitchen.

I sat up, tugged my T-shirt over my head, and tossed it on the floor. I'd nearly forgotten he'd seen me shirtless already.

"I want you so much I'm hurting." He flipped open the button on his jeans and unzipped them just enough to allow himself some room. "But not tonight."

"What?" Panic exploded inside me. Maybe I misread what he wanted. Maybe he didn't want to sleep with me.

"I don't want our first time to be after I've … not been at my best. I don't want you to have sex with me because you're emotional and need someone. I want it to be more than that, Tensley."

I blinked at him as though he'd just grown another head.

He leaned over and trailed gentle kisses up my stomach, stopping between my breasts. His minty breath tickled my skin. He must have borrowed my toothpaste, which meant he'd planned on kissing me. Or at least he'd hoped to.

"What do you want me to do?" he asked, desire burning in his eyes.

I stared at him, speechless.

"Let me touch you, caress you, savor and taste every inch of you with my mouth. I want it to be all about you tonight. I want you to come so many times, you can't stand up. Then I want to hold you while you sleep. Is that all right?" He paused, waiting for my reply.

I nodded. *Yes, yes, and hell fucking yes.* Granted it wasn't sex, but I'd take it.

Layne flicked open the front clasp of my black push-up bra. My nipples hardened as the chill of the air danced across my skin. His fingers ran down my side, and I automatically arched upward. He took my nipple between his teeth and his tongue expertly twirled it around in his mouth. His left hand cupped my other breast, and I grabbed the bedspread, bunching it together in my hands so I wouldn't scream his name.

Without a word, he backed away, then undid my pants. The zipper being pulled down was the only noise in the small room other than our labored breathing.

"I can't wait to taste you." His voice was gruff with need.

Seconds later, I was naked in front of him. His eyes traveled over me as he slipped his hand in his jeans, adjusting them down enough for me to have a bit of a view. It was obvious he was uncomfortable.

"Layne, you don't have to wait. I want you inside me." My words rushed out in a whisper.

He released himself without a word and knelt down on the floor. He pulled me to the edge of the bed and spread my legs. Then he gently parted my folds.

"You're so wet. Jesus." His tongue swirled around my clit while he dug his fingers into the flesh of my ass cheek. My back arched off the mattress while I called his name. His finger plunged inside me while his mouth caressed my sensitive skin. He sucked and nipped, sending waves of pleasure through me.

"Go ahead and come for me." He pushed another finger in me, reaching the depths of my body.

I squirmed against him, grabbing handfuls of his hair as he continued relentlessly. An intense rush of euphoria washed over me as I released. While I was struggling to regain my breath, he peered up at me with a mischievous grin on his face. "Hang on."

He grabbed my waist and pinned me in place while he lowered his mouth to my core again.

"Layne! Wait. Oh my God. I'm too sensitive. I need—" My words cut off as my hips found the rhythm of his tongue again. He moaned as his hand released me and found my breast. I took his hand, holding it while he kneaded my flesh.

He pumped his fingers in and out of me, slowly at first.

"More," I pleaded. "Layne, I need you inside me. Please." I'd never begged before, but he'd turned me into a lust-filled crazy person I didn't know.

He ignored my pleas but continued to bring me to the edge several more times. When he was finished with me, I was limp with exhaustion. He'd touched me in ways I'd never even considered. My core ached from his mouth and fingers, and a lazy smile eased across my face.

He joined me on the bed, wrapped me in his arms, and placed a kiss against my forehead. "I'll be right back."

I watched him as he stood and fastened his jeans, then he left the room. I grabbed my T-shirt and tugged it on while eyeing the floor for my panties. I retrieved them and slipped them on. My room smelled like sex even though we hadn't gone that far.

"How are you doing?" Layne closed the door behind him, then crawled into bed next to me. "Come here." He pulled me close to him and my head settled on his chest. "I can stay until you fall asleep." His fingers toyed with a strand of my hair.

"You don't have to go. Stay. Stay with me." I looked up at him, and his beautiful blue eyes connected with mine.

"Are you sure?"

"Yeah." I'd never asked a guy to spend the night before. I was definitely in new territory.

ALTHOUGH I KNEW it was real, I almost thought I'd dreamed the previous night. Reaching for Layne, I found his side of the bed empty but still a little warm. The sunlight filtered through my curtains, and I sat up, rubbing my eyes. It was nearly nine, which meant I had plenty of time to shower and get to Benji's.

My heart filled with excitement. I hadn't seen him since the attack. The fresh aroma of coffee tickled my nose, and I tossed the covers off me and dressed quickly. I wondered if Layne had made a pot or already gone back to his place.

I flung my bedroom door open and pattered down the hall in my bare feet. I poked my head into the kitchen and came to an abrupt halt.

"Morning," Avery said, picking up her cup and winking at me.

My eyes narrowed at her as I spotted Justin near the sink and Layne pouring a cup of coffee near the fridge. *Shit.* We weren't alone like I'd hoped, which meant Avery would ply me with a million questions.

"It's not what you think," I said under my breath as I walked past Avery.

She smirked and tossed me a wink. "Mm-hmm."

I willed myself not to roll my eyes while I approached Layne. My heart hammered against my ribs because I started to wonder if he regretted what had happened. *Fuck.* I wasn't sure how I would handle it if he did.

"Here." Layne grabbed a cup and filled it with steaming black liquid for me. He kissed me on the cheek and sat it on the counter. I could feel Avery's stare burning a hole in my back, but I refused to turn around and look at her.

I beamed at him. "Thanks." Maybe this was a good sign. It was definitely better than him dashing out the door and never hearing from him again.

He brushed a stray hair off my face, his eyes filling with concern. "Did you get some sleep?"

"I did. How about you?" I blew on my java, wishing I could tell him how nice it was to have him there, but I didn't want to say anything embarrassing in front of our audience.

He leaned over, and his warm breath grazed my ear. "It was the best night's sleep I've had in years." He tucked my hair behind my shoulder "Do you have plans today?"

I white-knuckled my cup so I wouldn't spill the hot contents all over the floor. It was crazy how he could turn my body into a blubbering, hormonal mess that would willingly roll over for him with a few little words.

I cleared my throat, steadied myself, then took his hand. "We'll be back in a bit," I said over my shoulder to Avery and Justin. I knew they were thinking that we were going to my room for a quickie, but we weren't. At least not that I was aware of.

"Sorry. I didn't want to discuss anything in front of Avery and Justin," I said, closing my bedroom door behind us. I took a sip of my coffee, then set it on my small desk next to my economics book. "I'm going to Benji's. It's the first time I'll see him since we were both in the hospital."

Layne sank down in the chair near the window. "That's great. I know you miss him."

I crossed the room and sat on the edge of my bed. "I do. He's my best friend, and my heart is broken over what happened. I know he needs me to be strong, though."

"Sometimes being supportive of someone means grieving together. You can't limit the time on the process."

"No, nor would I. At least not on purpose. I was just hoping he would be able to come back home. I mean here."

Layne's eyes flickered with compassion. "Can I see you later tonight?"

A smile eased across my face. "I'll be home around eight thirty if you want to come over."

He stood and held his hand out to me. In one swift motion, he pulled me off the bed and flush against his muscular body. "I'll be here." His head dipped down, and his lips brushed across mine.

"Are you for real?" I whispered, afraid I was breaking the moment.

A raspy chuckle rumbled through his chest. "You better believe it." He deepened his kiss, and everything around me floated away as I melted into him.

I wanted to ask him where our relationship was headed, but I didn't want to push him due to my desperate need for parameters, but I'd also lost too much to chance in my life already. This conversation was meant for my bestie.

I thanked the Uber driver and stepped out of the car. There weren't many brick homes in Spokane, but Michael and Marilyn owned one. It was a mansion. Well-trimmed hedges lined the sidewalk. The maple trees had turned a gorgeous red, and the sunlight provided a gold halo around the leaves. Autumn was breathtaking.

My black midcalf boots scuffed the steps as I approached the front door. For whatever reason, my heart was pounding double time. I had no idea why. I'd been to Benji's childhood home a lot. Maybe it was the realization that I would see him in a wheelchair, or maybe it would finally dawn on me that he wasn't moving back in with us. Regardless, I needed to put on my brave face and be there for him. I rang the doorbell and waited.

Marilyn opened the door and waved me in. "Hi, hon!"

I stepped foot into the marble entrance and gently closed the heavy mahogany door behind me. The sunlight glistened off the chandelier from the window, casting light in every direction.

Marilyn looked stunning in her black slacks and red blouse. The only reason I knew something was amiss was because of the circles beneath her brown eyes. "We've missed you so much," she said, wrapping me in a warm embrace.

"You too."

We released each other, and she hung up my jacket in the closet. Suddenly self-conscious, I smoothed my navy-blue sweater and skinny jeans. Marilyn was so classy, and I often felt underdressed around her. "How is he?" I asked softly in case Benji was nearby.

A conflicted look pained her face while she took a moment to collect her words. "Some days are better than others. He wants to hurry the healing process along and get adjusted, but there's no such thing. You can't rush the recovery, no matter how difficult it is."

"I would too. I'd do everything in my power to figure out my new normal and whatever that looked like."

"Don't let him talk you into anything you don't want to do, like move back with you and Avery." She touched her pointer finger on my nose and grinned. "I made coffee and lunch. Benji will order something for you guys to eat later." Her heels tapped against the floor as I followed her into the kitchen.

No matter how many times I'd been inside Benji's house, I was always overwhelmed by the beauty of it. The marble entryway flowed into a hall that passed the hand-carved stair railing leading upstairs, but now there was a lift for Benji. Marilyn and Michael's bedroom was on the main floor along with the living room, dining room, formal dining room, kitchen, and home office. White triple-crown molding accentuated every room, including the upstairs.

I didn't miss the rearranged furniture in the living room as I passed by. I assumed that wouldn't be the only space that had been reorganized to accommodate Benji's needs.

We entered the black-and-tan granite-and-stone kitchen. As always, it was immaculate. The stainless-steel fridge hummed quietly in the background as my gaze immediately landed on

Benji's. He looked as gorgeous as ever in his navy-blue-and-white-striped polo and jeans. His eyes had lost some of the spark they'd held before the attack, but I had expected more signs of his emotional and physical trauma. Overwhelmed with emotion, I didn't give a fuck if he was in a wheelchair or not. I flew across the room and wrapped my arms around him. He laughed and pulled me into his lap. Normally, I would have been embarrassed to sit on a guy's lap in front of his parents, but this was the best way to get close to Benji, so I didn't protest.

"Hi, babe." He placed his hand against my cheek and flashed me his million-dollar smile.

"I miss you so fucking bad," I whispered, tears streaming down my face.

"God, you too." He gave me a quick peck on the lips, and I laid my head on his shoulder.

"Am I hurting you?" I prepared to hop off his lap if I was.

"Nope, it's all good." He tightened his arms around me, holding me while I sniffled. "Mom and Dad left the room to give us some privacy."

My head popped up off his shoulder, and I placed both hands on his cheeks. "I just want to sit here with you all day. I can't describe the hole in my heart since you've not been at home, Benji." I hiccupped on the words, my tears running faster. "I should have told you not to park behind the comedy club. I should have fought harder when we were attacked. I should have—"

Benji placed his finger over my mouth. "Shh. It's okay, Ten. I don't blame you at all. It wasn't your fault. We've parked there before without any problems. Unfortunately, my attention was on Thomas and it never occurred to me it wasn't safe. Hell, I even blamed myself, but I'm not going to waste my time. Nothing I did gave those monsters permission to hurt us like they did. Not one damned thing."

Relief washed over me. I was so proud of Benji for not

blaming himself. In my mind, he'd done nothing wrong. Maybe if he wasn't torturing himself, I could forgive myself as well.

"Thomas." A growl escaped me. "Has he reached out to you at all?"

"Yeah, but I told him I wasn't interested in talking to him."

"Because of your wheelchair or because he's a full-on scummy, slimy douchebag?"

Benji cleared his throat. "Honestly? Both. You're the first person I've seen other than my parents." Sadness clung to his words.

"Don't you ever tell me you won't see me again. Under no circumstances will I accept that, Benji Parker! It's been hell for you, and I get that, but dammit, don't you ever leave me like that again." New tears spilled down my face while I chastised him, feeling slightly guilty for making the issue about my feelings.

"I know. And part of it was the pain pills. I was loopy as fuck, but I promise I won't shut you out again. If I'd been honest with myself, I needed you. I needed you next to me in bed, talking to me, helping me rebuild my future. I was scared and ashamed."

"No." I shook my head vehemently. "Never feel ashamed for who you are. Ever. I'm here now." I wiped away my tears and smiled. "I'm done blubbering. I want to hear everything you've decided to do and how I can help ... to bring you home."

Benji chuckled. "There's my girl."

"He wants to play basketball," Michael said, entering the kitchen with a wide grin on his handsome face. Michael's casual clothes were as nice as Marilyn's. His light-blue-and-white button-down shirt was paired with black slacks and matching loafers.

"What?" I asked, jumping out of Benji's lap. I could sit with him after his parents left.

"Yeah. Why not? I love ball. I just need to find out what I'm good at while sporting new wheels." He patted his wheelchair.

"I think that's amazing!" For the first time in weeks, a flicker of hope sparked to life in my chest.

"Kids, we've got to head out. There's money on the counter for dinner and to rent some movies or whatever you want to do. Just stay here for tonight, though."

Fear flickered across Michael's face. He and Marilyn had been through hell and back, and I couldn't imagine how difficult it was to leave Benji at the house for the first time.

"Promise. We're going to be fine," I assured them, flashing them a warm smile.

"We'll give you a ride home later so you don't have to pay an Uber," Michael said, leaning down and giving me a fatherly peck on the cheek. "Son, you call if you need anything." He squeezed Benji's shoulder, then left the kitchen. There was no mistaking the tension in his body.

"Shit," I muttered under my breath. "It's hard for them to leave you."

Benji held up a finger, signaling for me to wait. The moment the front door clicked shut, he threw his hands up in the air and released a loud whoop.

I nearly jumped out of my skin then giggled. "You fucking scared me!"

He rolled his wheelchair forward and laughed. "Man, I've not been able to do anything without them breathing down my neck. I can get myself to the bathroom, but nooo. Mom's gotta be right there, helping and watching every move I make." Benji rubbed his face, frustration rolling off him in waves.

"Oh no. I'm so sorry." My shoulders slumped. "I hadn't really thought about that. Fill me in. But first, are you hungry? Your mom has all this food for us." My mouth watered as I eyeballed the club sandwiches, pickles, and chips. "I can bring the plates to the living room or wherever you're the most comfortable." I grabbed a pickle spear and took a bite. The loud snap and crunch filled the kitchen.

"Vlasic," I said, wiggling my pickle at him like it was a cigar. I gave him a little wink, then laughed, trying to lighten his mood.

Benji barked out a laugh and smiled. "Yeah. I've got more space in there, plus the TV has Netflix and Amazon Prime in case we want to watch a movie. Hell, we might talk all day and not watch a movie. Honestly, I don't care what we do. I'm just so fucking happy you're here." His eyes misted over with his confession.

"Well you're stuck with me, and after you fill me in on your new plans, I have a few updates for you as well."

"From how your face just lit up, I'm going to take a wild guess that things got hot and spicy with a Mr. Layne Garrison?"

Although I couldn't see my cheeks, I felt them turn crimson. "I don't know what the hell I'm doing, Benji. I think I'm in way over my head." I slapped my hand over my mouth then dropped it. "No more." I waved my finger, emphasizing my words. "You first. We can talk about Layne later." I picked up our plates and made my way to the living room with Benji right behind me. I set the plates on the coffee table while Benji parked his chair at the end of the couch.

"I guess I'm a little hungry now that you mention it."

"Do you have a TV tray, or is your lap all right?"

He patted his legs. "I'm good right here."

I handed him his plate, slipped off my boots, and settled in on the black leather couch next to him. My focus landed on the family photo hanging above the stone fireplace. Michael, Marilyn, and Benji were beaming. The picture was one of my favorites. Not only was it full of color, but it was obvious they were happy. There was nothing fake about the love they had for each other.

"So there's something that happened this morning that I've not told anyone yet," Benji said before taking a bite of his sandwich.

I tucked my legs beneath me, giving him my undivided attention. "Really? What?"

"My dick got hard as a rock."

Although we'd talked about a lot of things, Benji's cock hadn't been one of them.

"Dude!" I said, pointing at him. "Does this mean you can still have sex?"

"Hell fucking yeah. My shit still works!" He pumped his fists in the air, laughing. "Seriously, we weren't sure what was going to happen. I might regain some of the feeling in my legs too. And if I get even tingles back, then who says I can't walk again?"

I picked up my sandwich and took a bite. "How positive have the doctors been?"

"Meh," Benji wiggled his hand from side to side. "So-so. There are a lot of complicated medical terms, but they're not a hundred percent sure what's going to happen. It's not as cut and dried as if your spinal cord was crushed. I think the big thing they're trying to avoid is getting my hopes up for nothing."

"Yeah. I mean, they have to err on the side of caution, but I can't imagine how difficult that would be for you."

"Honestly, the hope that I might walk again gets me through the shitty and emotional days, and a hard dick helps too." Benji snickered. "For now, as I've already mentioned, I'm looking into sports. It will keep me fit mentally and physically. I'll pick up school next year when I'm more comfortable leaving the house and getting around."

"I'll help you." I waved him off as though it weren't a big deal, but we both knew I couldn't be with him every minute of the day.

"Yeah, and what if you're sneaking off with Layne, and he's giving you the ride of your life?" His expression grew serious. "Will you walk away and wheel me around?"

My lips pursed together. "Um, what? I think you're assuming we're sleeping together, so lemme stop you there."

His eyes narrowed while he assessed me. "Really?"

Taking another bite of my sandwich, I shook my head. "Ugh. Dammit. Avery has been texting you, hasn't she? She just assumes something happened because he spent the night after he woke up from his drunken oblivion."

Benji moved his plate to the table then placed his elbows on his knees and cupped his chin in his hands. "Do tell, and don't you dare leave anything out. Until I can find a new boy toy, I'm going to have to live vicariously through you. Just don't leave me high and dry."

I rolled my eyes. "If I do sleep with him, you most certainly do *not* get all the deets. That's private. Besides, I've already told you he's"—I moved my pointer fingers apart—"this big."

Benji choked, his mouth gaping open. "You're not stringing me along? Like you're serious?"

I nodded. "Yeah. As I said to Avery, no wonder Chloe stayed with him. Biggest peen I've ever seen." I buried my head in my hands and giggled.

"So no sex?" Hope laced his tone.

"No, but ..." My core throbbed with longing for Layne. I couldn't wait to see him again that night. As soon as the thought crossed my mind, the fear crept in. What if Layne went home, reconsidered what had happened, and ghosted me? Butterflies ran rampant in my stomach. I wasn't so hungry anymore. I moved my plate to the coffee table and sat on my hands.

"Ten? You only sit on your hands when you don't want someone to see you scared or nervous. What's going on?"

"I'm terrified." The confession left my mouth before I realized it.

Benji pulled on my arm, freeing my hand and taking it in his. "Talk to me."

I swallowed. There was nothing to be afraid of. Benji was my best friend, and I trusted him. That was not what was difficult. Admitting my feelings out loud made them real, and I wasn't sure if I was ready for that yet. "He admitted he cared about me and is interested in something deeper. We kissed, and I was the one that wanted sex, but he said no."

Shock registered across Benji's handsome face. "Wait, what?"

"Layne said that he didn't want our first time to be after I'd found him drunk and learned how fucked up he was over losing his daughter."

Benji released a low whistle. "The dude's got it bad."

An anxious fluttery feeling descended on me. "What do you mean?"

"This is your first relationship, right?"

I nodded.

"Get used to it. He's head over heels for you. If he'd just wanted to get laid, it would have happened last night. The fact that he wants it to be special means you own his heart already."

I chewed my thumbnail, doubting his words. "Are you sure?"

"Oh girl, yes. I have no doubt."

Silence filled the room. The only noise was from the running HVAC unit.

A messy ball of excitement and fear wedged itself in my throat. "What am I going to do?" I croaked.

"Tensley," he started, his voice low and serious. "Let this man love you."

13

Benji's words bounced around in my head for the rest of the day. What if he was wrong and Layne broke my heart? I didn't know how I would come back from that. Life had dealt me shit over and over. I wasn't sure if I had it in me to let someone get close to me other than Benji and Avery.

At eight thirty, my doorbell rang. I peered through the peephole, then opened the door.

"Hey," Layne said, a kind smile on his face. "I brought Chinese, including your favorite, sweet-and-sour chicken."

"You don't have to bring me food every time you show up." My lips pursed as I reconsidered my comment. "I take it back." I laughed. "I'm starving, but you should let me cook for you some evening." I moved out of the way, allowing him inside the living room.

His eyebrow rose slightly. "You cook?"

"I do. I'm certainly no sous chef, but I can make a mean meatloaf, beef stroganoff, and a few other things. Ya know, if any of that sounds good." I made my way into the kitchen and grabbed us some plates.

Layne sat at the island and pulled the containers out of the bag.

"It smells wonderful. Benji and I talked so much, we hardly ate anything."

Layne paused, his attention landing fully on me. "How is he?"

"Under the circumstances, he's doing pretty well. Benji's a fighter, and he's determined he's going to walk again." I grabbed a few forks from the drawer and waved them around. "But his dick works, and that's the most important thing right now." I couldn't hide my grin.

Layne laughed. "That's probably the best thing that's happened to him since the attack."

"Oh yeah. I mean normally we don't discuss his anatomy, but he was excited. I think when you realize you may never have sex or make love to a significant other again, that would be really difficult." My voice trailed off with my realization, and I sat down next to Layne. "Sorry. I guess talking to you about Benji's peen isn't appropriate."

"It's fine. The circumstances are different than just saying, 'Hey, Layne, I want to chat about Benji's penis.'"

A laugh bubbled out of me, relieving some of the awkwardness of the topic.

Layne smiled, then it quickly faded, and his face clouded with sadness. He trailed his fingertips across my cheek and down to my mouth. His thumb gently pulled on my bottom lip. His lips brushed mine, and he cupped my face, peering deep into my eyes. His expression was determined and sincere. "If I couldn't make love to you, I'm not sure if I could handle it."

Our gazes locked, and my emotions started to spin out of control. "What ... what are we doing, Layne? When you say things to me like that, I don't want to misunderstand where you are in this, whatever this is between us."

His hands dropped to his lap, and a small flicker of fear danced across his face.

I hadn't meant to break the mood, but I couldn't fully give myself to him until I knew what his intentions were. "I'm sorry," I muttered, embarrassed. "I shouldn't have pushed you."

"You didn't. I should tell you something else, though," he said gently.

I hopped off the barstool and paced. "Is there something wrong? Layne, I don't think I can deal with anything else right now." I placed my hands on my hips and continued walking around the small kitchen.

"Hang on." Layne reached out and pulled me to him. "It's not bad. I didn't mean to scare you."

I took his hand and guided it over my racing heart. "Then tell me. Please."

"When I broke up with Chloe, she was obviously pissed I'd called her out in front of her friends for what they had done to you. She was screaming at me at the top of her lungs." He shook his head, most likely reliving the day. "Chloe accused me of cheating on her. And before you ask, no, I never did. Ever. I'm not that guy."

I released a breath I hadn't realized I'd been holding. A cheater was off the table for me.

"But I had developed feelings for another girl by then. It's why I was going to end it with her. Not only was she a raging lunatic, but there was someone else I wanted to spend time with."

I let go of his hand and dug my fingers into my thigh as panic jabbed at me. "Who?"

"Since the beginning of high school, no matter how hard I tried, my heart continued to go back to one girl ... you."

I gasped. "What? Me? No, Layne, you're wrong!" I pulled away in shock. "I was homeless, and I didn't always have clean clothes or money. We're from two different worlds." My words came crashing down on me like a hurricane ripping through a city.

Layne allowed me to step back. "That's not what I saw." His

voice was sweet and gentle. "I saw a highly intelligent, beautiful girl who had a pure heart."

I snorted loudly. "This heart isn't pure, Layne. I think you're remembering someone else."

"Were you the girl that told me she couldn't stay and study for our biology test because you needed to cook dinner and bathe the younger foster kids at home?"

"Yeah."

"Were you the girl who stopped James Rickly from beating up a kid who had worn the same pair of pants three days in a row?"

"Yes."

"And what about you hiding food in your locker? Was it for the younger foster kids?"

I nodded again. "How did you know?"

"Because every afternoon between sixth and seventh period, I made sure I walked by while you were at your locker. I needed one last glimpse of you for the day before I headed home."

Sinking back onto my stool, I stared at him, speechless. "If you'd really known me—"

"I do know you. I've known you for years. I've watched you and adored you from across the cafeteria." He chuckled. "That was romantic, huh?"

I smiled shyly. "Why didn't you say anything to me about it?"

He gave a half-shrug. "I thought about it all the time. Then Chloe showed up, and as you know, we dated for a while. I did care about her, so I just assumed I'd gotten over my crush on you. But then our senior year, you were in my English lit class, and that was it for me."

"Can I ask you what happened with Chloe after you broke up with her?"

Layne sighed, grief evident in his smoky-blue eyes. "I broke up with her, and I had planned on waiting a few days before I located you. I'd intended to apologize and see what I could do to help, but Chloe showed up at my house the next morning before school. She was pregnant." He paused, rubbing his face with his hands as though it would erase the pain of losing Nicole. "She thought I'd take her back, but I didn't. I did support her through the pregnancy, the doctor's appointments, and I got a job at the grocery store. All my money went to Nicole, as it should have." He looked away briefly, then back to me.

"I don't know a lot of guys who would have done that. I mean taken responsibility," I whispered.

"There was an innocent baby involved, and although I couldn't stand Chloe, I wouldn't make my child suffer."

My brows creased. "Layne, the night I found you drunk and out of it, you kissed Chloe, not me. At first anyway. But did you still love her? Even a little bit?"

Layne took my hands in his. The heat from his skin consumed me. "I cared about her because she was the mother of my daughter. Although I didn't particularly like her, it's a bond that I'd never had with anyone else. Her death fucked me up a lot, though. We'd shared good and bad times, and even when I thought she was cruel and heartless to you before the baby was born, I had to make the best of the situation for Nicole's sake. Sometimes a man has to realize it has nothing to do with the mom—it's all about the kid. You make nice, you're respectful, and you show your child what it's like to be a good father."

"I'm so sorry." More than anything, I wanted to kiss his pain away, but there was nothing I could do.

"To answer your question, finally, I want to be with you. I'm not dating anyone else. In fact, I haven't since I lost Nicole. I'm not sleeping with anyone either, and no one has my heart except you. I'm willing to take a chance on us." He tipped my chin up with his finger. "My only concern is that my emotions are probably ahead of yours, and I'm worried I'm going to say or do the wrong thing, move too fast. I can't lose you. After all this time, you're finally next to me."

"I'd rather just know so I'm clear. Otherwise, I'll run myself fucking crazy, wondering how you feel, or if I've said something wrong, or if you're going to walk out that door and never return." I wrung my hands together, trying to calm my overactive anxiety and trust issues that were plaguing me.

His eyes bored into mine, and silence descended over us. "I'm in love with you, and I have been for a while."

Shock rippled through me. "My entire life has been filled with empty words and promises. If you really love me, then show me. Make love to me, Layne. Let me give you everything I have to offer, the one thing I've never willingly given to anyone before."

He swallowed visibly. "I don't want to rush you. I know some of your experiences haven't been consensual, and there's no way I'd ever want to hurt you."

"Show me," I demanded quietly.

In one quick motion, Layne stood and swept me into his strong arms. "Is anyone else home?"

"No," I answered breathlessly.

"Good." He carried me to my room and gently placed me on the bed. He kicked off his shoes, closed the door, and flipped the lock. Then he quickly shed his dark-burgundy polo shirt and tossed it on the floor, exposing his muscular chest. I rolled over on my side and reached out to run my fingernails down his abs. He was beautiful, absolutely delicious. Leaning over me, he took my mouth with his. I threaded my hands in his hair and pulled him to me. I wanted to feel every inch of him.

He fumbled with my pants and sat up while he pulled them down my long legs. Then he stood and dropped his jeans. His thick shaft bobbed free. Although I'd seen him before, he hadn't been hard when he was passed out in my bed.

"Dear God," I muttered, staring at him.

His brows knitted together. "Are you all right? We can stop."

I shook my head furiously. "No. I want to be with you."

He pulled my black shirt off and unhooked my white bra. His eyes darkened as he tentatively slipped the straps off my shoulders. Cupping my breast, he leaned me onto the bed as our gazes locked.

"Hang on." He picked up his jeans and grabbed his wallet out of his back pocket. A second later, he produced a condom.

"Thank you. Maybe to a lot of girls, using protection wouldn't mean anything, but you just showed me you care about me."

"You have no idea how much." He rolled it on, then focused on removing my panties. After removing them quickly, he tossed them to the floor where they joined the rest of our clothes. For the second time in my life, I was naked with someone I cared deeply about. The first time had been the other night with Layne.

"I need to taste you," he whispered before disappearing between my legs. Layne wasn't wasting any time—he went right for my sensitive bud. His tongue skillfully worked its magic while I moved against his mouth.

"That's it, baby," he said.

I wasn't sure if Layne was incredibly talented in the bedroom or if my emotional attachment made his touch that much more intense. Regardless, I was putty in his hands, and he could make me do anything he wanted, including come in record time.

"Layne!" I cried, stars exploding behind my eyes.

He wiped his mouth and smiled while he kissed a trail up my stomach and to my breasts. He nipped and sucked my nipples, giving each of them equal care as he settled his hips between my legs. His long member rested on my waist, and butterflies broke out in my chest. He rolled over slightly and guided his dick over my swollen clit, and his eyes fluttered closed briefly.

"I've thought about this so many times," he confessed. He kissed me passionately before I could respond. The tip of his cock paused at my entrance, and in one smooth, gentle motion, he buried himself inside me.

My fingernails dug into his back as a cry escaped my throat.

"Are you okay?" He stilled, waiting for me to reply.

Before I knew it, my chin trembled, and tears slipped down my cheeks. "I need a minute."

"Dammit. I hurt you." His lips brushed against my damp face.

I shook my head. "No. I mean, it's been a while, and you're bigger than ... I didn't take this step lightly. It's the first time I've willingly been with someone. Before I left Arkansas, it had always been forced on me or for survival, not because I wanted it." I dried my face with the back of my hand.

He kissed the tip of my nose and made eye contact with me as his thumb stroked my lower lip. "I love you," he whispered.

More fucking tears escaped. I'd never experienced such a deep connection to someone, and it was overwhelming me. His touch, his words, his gentleness left me speechless, yet wanting more: more of him, his mind, his soul, and his body. In return, I would willingly give him everything inside me. No more walls, no more hiding. Just him and me.

"I love you so much," he whispered again. "I won't hurt you. Just let me love you."

I'd never felt so wanted and cherished. Layne had just given himself to me. For the first time, I held someone's heart in my hand, and I swore I would protect it. There was no turning back. He'd unlocked all the emotions I'd kept tucked away. Layne Garrison held the key, and all I needed to do was say yes.

"Yes," I whispered.

He moved tentatively inside me and I leaned up to kiss him. I ran my hands up and down his back, my fingers dancing over the rippling muscles in his ass.

"You feel so good," I said, relaxing into him.

He picked up the pace as our bodies and hearts continued to connect. All the pain of the past and all the fear of the future simply slipped away while I surrendered to this man. I rocked my hips against him, and sweet sensations spiraled through me.

"Layne," I moaned. "I ... I ..." I wrapped my legs around his waist, pulling him deeper inside me. "Oh God. I've never ..." I panted. "Oh …" I clawed at his skin, my body igniting from the very core of my being. My pussy clenched tightly around him, and my head tilted back as I screamed his name.

"Jesus," he cried, shuddering and tensing as we climaxed together.

Satisfied emotionally and physically, I went limp, and so did he. He planted kisses on my neck, chin, and mouth. We locked gazes, and I melted.

"I love you, Ten."

"I'm falling for you too. But I'm scared out of my head. Please don't break my heart."

"I promise." His entire face lit up with his gentle words.

"Besides, you're the first man that's ever made me come during sex." I giggled as Layne grinned like a happy fool.

14

Layne tossed the condom in the trash can near my window, then crawled back into bed next to me. "Come here." He wrapped his arm around me.

I nestled my head on his chest, loving the soft rise and fall of his breathing. It was calming and peaceful.

His fingers toyed with my hair, and for a painful moment, my butchered flagpole haircut flashed before my eyes. Pushing the memory out of my mind, I reminded myself that he'd seen me at my worst, yet there he was next to me.

"Have you ever considered trying to find your family?" he asked.

I propped up on an elbow and stared him down. "That's a really intense thing to ask me right now."

"I didn't mean for it to be. I've been meaning to ask you, but I didn't want to step on your toes. If you wanted to do Ancestry.com or something, I'd do it with you. I hear the results are posted online, and I'd love to be a part of you reuniting with your family. If that's what you want, I mean."

"Really? Why?"

His jaw tightened briefly. "Because I'd give anything to have

Nicole back, and if you have a chance to find your mom, dad, cousins, aunts, and uncles, I'd encourage it. And if you wanted to find out who they were but not meet them, that's all right too. I just know how important my family is … was. I wanted to offer to help was all." He stroked my hand with the pad of his thumb while he spoke. Then his eyes clouded with regret. "Maybe it's not the best idea I've ever had."

"No, I get it. You've lost part of your family, but you still have a loving and supportive mom and dad. It wasn't like that for me. Dad skipped out when I was three years old. I never heard shit from him. He made his choice."

Layne twirled a strand of my hair around his finger. "What about your mom?"

"My mom sold me to her dealer for heroin." The door of my heart slammed shut as the words left my lips. I'd never been able to forgive her for it.

Layne bolted upright in bed, a look of horror twisting his face. "Shit. I had a really bad idea, babe. I'm so sorry. Your mother doesn't deserve to see what a beautiful and wonderful woman you've turned out to be. Holy fuck." He ran his hands through his hair, his mouth opening and closing as if he were struggling for something positive to say, but the words were beyond his reach.

"You didn't know." I sat up next to him and pulled my knees to my chest, the dark-green sheet still covering me. "I was twelve," I whispered, unwilling to look at him. "Mom was jonesing really bad when her dealer showed up at the house with a fix, but then she admitted she didn't have any money. Before I knew it, he'd slapped his big, gruff hand over my mouth and jerked me out the front door. I never saw Mom again." My words fell flat and lifeless, almost as though I hadn't been the one to live the trauma. I wasn't sure if it was normal to shut down in that way or not.

Layne's breathing came in short bursts as he clenched his hands into fists.

"He tried to rape me, and I fought him with everything I had. He beat me to a bloody mess, then raped me. I was in and out of consciousness the entire time. When he was finished, he tossed me in a dumpster full of trash. I didn't even know where I was, nor did I care, but it was the first night I prayed to God to let me die. He ignored me. I stopped praying after that."

Layne pulled me into his lap, enveloped me in his arms, and rocked us slowly. I wasn't sure if he was comforting himself or me. I'd lived with what had happened to me for years, but he'd just heard it for the first time.

"I swear to you, Tensley Bennett, I will never allow someone to hurt you again." His voice was stern and protective.

I didn't reply because, although I understood where his heart was, I knew shit happened that was completely out of a person's control, and so did he. We were both living proof.

We held each other for a while, allowing the silence and the nightfall to comfort us. Maybe sharing the agony of the past would allow us to heal. Even if it didn't, no one had cared enough to share the weight of the pain and memories so deeply and intimately.

Finally, I wiggled off his lap and gave him a quick peck on his mouth. "Thank you."

He placed a kiss on my forehead and leaned back. "Anytime."

"I have to pee." I gave him a reassuring smile that I was okay and bounded out of bed. I scooped his shirt off the floor and slipped it on. It hit me midthigh, just enough to keep my ass covered if Avery was home. "Do you want anything to drink? A soda? Beer? Um, our dinner?" I giggled. "I totally forgot the food is on the island. If you want to eat in here, we can. I'm happy to warm it up and bring it to you."

"That sounds fantastic. A beer sounds good too." He licked his lips as his eyes greedily scanned my body. "I'd love dessert as well."

I gave him a playful wink. "You got it."

I hummed happily under my breath as I made my way down the hall. I hurried to the bathroom and quickly relieved myself. My core throbbed from the intense sex, but it didn't stop me from wanting more. After I washed my hands, I poked my head into the hallway and noted that Avery's door was closed. Although I didn't hear anything, I wasn't sure she if was in there or still gone.

I tiptoed down the hall just in case. The last thing I wanted was to run into Justin. I would die of embarrassment. I ducked into the kitchen, darted to the fridge, and threw the door open. I grabbed two beers and popped the lids off. I took a big swig and grinned. It had been one hell of a night, and for the first time in years, I was happy. Shit, I was finally in love. A silly grin spread across my face.

A loud bang and shouts filled my house, and a scream ripped through my throat as men dressed in black filed into my living room. "FBI! Hands up!"

"What the literal fuck?" It happened so fast, I barely had time to process that guns were trained on me. The beer bottles slipped from my grasp, crashing to the linoleum floor.

Heavy-booted men scattered through the rooms and down the hallway.

"Layne!" I shouted, attempting to give him a heads-up. Surely, he'd heard the commotion, though.

"Hands behind your head!" the agent yelled at me, his authoritative voice sending chills down my spine.

"Tensley!" Layne rounded the corner in his jeans and no shirt, halting when he realized a weapon was trained on him.

"On the floor!" another agent commanded.

"Layne, what's happening?" Terror traveled through me, and my body began to shake as I kneeled in the spilled beer and shattered glass. My eyes cut over to Layne, a sob escaping my throat.

He slowly sank to the floor, his hands in the air.

What the hell? What is going on? There was no reason the FBI should be in my house. Other than stealing food to eat when I was younger, I'd never broken the law. Even with all the insane activity around me, a horrifying thought gnawed at me then materialized fully. *Layne.* He was the only new person in my life, and I'd only reconnected with him a few months ago. There was no way the FBI could be after Benji or Avery. They weren't even home. *Oh my God.* I'd just fallen in love with a criminal and had no fucking idea.

15

My mouth clamped shut as the cruel reality stomped on my heart. Layne didn't love me. He'd used me to hide from the FBI and cops. *But what did he do?* I struggled to breathe above the panic running riot inside me. I'd been so stupid to trust him.

"No one else is here," one of the agents reported.

I refused to look at Layne, but kept my focus on the front door, which was wide open, causing the cold air to rush into the living room. The blue and red cruiser lights cut through the black night.

A police officer stepped inside, eyeing the situation skeptically. "Bring them down to the station."

"Sir! Please. We will fully cooperate, but can my girlfriend get her pants? She's only wearing my T-shirt," Layne explained, his words full of concern.

Usually, I would have been embarrassed, but I didn't even care. All I wanted were some answers.

"I'll escort you to grab clothes and shoes, but don't even think about running," the officer replied curtly.

Layne nodded. "Can I stand?"

The cop walked over to him, stared long and hard, then gave him permission.

Layne stood slowly, then the cop's boots scuffed against the hallway as he escorted Layne to my room. I remained still, kneeling in the beer and shards of glass, but the pain was nothing compared to what Layne had done to my heart.

Less than a minute later, Layne and the policeman returned. Layne had slipped his shoes on, but I had his shirt.

The cop strolled toward me, holding my items. His badge read Officer Hazelwood. "Get up." His voice was clipped and rude. "Get dressed."

I blinked rapidly at him. "Here?" I squeaked. "While you're staring at me?"

Officer Hazelwood cleared the FBI from the room. "Patrick!"

A female officer appeared at the edge of the kitchen. "Sir?"

"Keep an eye on her while she gets some clothes on, then bring her in."

I gulped, not because another female would see me naked, but because I was being brought in. My faced burned.

"Get used to it, honey," Officer Patrick said, standing in front of me, her hand resting on her gun. "If you're booked, you'll never have privacy again."

Jesus. What did Layne get me into?

"I bounced around foster homes for six years. You lose dignity real fast. So you staring at me doesn't faze me. I don't know what's going on, but I haven't done anything wrong."

"Save it," she said, her tone harsh and unfeeling.

I shed Layne's T-shirt and stood unashamed in front of Officer Patrick. "Layne will need his shirt. If you'd be so kind as to make sure he gets it, I'd appreciate it," I said softly. Although I was a bundle of nerves, I was furious and terrified all at once. I just couldn't allow my mouth to get me in more trouble than I already was.

The officer tossed my clothes on the floor, and I scrambled to pick them up and dress myself. After I slipped my shoes on, she spun me around and slapped cuffs on me. Before I realized it, I'd been read my rights.

I clamped my mouth shut. I needed a fucking lawyer, and I had no idea why. There was only one call I could make, and I knew exactly to whom it needed to be.

Officer Patrick escorted me outside, down the porch steps, and into the back of a police car. The door slammed closed, and I scanned the scene. Layne stood helplessly in the middle of the lawn, handcuffed.

"I love you. Don't talk. I'll get you a lawyer," he mouthed.

His words splintered my heart. No way would I trust a word he said ever again.

I had a front-row seat to the drama unfolding in my yard. The FBI had started to load up and pull away. Although I felt anything but calm, I needed to stay focused. Even if Layne was a criminal, shit was really bad for the FBI to storm into my house like that.

Twenty minutes later, two officers hopped into the front seat and drove to the station.

"I want to call my attorney. I won't tell you anything until I've spoken with him first," I said.

"That's your right," Officer Hazelwood said while driving.

I leaned back in my seat and attempted to steady my breathing. My head was pounding from being scared shitless, but a slow-burning anger was simmering inside me too. Layne Garrison would regret ever messing with me.

HOURS ROLLED by before I was allowed a phone call. I'd declined anything to drink, so I sat alone with my thoughts in the tiny room with white cement blocks and no windows. I assumed Layne was in a little space similar to mine.

As much as I hated to, I called Benji. I knew his parents could help with a lawyer. I would work my ass off to pay them back, but I also doubted they would think I'd done anything wrong other than fall in love with a piece of shit.

Before an attorney arrived, the door swung open, and a handsome, well-dressed man stepped inside. His green eyes, offset by his dark complexion, caught me off guard. His chiseled jaw, perfectly proportioned cheekbones, and full mouth left me mentally panting. These people were nuts. They had to have hired an actor to pretend to be a detective because this guy was way too pretty. Maybe they thought I would roll over and spill my guts because he was possibly the hottest guy I'd ever seen.

"Victoria," he said, pulling out the chair across the table from me.

I pursed my lips and crossed my arms over my chest. That wasn't my name, and they needed to get their facts straightened out.

"I'm Detective Jacobs." He folded his large hands on the table and had the audacity to smile at me.

This isn't a party, dude. Go sweet-talk someone else.

"I understand you lawyered up, and he should be here shortly. I spoke with Michael and Marilyn Parker, who insisted they wait here at the station for you."

I heaved a sigh of relief. Help was on the way.

"I also learned that you and your friend Benji Parker were brutally attacked a few months ago. I wanted to let you know the men who were responsible will be charged with first-degree aggravated assault and first-degree attempted rape. Hate crimes are not taken lightly in Washington, plus it's a federal offense. They will pay for what they did."

"Really? Oh my God, that's wonderful news!" I slapped my hand over my mouth. *Dammit.* He was good. He was trying to connect with me so I would confess to whatever crap I didn't do.

"I thought you'd appreciate having that information. Michael, Marilyn, and Benji also know."

At least the attackers weren't able to walk away after what they'd done to Benji, but neither was he.

He raised one beautifully arched brow at me. "Now, why don't we cut all the bullshit and just have a chat?"

The door swung open, startling me.

"You're not harassing my client, are you?" A stunning man with beautiful blue eyes closed the door behind him. He smoothed his red tie, which complemented his expensive black suit, and walked toward me. I'd heard the term silver fox before, but I hadn't seen any until now. *Jiminy Christmas. Where do they hide these men?*

Detective Jacobs flashed a reassuring smile at my new lawyer. "No. I was just giving her some good news concerning the men who assaulted her and her best friend a few months ago."

My attorney harrumphed and sat in the seat next to me. His kind blue eyes searched mine. "Are you all right? Were they coercing you to talk? Were you manhandled at all?"

"No, sir. I'm okay. I just don't understand what's going on."

"My name is Franklin Harrington. Michael and Marilyn retained me, so I'm at your service." *Why does the name Harrington sound so familiar?*

He patted me on the back and gave me a gentle smile before he turned toward the detective. His expression morphed into something more eager, as though the hunter had just become the prey, and his laser focus homed in on Detective Jacobs.

I almost giggled, partly out of nerves, but also because I knew that Michael and Marilyn would never screw around with my life by hiring a shitty attorney. I owed them big.

Franklin rubbed his chin, then folded his hands on the table and mimicked Detective Jacobs's body language. The tension was palpable in the little room, and I struggled to suppress my leg from bouncing.

"What's this about?" Franklin asked. "The FBI storms into my client's home for what exactly?"

The detective didn't flinch as he responded. "We had probable cause."

"I certainly hope you can back it up, because if not, my client will sue the department for breaking and entering, invasion of privacy, sexual assault, and anything else I can think of. I'll have you all so buried in paperwork, you'll never see another vacation."

Damn. Franklin wasn't playing.

Detective Jacobs slapped a manila envelope on the table and slid it to me.

Franklin gently moved my hand away and pulled it toward him. "Don't say a word until you and I have an opportunity to talk. Let me handle everything until you're released."

I nodded my agreement, secretly relieved he was taking care of me.

Franklin moved the folder, blocking my view, and opened it. His expression never changed as he sifted through the contents. When he was finished, he slapped it on the table and slid it toward me. "What's this have to do with my client?"

I lifted the flap of the envelope and peered at the pictures. The color drained from my face as I sifted through the first three, then set them down. My stomach churned, and I willed myself not to vomit.

The detective leaned back in his seat, his eyes never leaving me. "Does the name Jack Flannery mean anything to you?"

I racked my brain for any recollection, but I had no clue who Jack Flannery was. In fact, no one had mentioned his name to me in the past or recently. With each second that ticked by, I was growing more and more confused.

"Of course it does," Franklin retorted. "He's on the national news for murders in eleven states."

Fuck. Murder? Eleven states? I dug my fingernails into my leg.

My yoga pants didn't provide any protection from the self-inflicted pain. Under no circumstances could I say anything. This had suddenly become more serious than I'd speculated. Terror ripped through me.

What if Layne used an alias? What if Layne is Jack Flannery? Have I just given my heart and body to a serial killer?

16

No matter how hard I tried, my breaths came in short bursts.

Franklin turned toward me, his eyebrow arching. "I need some time with my client."

Detective Jacobs grinned like he'd just caught the mouse he'd been hunting. "You got it." He stood and left the room.

"Tensley, there are cameras in here, but I need to know if you're all right."

I fanned my face as beads of perspiration trickled down my spine. "What if—"

"Whisper it in my ear." Franklin leaned into me.

"Is my boyfriend Jack Flannery? Did he murder people? I thought his name was Layne Garrison." Tears streamed down my cheeks, and I buried my face in my hands as the harsh reality squeezed the life out of my heart, and I broke into sobs.

Franklin patted my hand. "I have a son and daughter your age. I'd do anything for them, protect them from any harm. In fact, I have, but that's a story for another day. You might actually be familiar with the music group August Clover."

"What?" I hiccupped. "They're one of my favorite groups.

You're Hendrix Harrington's father? And you know Gemma?" For a moment, my mind was distracted from the hell I was in the middle of.

He chuckled. "I am."

Then I realized he and Hendrix looked nearly identical except for the height, hair length, and age. My tears and anxiety began to settle down the more he spoke.

"I helped Gemma with some difficult legal issues concerning her father. I didn't represent her because I was too close to the situation, and it occurred in Louisiana. Normally, I take on cases concerning adults, but over the last few years, I've found some great kids in hot water, and it wasn't of their own choosing. If you've kept up with Gemma's story, you know she's doing very well now. I can't divulge the details to you, but I'm not opposed to connecting the two of you. She might be of some valuable support."

I frowned. Although I would wet my pants if I met Hendrix and Gemma, I didn't understand how it all came back to me. I was familiar enough with distraction techniques used to help someone calm down, but now I was incredibly puzzled.

"Okay. But I don't know why I'm here." I leaned into him and whispered, "Are you saying Layne isn't a murderer?"

"I can't answer that yet, but we're going to find out. Are you okay moving forward? If so, I'll step out, grab you something to drink, and invite the detective to join us."

I swallowed hard. I wasn't sure if I was ready to hear the truth. "Yes. Thank you. Something to drink would be great." I offered him the best smile I could muster.

Drumming my fingers against the scuffed wooden table, I did my best to remain calm. Franklin seemed like a good guy who cared about helping me. Plus I trusted Michael and Marilyn. Although my pulse had kicked into overdrive, my tears had dried, and I felt a little more settled.

Five minutes later, Franklin strolled back in with the detective on his heels.

"Jack Flannery," Detective Jacobs began, "is wanted in eleven states. We tracked him here." His green eyes landed on me, sending shivers over my body. "To your house, Victoria."

The cops knew Victoria was no longer my legal name. They were trying to rattle me, and it was working.

"That's not her name. If you're interested in someone named Victoria, we're done here." Franklin began to stand. I looked at him wide-eyed, wondering if it could really be that simple.

"Not so fast, Franklin." The detective held up his hand. "When she was read her Miranda rights, she was addressed by her legal name. However, Victoria Alison Benton was her birth name, and she is the daughter of Jack Flannery."

"What the h-h-hell?" I sputtered, my mouth gaping open in horror. "No. I don't even remember my father. He married my mom, and his name was Bart Benton. He took off when I'd barely turned three. I never saw him again." Desperation and shock rippled off me as I looked at Franklin.

"Let me handle this," he reminded me calmly.

They were wrong. I was in no way related to a monster that could murder someone, much less multiple someones in eleven states. *Shit.*

"Do you have proof, or are you guessing, hoping something will come together?" Franklin asked, leaning back in his chair and crossing his legs. Confidence radiated off him.

I literally wanted to hide behind him.

The detective retrieved a photo from the inside of his cheap suit pocket and slid it over to us. Franklin and I both bent over the photo, and my insides twitched. It was my house. A strikingly handsome man who looked to be in his mid-fifties was slipping inside the tool shed. It was too dark to make out a lot of the details, but he was tall and well-built. His hair was thinning slightly on the top, but I couldn't make out what color it was. There was no mistaking that it was my home, though.

"Your girl here is hiding a serial killer," Detective Jacobs said, "with her boyfriend's help."

"What? I ... no! I don't even know who that man is. Yes, it's—"

Franklin patted my hand to silence me. He leaned his elbows on the table and smiled. "Have you seen this man enter Tensley's home? Have you seen her answer the door and slip him inside? Or her boyfriend? When was this photo taken?"

"Six weeks ago."

Franklin chuckled. "You've got nothing, or you would have moved in faster. For all we know, he had no idea whose house he was at. Or maybe he did, and he wanted to keep tabs on her for whatever reason. But unless you can prove that my client aided and abetted a criminal, we're leaving." Franklin motioned for me to follow him. "If you need anything else, feel free to contact me." He tossed a business card on the table then gently placed his hand on my back and guided me out of the door, leaving the detective alone in the room.

"Tensley," Franklin said once we were in the hall, away from anyone, "is Jack Flannery your father?"

My eyes brimmed with tears as I shrugged. "I don't remember him."

"How do you feel about a DNA test to at least be sure? Regardless if he is or isn't, he's been on your property, and you're in grave danger."

"Can we talk somewhere else? I have questions, and I need to see if Layne is all right. I thought ... I thought the FBI was after him." I covered my mouth with my hand, attempting to hold back the tears. I was so relieved that he was still my Layne, at least for the moment. I assumed he'd learned about Jack Flannery as well, and that most likely changed everything between us. There was no way Layne would want to date a serial killer's daughter.

"It's a little after midnight, but everything is fresh in your mind, and I now have the file with all the information I need. Let's wait for Layne to be released, then I can take you to my office."

With every step toward the exit, my pulse picked up pace. I couldn't even imagine what Michael and Marilyn would think. But as we rounded the corner, I found them pacing and holding hands.

The moment Marilyn saw me, she rushed to me and hugged me hard. "Are you all right?" She grabbed my shoulders, scanning me for anything amiss.

"I'm physically fine. And thank you for sending Mr. Harrington. I promise I'll repay you."

"Don't you even worry about it. He owes me one," Michael said, shaking Franklin's hand and smiling.

"Happy to help," Franklin said. "We might have an interesting road ahead of us."

"Tensley?"

I whirled around, my stomach twisting into knots.

Before I had time to speak his name, Layne bolted to me, picked me up off the floor, and hugged me. "Babe, are you okay?"

"Yeah," I whispered. "Are you?"

He gently lowered me to the ground and kissed me. "No one laid a hand on you or bullied you?" He smoothed the hair from my face while he quickly assessed me.

I shook my head. "Do you know? Did they tell you why the FBI showed up?" Showed up was an understatement. It would've been more accurate to say they charged in like a fucking bull that was mad as hell.

"Yeah, and I don't know the entire story, but this changes nothing. I don't give a shit who your father is. I love you. You don't have to say it back until you're ready, but I want you to know you own my heart." He leaned down and kissed me again. "I'm right here with you."

"Thank you," I whispered, my chin wobbling for the umpteenth time that night.

"Tensley, let's get everyone to my place. I'll make some coffee and we can speak openly," Franklin suggested.

"You can both ride with us," Marilyn said, wrapping a protective arm around my shoulders.

Layne held my hand tightly, giving me a reassuring squeeze, silently telling me that he wasn't going anywhere. I hoped like hell.

"Wait What about Benji?" I asked.

"My sister is with him," Michael piped in. "But he'll be on pins and needles until he knows you're okay."

I directed my attention to Franklin. "If I don't discuss any details with him, can I at least call and let him know I'm okay?"

"Of course. I've known Benji since he was ten. He's a great guy, and I trust he can keep things under wraps. But for now, just tell him you're all right and will give him more information as soon as you can."

"Thank you."

We left the police station together, and Layne continued to place soft kisses on the back of my hand. We slipped into the back of Michael's Lexus SUV, and I called Benji the moment we were on the way to Franklin's.

"I've been going crazy for hours. What the hell happened?" Benji asked as soon as he answered the phone.

"I can't tell you anything yet. Besides, we're still trying to figure it out ourselves. But I'll fill you in as soon as I can. We're on our way to Franklin Harrington's house to discuss the next steps." I blew out a huge breath and rubbed my forehead. I'd been through a lot of shit in my life, but this might have topped it all. "Maybe I'll be able to tell you more tomorrow. I'm safe, though. I just wanted to let you know."

"Thank you. I'm glad you called. And seriously, Ten, try to stay out of trouble until tomorrow, will ya?"

"I'll do my best." Benji didn't evoke a laugh from me, but I did smile. I tapped the red End Call button and reached for Layne's hand.

Marilyn eyed us over her shoulder. then smiled. "I see you two figured out your way to each other."

Layne kissed the back of my hand. "Yes, ma'am."

"I'm pleased to hear it." Her face grew serious as she twisted around in her seat a little more. "If you hurt her, you'll have Michael to deal with, but even worse ... me."

"I understand."

The moment Marilyn turned around, Layne sank into his seat slightly and rubbed his eyes. He peeked at me and winked. Maybe he was processing the fact that Marilyn had basically threatened his life if he screwed me over.

I was just thankful I had some type of parents in my life that loved me. If I'd ever doubted Michael and Marilyn, I didn't after that night.

Michael took a sharp turn off Division and continued to follow Franklin's car.

"How long have you known Mr. Harrington?" I asked.

"Michael and I were friends with his wife, Janice, before they met. They divorced for a while but recently worked things out. Franklin has had his share of life and bad choices, but he's done a remarkable job at repairing the damage. He's very well-respected in Washington."

"He mentioned his son, Hendrix."

A broad smile eased across Marilyn's face. "He's an amazing young man and doing so well for himself. Franklin said the band will begin a new tour soon."

"I love August Clover!" I covered my mouth with my hand, realizing my voice had been too loud for the confined space.

"Wait, your lawyer is *the* Hendrix Harrington's dad?" Layne's eyes widened with the realization.

"Yes!"

His face lit up. "Holy crap. I've followed their success since the band was formed. I had no idea you liked them."

"My fave. And, oh man, Gemma's voice is amazing. She and Hendrix complement each other so well." I released a total fangirl sigh right next to my boyfriend.

"Have you heard Cade's new song?" Layne asked.

"Oh my God, it's so so good."

"I'm taking you to a concert after all of this is over. Maybe it will give us something to look forward to while Franklin figures all of this out."

I nodded, reality weighing heavily on my shoulders again. "I'd love that."

We fell into a heavy silence until Michael pulled into a long, curved driveway and parked in front of a mansion.

"Holy shit," I muttered under my breath, then chastised myself for swearing around Michael and Marilyn.

17

It was almost one in the morning when we all filed into Franklin's house. I thought Michael and Marilyn's home was luxurious, but Franklin's stole my breath away.

"Come on in," Franklin said, keying in the code and stepping inside. "Janice is asleep, but she won't hear us."

Michael patted Franklin on the back. "I'm looking forward to your Christmas party this year. I wish we were here on better circumstances and catching up with our friend."

"Is anyone hungry or thirsty? I have a full bar, snacks in the fridge, and soda."

I held up my hand sheepishly. "I'm starving."

Layne chuckled and slid his arm around me. "My girl can eat."

Franklin grinned at me. "Aww, then you should meet Mac."

My eyebrow arched. "Mac?"

"Mackenzie, but we call her Mac. She's my daughter, and when she's stressed, she can eat like no one I've ever seen. She's petite, so at least she can get away with it. I, on the other hand, couldn't." Franklin patted his flat stomach. "Follow me." Franklin locked the door behind us, then turned on his heel and guided us into the kitchen.

I stared at the black-and-white swirled marble that not only graced the entrance but expanded down the hallway as far as I could see. Massive decorative pillars marked the opening of a formal dining room on the left, and a more casual living area was to our right. A mahogany staircase led upstairs.

It was rude to gawk, but as we entered the kitchen, I did just that. A rich, deep brownstone covered the wall and accented the stove and oven, and the dark cabinets complemented the tan marble countertops. The large stainless steel refrigerator took up most of the wall. It could easily have fit three standard-sized fridges inside it.

"Please, we will be here for a while, so let's get everyone comfortable." He opened the fridge and began pulling out beer, iced tea, and soda. Next, he took out a large dish. "Ruby made this today." He lifted the lid and eyeballed it. "Oh, it's her taco casserole. It will melt in your mouth. Who wants some?"

We all stared at each other, then agreed we could eat. Franklin popped it in the oven for twenty minutes while we grabbed drinks, plates, and silverware. I sat at the bar while Marilyn and Michael settled in at the little table in the breakfast nook. Layne slid onto the seat next to me, rubbing his hand in small circles on my back. If my anxiety wasn't so high, I would probably have fallen asleep.

Franklin grabbed a tan dish towel from the oven handle, wiped his hands off, then leaned against the kitchen counter, facing us. "While this is cooking, we can start discussing details."

We nodded, allowing him to lead the conversation.

"Here's what I know about this case so far. It's huge. Jack Flannery has crossed eleven states, murdering two to three women in each one that the FBI is aware of. What makes this case so interesting is that he's not targeting prostitutes or young girls who are on the streets. His victims are professional women who have money. They're educated, smart, and don't easily fall for someone asking for help to find his lost puppy. Jack's a good-looking guy, so that helps. He's meeting these people at business conferences, fundraisers, and political events. He's sharp and cunning."

Shivers ripped through my body. That man had been on my property. Regardless if we were related or not, he was dangerous. *How can I sleep there again? Shit. Is Avery there alone?*

My eyes widened with fear. "Excuse me, but I have a very gorgeous roomie that I live with, and I need to make sure she's not alone at our place tonight."

"It's already taken care of, hon," Marilyn said behind me. "Benji told her she needed to either stay with Justin or her family tonight. No one is at your house."

I sank in my seat, relieved. I couldn't believe it had taken me that long to consider Avery's safety.

The oven timer buzzed, and Franklin removed the casserole. He continued to talk while he cut everyone's pieces and placed them on plates for us. "This next part is going to get detailed and gruesome. So for now, Tensley, why don't you tell me what you do remember about your father while we eat?" He put a plate in front of me then Layne.

It smelled heavenly, and my mouth watered from anticipation.

"Thank you," I said, digging right in. Grabbing a napkin off the counter as my eyes rolled back in my head. "Amazing."

Everyone laughed, and I was thankful for the lighter mood, even if it was only briefly.

I speared another bite with my fork, grateful for the warm, delicious food. Sometimes the little things were all it took to make me happy.

"I don't remember much about my father. I'd barely turned three when he took off. I don't even remember what he looks like. I know that doesn't help, but I can't imagine that I'm related to this Flannery monster. I mean, people have pissed me off, but I've never harmed or killed anyone. If my dad was a murder, isn't it ..." I frowned, searching for the right word. "Genetic? I don't know. Maybe it's just my opinion that their brain is broken. It's not firing correctly or something. I wouldn't go so far as to say nothing is wrong with me, but not like that."

"You're not necessarily incorrect, but there are several theories floating around out there." Franklin took a drink of his soda and pursed his lips into a thin line. Apparently, he wasn't hungry. "Are you open to a DNA test?"

I put my fork down. Shit was getting real. "Yeah. I'll do it." I glanced over my shoulder at Layne, who placed a gentle kiss on the side of my head.

"How long does it take?" I asked.

"Not long at all. The results can take up to two weeks, but I have a friend who can push it through faster, and we could have the results in forty-eight hours, possibly sooner."

"That fast?" I squeaked. My stomach churned. What if I was wrong and Jack Flannery, the serial killer, was my father? Shit. Even Luke Skywalker's father would look like a good option compared to Flannery.

"The sooner the better. The DNA results won't clear or convict you since the FBI has photos of him on your property. It will, however, give us something to work with. If you're related, it might explain why he was in your shed. We would then assume he would come back. I realize it's going to be unnerving for you, but once we clear you of hiding him, the accusations will be all over. It will be worth a few difficult days."

"We'll be with you. You have our full support," Michael added.

I stared at my clean plate, wondering how my life would change and hoping this would all be a memory that would fade into the night.

Franklin collected our plates and ran water over them in the sink. "Why don't we move into my office?"

I grabbed my beer and hopped off the barstool. Layne took

my hand, his fingers threading through mine while we followed everyone past the living room and down a long hall.

Franklin's office was at the back of the house. "Have a seat wherever you like." He sat at his desk.

I chose one of the black leather wingback chairs in the corner. Layne settled in next to me while Michael and Marilyn sat closer to Franklin's desk.

The mahogany wood from the staircase continued into his office. Several bookshelves held law books and pictures of him with a beautiful woman whom I assumed was his wife. My face lit up as my eyes landed on Hendrix and Gemma. A gorgeous dark-haired girl stood next to them. I suspected it was Mackenzie, his daughter. They looked so happy. I wanted that. I wanted to belong to a happy family. *Maybe someday.*

My attention was pulled away as Franklin began to talk again. "The FBI finally caught a break in these murders when they found a few spots of blood that didn't match the last victim. It was then they identified the killer. Jack's been on the run since. He knows he's being watched, so I hope that stops his killing spree, but I doubt it. He loves the game. Jack builds a friendship with these women after meeting them at a conference or event. He continues to attend events and establishes a connection. Once they trust him, he invites them for drinks at his place. They never see the light of day again. He's a cruel, sick bastard."

Franklin cleared his throat and took a deep breath. It was the first time I'd seen the case get to him. "In some instances, he prepared a soundproof room and suspended them from the ceiling with meat hooks in their skin."

I gagged. "What kind of person does something like that?" I grunted, clutching my stomach. I suddenly regretted that I'd wanted to eat before we discussed details.

"That's just the beginning, I'm afraid. When the victims have been found, they've been … filleted and put in a wedding dress.

At some point, he's had sex with them, but I don't know if it's pre- or postmortem."

"Dear God," Marilyn said, the color draining from her face.

Michael clutched her hand, visibly upset.

I swallowed multiple times, forcing back the bitter bile that threatened to come up. Jack Flannery was one sick fuck.

"Sir, she can't go back to that house. No one can. He knows where she is, and if anything happened to her …" Layne pinched the bridge of his nose. "It just can't happen." His voice cracked with a combination of fear and anger.

"How long have you two been together?" Franklin asked, compassion filling his handsome face.

"Very recently, but we've known each other since high school," I responded, giving Layne's hand a gentle squeeze. I glanced over at him, and his blue eyes were filled with worry.

"Then it sounds like our first priority is to keep you two safe so you can enjoy your future together. Do you have someone you can stay with?" Franklin directed his question at me.

Tears filled my eyes as I looked at everyone in the room. "I …"

"She's staying with us. Both of them are," Marilyn said. "Benji will be thrilled to have you all under the same roof. He's been lonely anyway."

I tucked a stray piece of hair behind my ear with a shaky hand. "Marilyn, I can't impose. We have no idea how long this might take."

"It's already decided," Michael added. "Layne, it would make more sense if you stayed with us as well unless you have a family you can stay with that you've not seen lately? We don't know if he's followed you to where you're staying now."

"I've been living with my uncle, but he's out of town for a few weeks."

"Oh my God, I visited you guys yesterday. I'd been at the Parkers' for hours. "If Jack is tracking me, then he might have seen me at your house. That would put everyone at risk. I can't do that." I dabbed at my forehead with my hand. I wasn't feeling so great. All the events of the night had me reeling.

Marilyn scooted to the edge of her seat, her eyes never leaving my face. "We have a security system and the means to hire bodyguards."

Michael nodded. "Correct. That's why we think it would be better for everyone to stay at our place. Besides, if you're all under one roof, you're easier to keep up with. If all of you are scattered, I'm afraid my wife won't get a wink of sleep. We need to remain functional. Sharp." His leg bounced up and down briefly. We were all scared.

I tugged on my lower lip with my teeth, analyzing the situation from as many angles as possible. "What if the bodyguards throw off everything? If I were Jack, the minute I saw them, I'd move."

Franklin pulled a business card from his wallet. "I have a recommendation: Westbrook Security. These guys are the best I've ever worked with. If you want them hidden, you'll never see them. Trust me—Pierce is your man." He handed the card to Michael.

"I'll call them tomorrow, then. At least for now, it's settled, and the kids will stay with us."

Marilyn gave us a sincere smile. "What good is a big house if it's not filled with fun and laughter?"

"Thank you," Layne said. "My main priority is keeping Tensley safe."

"It's now about all of you," Franklin added, leaning back in his chair. "All right. Let's get your bodyguards in place first, then someone can take Tensley downtown for the DNA test as soon as we can. I'll call my contact and see how fast they can test her and deliver results. Hopefully, we won't have to wait long."

"Thank you," I said. "For everything."

"You bet. You all get some sleep." Franklin continued some small talk as he escorted us to the front door.

A few minutes later, we were on our way to my best friend's house. I wondered if he would still be up even though it was late.

There was no way I would be able to sleep. I wouldn't admit it, but I might be afraid to close my eyes after hearing the details of Jack Flannery's murders. At least I could snuggle up to Layne, but even then, I didn't think it would slow my mind down from fucking with me.

My pulse continued to escalate on the ride to Benji's. Layne hadn't released my hand, and I was grateful. The last thing I wanted was to be alone.

MARILYN WAS a natural and gracious host. Layne and I kept our voices down as we ascended the tan carpeted stairs behind her in case Benji was asleep. I'd been in the house many times, but I was always struck by how much the Parkers loved their home. Family photos lined the walls and included Benji waterskiing behind their boat, attending reunions, and at Christmas parties. I'd been invited to the parties since I'd met Benji, but my insides twisted into knots when I saw the pictures because I knew it wasn't a facade. The love they shared and the bond they had were genuine, and someday I hoped to have those for myself. Until then, I counted my blessings that the Parkers included me in holidays and get-togethers.

"This is Benji's room. Layne, you'll be across the hall, and Tensley will be the last door on the left. Let me make sure the bathrooms have clean towels before you get settled. That way, if you want to … oh dear." Marilyn stopped midway down the hallway and turned toward me. "I'll get you some pajamas, Tensley. We look about the same size. I'm probably a little bigger, but I don't think you'll drown in them. Layne, you can probably borrow a clean shirt and shorts from Benji. I'll make sure we grab you both fresh clothes tomorrow."

"Thank you again, Mrs. Parker," Layne said. "I'm happy to help with anything around the house too. I'm a neat guy, so I won't make a mess or be in the way."

My heart expanded with an array of emotions: love, appreciation, respect, and awe. Layne had been through so much, but he'd remained kind and respectful. I didn't know how he hadn't closed off the world after losing Nicole. Or maybe he had, and I just hadn't been around to witness it.

Marilyn patted him on the cheek and beamed at him. "I knew the first time I laid eyes on you that you were a good man. You'd have to be in order to win Tensley over."

My cheeks flushed with her words. Although she was paying Layne a wonderful compliment, she understood it was difficult for me to allow new people into my circle, much less a boyfriend.

A little after three in the morning, Marilyn left and returned with clean clothes for us. Not only had she brought me something to sleep in, but she'd also provided me with a fresh pair of jeans and a polo shirt. She'd even included a brand-new pair of underwear with the tag still on them. They were from Saks Fifth Avenue. As soon as she disappeared down the stairs for the night, I grabbed Layne's hand and dragged him down the hall to my room.

"I want to see if Benji is awake, but first ..." I flipped on the light, stood on my tiptoes, and kissed him. His arms encircled my waist and pulled me flush against his muscular body. "I need a distraction right now." Frantically, I fumbled with the button and zipper on his jeans and tugged them down. I wrapped my fingers around his hard dick and sighed while I stroked him.

"I like the way you think." He groaned before his lips crashed down on mine.

In record time, my pants and panties were around my ankles. I stepped out of them, and Layne spread my legs.

"You're so wet," he whispered against my ear.

I moved his hand and slid my fingers along my wet slit, then I rubbed my juices along the tip of his cock.

"Oh my God, that feels good."

We'd only been together once, but I wasn't in the mood to make love. I wanted him to fuck me. And I wanted to make him come harder than he had in his entire life.

I brushed past him and crawled onto the bed on all fours, my ass tipped in the air. I tossed him a look over my shoulder and grinned.

Layne kicked off his jeans and waited for my next move.

I rolled over and shed my shirt and bra. "No touching. You can only watch." I pulled my bottom lip in between my teeth and traced a trail down my stomach with my fingertips.

He laced his fingers behind his head and sucked in a sharp breath, his heated gaze never diverting from my body. My hand slipped between my legs, and I spread my folds apart for him, gently circling my throbbing clit. Layne grabbed his hard dick and squeezed.

"No touching. That means you too." An impish grin appeared on my face while I eased a finger inside myself, then two. I moved my hips to my own rhythm, pleasure mounting in me. My other hand tweaked my nipple, and Layne looked like he was about to explode. I moaned, throwing my head back as I pleasured myself, and he watched. This was sexy as hell, and I would happily watch him as well. But right then, I needed him to finish me off.

"I need you," I said, removing my fingers from my sensitive flesh.

In two long steps, Layne was on his knees, greedily sucking and licking my pussy. His fingers clutched my ass cheeks, holding me in place while his tongue slid inside me.

"Oh yeah." I grabbed his shoulders, digging my fingernails into his skin while I willed myself not to come. *Not yet.* I wasn't ready for his hot, wet mouth to leave me. My hips wiggled beneath him, my orgasm seconds away. His hands wrapped around my waist, pinning me in place.

"Dammit, Layne." The moment I spoke his name, he sucked my bud harder and pumped his fingers inside me.

Black dots floated behind my eyes as I exploded. I clutched at the cream comforter and clamped my mouth shut so I wouldn't scream.

I whimpered as Layne stood and rummaged in his wallet for a condom. He expertly rolled it on while I waited impatiently. I needed to find out if and when he'd been tested so I could get on the pill and not deal with the condoms.

His blue eyes connected with mine, and he pulled my hips to the edge of the bed, then shoved deep inside me from a standing position. Thankfully, the bed was a perfect height for us.

Layne spread my legs wider, picking up the pace. He leaned over, pulling my nipple between his teeth. Although it hurt a little, it felt good at the same time. I liked it, at least from him. His mouth covered my breast while he thrust inside me. He slowed, then smiled at me, his eyes dark with desire. "Stand up." He backed away so I could.

"Turn around." His voice was gruff and demanding.

Chills shivered down my body. I had needed him to take control tonight.

"Bend over the bed and spread your legs."

Jesus, this wasn't his first rodeo for damned sure. I nearly orgasmed with his order alone.

His hand ran over my ass cheek and squeezed. He parted my soaked folds again, then ran the tip of his dick up and down my slit.

"Take me anywhere you want," I whispered over my shoulder. "Just fuck me hard."

Layne's eyes widened, and he eased inside my pussy. He grabbed my hips and forcefully moved me back and forth over his cock.

"Harder," I whimpered, pain and pleasure swirling in me.

"Ten," he gasped, pounding me. One hand massaged my breast as we frantically fucked the awful night away. He tugged hard on my nipple, and I bit my cry back.

"That's it, baby," I said, encouraging him. In the back of my mind, I knew we were having sex in someone else's house, which meant we had to be quiet. But I needed anything I could get to erase the earlier events, even if just for a few minutes.

Layne pulled out, then shoved inside me again. My body lurched forward from the impact, but he grabbed hold of my hips again, steadying me.

"I can't last much longer." His words came in quick, short bursts. His hand slipped between my legs and teased my sensitive bud between his fingers.

With a sharp pinch and pull on my clit, I couldn't hold out anymore. My body went into a full-on frenzy of intense pleasure. I slammed back into him while my core tightened around his shaft, and I released. Bliss didn't even come close to what he'd made me feel. His grunts and shudders followed mine, then I collapsed on the bed with him still inside me. Layne's weight landed on me, crushing me momentarily before he pulled out and rolled over onto the mattress.

I turned my head, eyeing him wearily. We hadn't really discussed what was and wasn't off-limits in the bedroom, and I wondered if I'd pushed the boundary by telling him he could fuck me any way he wanted.

Layne removed the used condom and walked into the bathroom to discard it. I'd been so eager to have him all over me, I hadn't paid that much attention to the room. The king-size bed held two small cream and three larger black throw pillows, and I realized the comforter was feather. I sank right into it.

I sat up, grabbed a pillow, and leaned against the oak headboard. My eyes took in the room. There was a six-drawer dresser with a mirror and two matching nightstands. A vase of fresh pink and red roses rested on the corner of the vanity, but what really added life to the room was the picture of oak and maple trees lining a dirt lane. The trees displayed the most magnificent red and golden autumn leaves. A fence ran along each side of the path as the fog settled in the edges of the land. It was stunning.

"Are you all right?" Layne asked, leaning against the door frame.

My eyes greedily raked over his nakedness and every muscle in his arms, chest, abs, and legs. I'd never seen anyone so edible in my life. My core throbbed with need again.

"Why?" I wondered if we needed to discuss the rules of our sex playground.

He strolled over to his clothes and picked them up off the floor. "Do you want yours?"

"Yeah. I guess I should in case someone knocks on the door or something. I mean, it's highly unlikely at three forty in the morning, but still." I'd opted to wear my yoga pants instead of the pajamas Marilyn had given me. I would save them for after my shower.

We dressed in silence, my anxiety toying with my emotions. Layne's gaze fell on me, then he sat on the opposite side of the bed.

My breath hitched. "Did I do something wrong?"

"What? No. Not at all." He shook his head. "I'm just tired."

I rolled the blankets down and crawled beneath them. My head sank into the pillow, and a soft sigh escaped me.

Layne stood and faced me, rubbing his exhausted face with his hands. "I'm worried about you, Ten."

I sat up and folded my hands over my chest, attempting to contain my emotions from erupting. So much had happened that night. My chin wobbled as the terrifying information Franklin had shared with us about Jack Flannery assaulted my already overloaded mind. "What if he's my ... You're going to leave, and I can't blame you." My hands flew up to my mouth as a soft cry slipped from me. I'd just not had enough time to process all the shit that had gone down earlier that evening. Layne would leave just like everyone else in my life had.

"No, babe. No." Layne hurried to my side of the bed, sat down, and scooped me into his lap. "Ten, I love you. Nothing will change that. I've loved you for a long time, and I'm not going anywhere. Listen to me for a minute. After I lost Nicole, I escaped in every way imaginable—drugs, booze, and a lot of women." He paused, a fleeting look of guilt in his expression. He brushed a stray hair from my face then continued. "All I needed was to be told I was okay, forgiven, that I wasn't a horrible human for not being strong enough to outlast the tornado. You know I still struggle with it today and most likely will for the rest of my life." He visibly swallowed, dealing with his own darkness. "Babe, you've got a lot to deal with, and I'm all for a healthy distraction. Whatever sexual boundaries we decide are loving and acceptable for us in the bedroom, I'm fine talking about it. But not yet. You're too vulnerable, and I can't be the one that shatters the fragile exterior that's barely holding you together. You're strong, Ten. I've never met a stronger woman, but you can't carry this on your own. You're safe. *We're* okay, so please stop worrying." He placed a gentle kiss against my mouth. "We're in this together no matter how shitty it looks. You're. Not. Alone. Ever. Again."

I fought the tears that welled in my eyes. "What if ... What if Jack Flannery is my father? You can't tell me you'll not want to get as far away from me as possible. What if I'm just like him, and I don't know it yet?"

"They would have seen signs of it when you were younger— killing animals and shit like that. Don't let anyone tell you differently." He cupped my chin, and our gazes locked. A fire burned in his eyes. "DNA does *not* define you. Everyone who loves you knows your kind and generous heart, your spunk, your determination, and ability to determine right from wrong. Ten, it's all those things I fell in love with when we were in high school. You're the epitome of good. If you share DNA with Jack Flannery, in no way does that change who you are. You're good and loving, but most importantly, you're mine." He leaned his forehead against mine and kissed the tip of my nose.

His words sank deep inside me, unraveling all the fear, anger, guilt, and sadness from the past years. Before I could stop myself, my shoulders heaved, and quiet sobs shook my body. I curled into Layne while his hand gently stroked my back.

He held me while I cried. "I love you."

"I'm so sorry." I nearly choked on my words. "When the FBI showed up, I thought they were after you." I peeked up at him and my chest tightened. "Please don't be mad at me."

Layne's jaw tightened. "I'll be glad when you trust me completely, but I know it will take time. And why wouldn't you have thought the FBI was after me? Everyone in your life has lied to you and used you." He tipped my chin up with his finger. His gentle expression was full of the forgiveness I needed. "I'll show up for you again and again, and soon your heart will catch up to mine."

At some point, we slid underneath the blankets with our clothes on. Layne snuggled up to me, his strong arms wrapping me in a safe cocoon while I drifted off to sleep.

18

It was nearly one in the afternoon when I woke up. Layne had already left the bed, and my heart ached as reality weighed heavily on my shoulders.

Not ready to face the day yet, I burrowed under the blankets and closed my swollen eyes. The Saturday afternoon sky appeared as dreary as I felt. Although I'd agreed to a DNA test, I was scared shitless. Unable to shut my mind off, I opted for a long shower.

I rifled through the clothes Marilyn had so graciously lent me and headed toward the bathroom. I flipped the light on, then stared at the many button options. Fan, sink lights, shower lights, and heated floor. That sounded heavenly. By the time I was done drowning my sorrows under the hot spray, my feet would be toasty warm as they touched the tiles.

The double sinks with beige granite and a large framed mirror were gorgeous. A vanity was across from the walk-in closet, and next to that was a huge shower and the biggest jet tub I'd ever seen. I was pretty sure it would easily hold three people. My mind immediately turned to Layne and all the things I would love to do to him while soaking in bubbles. Although my hormones ran full speed ahead, my body was rebelling after the deliciously hard pounding he'd given me the night before. Sometimes I just needed it rough, and other times slow and gentle.

I pulled on the glass door handle of the shower, and my mouth gaped open. I shouldn't have been surprised, but I'd never seen so many showerheads or spouts or whatever wealthy people called them. A bench long enough for me to sit on and comfortably shave my legs butted up against the far wall. I would definitely take advantage of that, but first I needed to clean myself up. I reeked of sex, and I had more important meetings later that day.

A feeling of dread tugged at me as I turned the water on and stepped under the warm spray. I slammed my eyes shut and focused on the here and now. I was safe and loved.

"Safe and loved," I said over and over again softly. It was apparently my anxiety-reducing mantra. Between talking to myself and the rich scent of the apricot shampoo, the tight muscles in my neck began to relax. *Too bad I can't stay here for the rest of the day.* I applied conditioner to my long hair and let it soak in while I lathered up my body. Twenty minutes later, I stepped out of the shower, dried off, and dressed. Marilyn was right—we were close in size. The jeans were a little baggy, but I preferred the boyfriend fit anyway, so they worked fine.

After drying my hair, I slipped my shoes on and wandered down the hallway. Benji and Layne's doors were open, but I didn't see either of them. Voices carried up the stairs, and I followed them into the living room. Benji, Michael, and Layne were discussing a football game. A flicker of joy sparked inside me. My three favorite guys were not only spending time together, but they seemed to be enjoying it. Benji caught sight of me first. His faced morphed from excitement to concern, which told me he knew all the details of the previous night.

Benji waved me into the living room. "Hey, sleepyhead. I've been waiting for you."

I gave him a big smile. "Hey." No matter how shitty life was, I loved my best friend. "Guess you have roomies again for a few days, huh?"

"Thank God. I need some company." He flashed me a huge grin, alleviating some of the tension in the room.

Layne stood and kissed my cheek before we sat down next to each other on the couch. Benji cocked an eyebrow at me and shot me a *you got laid last night* expression, and I gave him the most innocent look I could muster. I knew damned well Layne and I had been super quiet.

"How are you doing this morning?" Michael asked from the leather recliner across from us while he took a sip of his soda. The heavy damask curtains were closed, and I suspected we were waiting for our new security guys to show up.

I shrugged, not sure how to answer him and not wanting to lie. "I'm not sure yet."

"That's fair." Michael gave me a tight-lipped smile.

"I'm so glad you're safe. When Dad called last night and told me what had happened, I was terrified," Benji blurted.

"It was definitely one hell of a night," I muttered under my breath.

"Tensley, you're awake." Marilyn waltzed into the living room with a soda and plate topped with a grilled cheese and veggie chips for me.

"Thank you! I did wake up hungry." I took a bite of my sandwich, and my tummy growled loudly.

"Everyone else has already eaten, so when I heard your voice, I tossed you something together." She leaned over and gave me a quick kiss on the cheek. Layne's arm tightened around my shoulders and I glanced at him. I almost melted into a puddle on the Parkers' plush couch. No one had ever gazed at me with so much love and adoration in their eyes before.

Marilyn sank into the chair next to her husband and sighed. "I realize you've not been up long, hon, but we have things to take care of today." She folded her hands in her lap then glanced at Michael.

"Pierce Westbrook will be here in about ten minutes," Michael explained. "He has three highly trained bodyguards with him. One will stay on the property, and one will discreetly follow us when we leave."

I stopped chewing. Franklin had mentioned bodyguards the night before, but ... I lowered my sandwich and focused on Benji's parents.

"We will all be safe, Tensley." Michael's voice and mannerisms were confident and reassuring.

"And if I'm not Jack Flannery's daughter, then what?" I peered up at Layne, wondering if I had put everyone I loved in jeopardy just because they were in my life. My hands turned clammy with the prospect, and I rubbed my free one on my jeans. Realizing I was no longer hungry, I put the plate down on the coffee table.

"Shit," Benji muttered. "No matter what she says, Ten is scared. She never turns down food."

"I'm not scared," I lied. "I'm not related to this monster. All I want to know is if we'll be able to go back to normal when the tests come back negative."

Michael rubbed his chin. "Until the FBI catches him, I'm afraid not."

"No. No." I shook my head adamantly. "I refuse for some crazy, sick—" I stopped before I dropped the f-bomb. "I won't allow him to dictate my life."

Michael held his hand up, halting me from continuing. "This is a moot point, Tensley. Until we have the DNA results back, we can't plan accordingly for your safety."

Dammit, he'd just played the dad card on me. Before I could object, the doorbell rang.

"I've got it." Michael stood, smoothed his khaki slacks and gray button-down shirt, then left the living room.

From the angle of where I was sitting, I had a pretty decent view of who was at the door. I leaned forward, attempting to get a better look. A dark-haired, well-built hottie shook Michael's hand, and I assumed he was Pierce Westbrook. As the other men stepped into the foyer, I realized they were all in black suits. *Men in Black.* I stifled a giggle. For a moment, I wished Benji and I were sitting next to each other so we could drool over the eye candy.

Michael led the men into the living room, and Marilyn stood. I didn't miss the subtle flush that crept over her cheeks.

"Everyone, this is Pierce Westbrook," Michael said, glancing around at us. "He owns the security firm."

Pierce stepped forward and shook our hands, smiling confidently. "It's nice to meet you all. These are some of my best men, and they will be discreet. You won't even know they're around. This is Vaughn Reddington." Vaughn shook our hands, and for the first time, I realized he had one blue eye and one brown eye. His short blond hair and angled jawline added to his distinct appearance. He was hot as hell.

I minded my manners, but I knew Benji, and I would definitely need some one-on-one time to discuss how fucking gorgeous these guys were. For starters, where in the hell had these dudes come from? Maybe there was a hot-bodyguard-cloning factory somewhere.

"This is Zayne Wilson," Pierce continued.

Zayne followed suit, introducing himself to us. I didn't miss the hint of a tattoo peeking out from his jacket sleeve or how his emerald-green eyes stood out against his dark hair.

"And Tad Murphy," Pierce announced.

"Nice to meet you," Tad said, smiling and shaking our hands firmly.

Never had I seen red hair and big brown eyes look so smoldering hot. Tad had an infectious presence that filled the room.

I was a hormonal mess. My brain realized the men were there

to protect us, but I was ready to pull Layne into the bathroom for a hot and hard quickie.

"I'm going to show everyone around the house and property," Michael announced.

I peered over at Benji. His eyes were glued to the backsides of the men as they left us. If the circumstances hadn't been so serious, I would have jokingly wiped the drool off his chin. I stifled a giggle with my arm.

"Well, they seem like lovely men," Marilyn gushed.

Layne leaned over, his breath tickling my ear. "I'm glad they won't be where you ladies can see them on a regular basis."

Flustered that I'd not been more discreet in my attraction to the bodyguards, I glanced up at him. "Oh my God. I'm sorry. I—"

Layne's chuckle rumbled through his chest. "Hell, even I noticed how gorgeous they all were. As long as I'm the one you're taking to bed, it's all good," he whispered in my ear.

"Always." I gave him a chaste kiss on the mouth since Marilyn was in the room.

"Have you heard from Franklin today?" I asked, attempting to focus again.

"Yes. Michael will take you downtown to meet him, then you'll follow him to take the DNA test. Although I know how powerful a man Franklin is, I'm still amazed at how quickly he can move things along. You should have your test results by morning."

I gulped. "Okay. I'm glad I won't have to wait long, and then we can resume our lives."

Marilyn's sad smile said otherwise, but I needed to hold on to what I could, even if it might not be accurate.

"I miss my drums," I said, leaning over and staring at Benji. "I need something to pound on. I wonder if Matthew could arrange for me to get in before the bar opens and blow off some steam."

Marilyn's eyes widened. "That sounds wonderful! In fact, let me call and see if they can let us have a private party for a few hours. Let's invite Avery and Justin. Benji, who else? This would be a fantastic way to have some fun while we wait for the results." Marilyn hopped out of her chair, grinning. Entertainment should have been her middle name, but I needed my drums, so I would let her plan anything she wanted to.

"Mom, I can give you a list of names to call, but let's keep it to twenty or so people. This is my first time in public since the attack, and I think I need to keep it small. Nothing big. Just let Tensley perform and everyone drink. Reality will sink back in soon enough." Benji eyed me, worry clouding his expression.

Marilyn clapped her hands together. "Perfect. Benji, while they're downtown, you and I can plan it. I'll call Matthew. I think Craig, the owner of Barney's, is out of town."

Layne cleared his throat. "Mrs. Parker, I don't mean to be disrespectful, and if Ten needs her drums, I'll do whatever I can to help. But there's a serial killer that might be stalking her. Why are we planning a night of fun in the middle of so much danger and chaos?" Layne's arm protectively tightened around me.

Marilyn's expression softened while she studied Layne. "Because laughter and love heal everything, and tomorrow is never promised." Her eyes flitted to Benji. Her face was a combination of grief and joy.

"Love you, Mom," Benji said.

"Love you too, baby." With that, she hurried from the living room to make her calls.

THE LATE-AFTERNOON NOVEMBER air had a chilling bite. The wind whipped my hair into my face as I hurried into the building along with Franklin and Michael. I'd hoped Layne would be able to attend the DNA test with me, but Franklin preferred we go alone in case we needed to discuss any confidential information. Michael was basically acting as my guardian even though I was twenty-one, so legally, it wasn't necessary. He was, however, housing Layne and me along with paying the security team, so I had no intention of kicking up a fuss that Layne couldn't tag along.

Franklin escorted us through an empty hallway and toward the back of the building, where we stopped in front of suite 122.

"Are you ready?" Michael asked, placing a comforting hand on my shoulder.

"No. But if this gives us some answers and peace of mind, it's worth it." I glanced at Franklin, who smiled kindly.

"We'll be with you every step of the way, and the collection of the DNA is painless. It's literally seconds of swabbing the inside of your cheek. It will take longer to process." Franklin opened the door for me.

"Thank you," I said, my Southern drawl slightly noticeable. "My accent shows up when I'm stressed or mad."

"It's understandable," Michael said. "Try not to worry too much."

Pursing my lips, I entered the sterile waiting room. Everything was white—white walls and white tile floor. The only décor that offered any contrast were the six black chairs. Franklin pulled his phone from his pocket and tapped the screen.

"We're here." He hit the End Call button, and before I had a chance to sit down, a middle-aged man in a white lab coat rounded the corner.

He extended his hand, and Franklin shook it vigorously. "Franklin, it's always good to see you."

"Albert, thank you for slipping us into your busy schedule. This is Tensley."

Albert turned toward me and grabbed my hand, shaking it with the same energy. "Franklin explained this is a rush situation, so I'll put it at the top of my list." His smile was reassuring.

Franklin gestured to Mr. Parker. "And this is Michael."

Michael extended his hand. "Thank you for helping us on the weekend."

After all the introductions, we followed Albert into another room that looked exactly like a doctor's office. He explained the cheek-swab test, and I took a seat, my attention bouncing between the three men.

"Open, please." Albert swirled the tip of the long cotton swab along the inside of my cheek then popped it into a tube and capped it. "All done. The hard part is the wait, but I promise the moment I have the results, I'll call Franklin." Albert patted me on the back.

"Thank you." My voice cracked with nerves.

Minutes later, we exited the building and hopped into Michael's SUV while Franklin waved and slid into the driver's seat of his Porsche 911.

The radio came on as Michael started the car, and he quickly flipped it off. "How are you holding up?" He pulled out of the parking lot and merged into the downtown traffic.

I shrugged. "I don't know. I'm not sure this changes anything, really. Jack Flannery was on my property … period. Unfortunately, that makes me a suspect in his illegal activities." I glanced out the passenger window, detecting a black Mercedes a few cars behind us. "I almost forgot the bodyguards were with us."

Michael glanced in the rearview mirror, nodding his confirmation. "They're good and discrete."

"I guess it makes me feel a little safer that they're around. Maybe Jack will stay away from us if he spots them." I inwardly cringed that I'd just used Jack's first name as though he were an old friend. "I'm ready for tonight," I said, changing the subject.

"I think it's a great idea, not only for you to play, but to get Benji out of the house. Everyone needs to relax and blow off some steam." Michael flipped on his turn signal then pulled onto Division.

"Will you and Marilyn stick around at Barney's tonight?"

Neither of them had seen me play before, and it would mean a lot to me if they hung out for a while.

"We will. Security will be outside of the building, but since it's Benji's first night out, we want to be there in case he needs to go home. If we do need to leave, I know Layne will be with you, but if you're both drinking, then call an Uber."

"I don't know if Layne will be drinking or not, but I am definitely downing some shots." I leaned back in the leather comfort of the passenger's seat and released a long sigh. "I miss Avery, so it will be great to see her. I guess her family has friends in town, and she's bringing their son, Ramsey, with her and Justin tonight. It sounds as though he's moving to Spokane from Montana or something like that."

"Good. Another friend to add to the inner circle." Michael kept his focus trained on the road while he spoke.

"We'll see. We're pretty tight." Thoughts of the test broke through my excitement of seeing everyone that night, and I quickly returned to our conversation.

"It's better to have a few people you can trust with your life than a lot of people you can't," Michael added.

"You don't have to tell me that. I learned the hard way in foster homes."

"Well, you have the support and a home now." Michael glanced at me. "No matter what the results are, Tensley, you have a family right here."

"Thank you," I said, swallowing the lump of emotions down that had lodged itself in my throat. "You guys have been the only real family I've ever had, and I don't know what I'd do if I lost you." Tears pricked my eyes, and I blinked rapidly, forcing them back.

Michael reached over and patted my hand as we pulled into the driveway. "Let's have a good rest of the day, shall we?" He graced me with an infectious smile and parked the car in the four-car garage.

I NEEDED LAYNE. The moment we walked into the house, reality hit me, and we didn't even have the test results yet.

I bounded up the stairs and down the hall.

"In here!" Benji yelled from the family room.

Backing up, I poked my head around the door. A seventy-two-inch TV hung on the back wall, and the soft brown leather sectional called my name. I'd always loved that room. On holidays, Benji and I would fill up on food and alcohol, then cuddle up on the couch and talk until the early hours of the morning. It was a nice break from the thin walls in our house.

"Hey, you guys are shooting pool?" The moment I saw the massive smile on Benji's face, I knew Layne was good for him. Benji had been cooped up in the house, shutting everyone out since he'd started the long road to recovery.

Layne bent over the table, allowing me a magnificent view of his tight ass and muscular legs. My head tilted, a smile easing over my face as Benji's eyes caught mine. He winked at me as Layne cracked the balls, sending the orange striped one into the corner pocket.

Benji shook his head. "He's kicking my ass."

I laughed and strolled over to my boyfriend. "Nice shot. You know pool is just foreplay, right?"

Layne gave me a lopsided grin while a light pink dusted his cheeks. Benji's laugh filled the room.

"Sorry," I mouthed with my back to Benji.

Layne slid his arm around my waist and pulled me to him. "How did it go?" he asked before placing a sweet kiss on my mouth.

"It was boring." I patted my hand against his chest and backed away. "Don't let me stop the game." I plopped down on the couch and propped my feet up on the armrest. "The test was done in under twenty seconds."

177

"Really?" Benji asked, moving his wheelchair into place for the next shot. I hadn't noticed it before, but apparently Benji had a booster seat. It brought his body up so he could actually reach over the table.

"Yeah. All we have to do is wait." I rubbed my forehead with the palm of my hand. "I'm glad your mom thought about Barney's tonight. I need to play some drums and get ripped. It's been a while."

Regret twisted Benji's face briefly, then a sad smile eased across his face. "It was the same weekend our lives changed forever. The last time we got ripped was at Barney's, actually. The next night was the comedy club."

Silence filled the room as we all stared at each other. No words were necessary. All three of us had been there that night. There was a distinct possibility that two of us wouldn't be in this room alive if it hadn't been for Layne, and we all knew it.

"Tonight will be about moving forward." Benji rubbed the unshed tears from his eyes. "You'll have your results, it's my first night out, and we're surrounded by family and friends. That's my focus." He inhaled, then that beautiful smile lit him up from the inside out. "We've got our entire lives ahead of us, and I'm looking forward to sharing the adventure with both of you."

Layne took his turn, tapping a ball lightly and sending it into the far-right pocket.

Benji shook his head. "Remind me to get him drunk before I play him again."

I couldn't suppress my giggle, then gave Layne a meaningful look. "It was the first night I saw you."

"Oh, I remember that very well," Benji chimed in, his mouth forming a big O. "You had my girl rattled to her very core. I'd never seen her so fucked up. Avery and I were ready to send you packing." Benji's chest puffed up with his words, his protectiveness not lessening just because he was in a wheelchair.

"I didn't mean to scare you, Ten." Layne pinned me with those smoky-blue eyes, and I nearly melted in my seat. "And I'm glad I saw you. I actually had no idea you were even out here, but we've talked about all of that already."

"And here we are." I hung my head upside down over the side of the couch, my long blond hair grazing the carpeted floor. "Never in a million years did I think we'd all be here together right now, discussing DNA results."

The cherrywood grandfather clock struck five, sending me jumping off the couch. "Shit. I forgot about that damned thing."

The guys laughed as they put their pool sticks away.

"Thanks for playing, man." Benji wheeled over to Layne and shook his hand. All the years of competitive sports they had played must have kept them in the habit of shaking hands.

"I should take a shower and find some clothes to wear for tonight."

"Oh, Mom told me to let you know that your clothes and toiletries were packed and brought over for you."

"Really? Who grabbed them from the house?"

Benji shrugged. "Maybe one of the bodyguards or something. I have no clue who had their hands on your panties." Benji snickered at his own joke.

"As long as Layne is the one taking them off, I couldn't care less." I winked at Layne then left the room.

"I think that was an invitation." Benji's voice trailed down the hallway, reaching my ears.

Giggling, I hurried into my temporary bedroom and jumped on the bed. My nerves were wound up tighter than Santa's belt on Christmas Eve. I chewed on my bottom lip, waiting to see if Layne was going to show up or not. A minute passed, but no boyfriend. I wrinkled my nose in disappointment, hopped up, and closed my door. At least I would have plenty of time to doll up for the night. I'd never cared before, but with Layne in my life, I wanted to look nice. Maybe I would even curl my hair. My mind wandered to his hands running through the soft strands and down my body, and my senses immediately heightened.

I grabbed my iPhone and made a beeline for the shower. Some music would put me in the mood for the festivities. I scrolled through Spotify and landed on my newest angsty playlist. The tunes were all about the drumbeats. The music floated through the speaker, and I placed the phone on the vanity counter. Steam filled the bathroom as I stepped out of my clothes and into the spray of hot water. I closed my eyes and allowed it to consume me, melting the stress from my shoulders.

"Can I join you?" The shower door opened, and Layne peered in, waiting for permission.

"Yes," I laughed, relieved. The whole wanting sex thing was new to me, and I sometimes struggled with the idea of being so vulnerable. I pulled him in and wrapped my arms around his neck.

"You're so beautiful," he said while he nipped at my earlobe and grabbed my ass cheeks.

"I didn't mean to embarrass you in front of Benji. I guess I'm used to not having a filter around him, and I didn't stop to realize it might make you uncomfortable."

"You're fine. I'm just getting to know him, and before you know it, we'll all be joking openly." His thumb traced my bottom lip, then he gently turned me around.

I leaned up against the wall and parted my legs. He cupped my breasts and tweaked my nipples while he rubbed his hard cock against the curve of my butt. "We'll have to wait until later tonight," he groaned. "I accidentally left the new box of condoms in my car. I bought some while you were gone today."

I turned to face him, pouting. My finger trailed down his chest to his stomach. "Guess we'll have to find something else to do instead." I sank to my knees, my tongue licking the stream of water off his abs. I glanced up at him while I took the tip of his thick shaft in my mouth.

"Ten," he gasped, his fingers threading through my wet hair.

I stroked him firmly while I gazed up at him. Water streamed down my face as I slipped him into my mouth, sucking him. His lips parted, and he cautiously moved his hips back and forth with me. I continued to stroke him as I gently sucked on his balls, eliciting a deep growl from him. He closed his fingers around my tit and kneaded my sensitive flesh. I picked up my speed, stroking him faster. My body reacted, and my pussy ached for him to fill me up. A whimper escaped me as he quickened his pace. My tongue swirled around the tip of his cock, and I dug my nails into his legs. I was so fucking turned on. All I had to do to was slip my hand between my thighs and I would come.

"Babe, if you don't want to swallow, then ..."

I pulled him out of my mouth and stood. "Thank you. Someday I will, but I need some time. For now, I want to watch you jack off on me."

"Jesus. That's fucking hot." He wiped the water from his face, his attention never leaving me.

I sank onto the bench seat and leaned against the wall. His eyes followed me while I spread my legs and slid my hand down to my throbbing center. "I need you inside me later tonight. Do you understand?" I asked, my tone demanding.

"Fuck this." Layne dropped to his knees and buried his face between my legs. He pulled my sensitive bud between his teeth and pumped his fingers in and out of my wet folds.

My back arched off the wall, and my hips ground against him. "Baby," I whimpered. "I'm going to come."

His tongue ran up my slit, then he stood and grabbed his long, hard cock, which I wanted in me so badly. His body visibly shuddered while he stroked himself, his eyes never leaving me while I touched myself.

"This what you want?" I asked, my tongue darting out of my mouth.

Layne's free hand landed on the shower wall, and every

muscle tensed. My entire being burned with desire as I watched him come. He was magnificent, strong, and sexy as hell. I'd never wanted to watch a guy get off before, but this was different. Layne loved me, and every moment of fun we had physically only brought us closer.

"Did you come?" he panted, dropping his hand from his cock.

"No. I guess I just wanted to watch you." A satisfied smile eased across my face. "I'll wait until tonight." I stood slowly, my heart fluttering in my chest with anticipation.

"I'll make it up to you. I'm sorry I forgot the condoms." He leaned his forehead against mine.

I stood on my tiptoes and kissed him. "This was perfect."

His arm wrapped around my back, and he cradled me against him as he deepened our kiss. Suddenly, it wasn't about the sex or the orgasms anymore—it was all about my heart. This man had walked into my life again after three years and was cracking through the wall I'd built around myself.

His tongue caressed mine, and I moaned softly into his mouth.

Finally, I broke our kiss. "I feel safe with you." My voice was so soft, I wasn't sure he'd heard me over the spray of the water. "When we're together, I feel like there's nothing we can't do, Layne. I … I've never felt like this before."

His hands cupped my cheeks.

I grabbed his wrists, staring into the depth of his eyes.

"I love you so much, Ten. There's nothing I wouldn't do for you."

"I know." And for the first time in my life, I really did.

19

I screamed like a little girl on Christmas morning when I saw Avery at Barney's. Although it had only been a few days since I'd seen her, it felt like years. She looked beautiful in her tight, dark-washed jeans, which hugged her curves, and a plum-colored, low-cut blouse. A one-carat diamond pendant dangled delicately from her neck.

She ran across the dance floor and pulled me into her arms. "You look amazing. A nice shirt and sex definitely agrees with you." She smacked me on the butt and giggled. Thank God I'd left Layne and Benji at the door when I'd seen her. She would have embarrassed the shit out of me in front of my boyfriend.

I'd opted for my favorite pair of black boots with a baby-blue top Avery had loaned me months ago tucked into my black Levi's and a wide belt.

"Are you all right?" I asked, breaking our hug. "No strange men have followed you?"

Usually, Avery would have made a big joke about my question, but not this time. Her face grew serious, and she grabbed my hand in hers. "I'm good. Dad or Justin have been by my side every single minute. But, like, you've got to fill me in on everything. All I know is that some crazy criminal dude was hiding on our property and we need to lay low until he's captured."

A slight frown creased my forehead. *Dammit.* They hadn't told Avery everything. "We'll get all caught up, but not tonight. I need to blow off some steam, and this is Benji's first social outing since the attack."

She grabbed my face with her hands and placed a firm kiss on my cheek. "I love you, Tensley Bennett! I'm not sure what the hell is going on, but nothing bad had better happen to you."

I forced a laugh. "I'm safe. I promise." My gaze drifted over to Layne, who had ordered some shots and grabbed us all a table. He and Benji clinked glasses and downed whatever they were drinking.

"Get Justin and meet us at the table. I know some more people are coming too."

Her smile lit up her gorgeous face. "He went to the bathroom, so we'll join you in a minute." I hadn't realized how much I'd been wrapped up in my own shit until I saw her. We would have to carve out some girl time soon.

On my way to the table, I stopped at the bar. Matthew greeted me with a warm smile.

"Can we get some music?" I asked, grinning widely.

"You bet. And what would you like to drink tonight?" He leaned on the bar, his fingers grazing mine.

I pulled my hand away. "What did Benji and my boyfriend order?"

My heart sank to my toes as Matthew's face fell. "Benji's your boyfriend?"

No wonder he looked so confused. I laughed and shook my head. "No. The tall guy with dark hair is. His name is Layne."

Matthew stilled for a minute, and his deep-brown eyes searched me. "Is he good to you, Ten?"

For the first time, I realized that Matthew had real feelings for me. He hadn't just been a fun and flirty bartender. *Fuck. How did I miss that?*

"Yeah. Very. We, uh, we knew each other from high school, but until he moved here and we had some time to get to know each other again, he was my sworn enemy." I attempted a lighthearted laugh. Awkward didn't even begin to describe how I felt at the moment.

"They had Redheaded Sluts."

Good grief. "Who in the hell comes up with names for these drinks?"

Matthew chuckled and rattled off the ingredients. "Since you're playing tonight, your drinks are on the house." He flashed a big grin at me then made me two.

"You're the best. Thanks." I downed one, then grabbed the other. "I'm going to head to the table with everyone, but I'll catch you later."

When I turned around, Layne's attention was glued to Matthew and me. His gaze drifted from me to our friendly bartender, and their eyes locked. Neither of them said a word, but I was very clear about what was transpiring between them. Layne was marking his territory: me.

I sidled up to Layne and kissed him on his full mouth. "Stop. Matthew is harmless."

"No guy that looks at you like that is harmless," he whispered against my ear. Goosebumps dotted my skin, and I remembered his promise to make love to me later that night.

"There's no competition." I slammed my shot down as "Cry for Me" by Camila Cabello filled the bar.

"Dance with me!" Avery said from behind me, tugging on my arm and pulling me backward. I released a loud whoop.

"Here's a show for you, Layne," Benji said, laughing into his hand.

Justin joined the guys at the table while Avery and I made our way to the small wood floor. Since only a handful of people had been invited, we had plenty of space. The alcohol warmed me as the music filled the bar. Avery whirled me around and we laughed together.

"Poor Layne," Avery yelled over the noise, her hand landing on my waist. "He's going to lose his shit when he sees us dance."

I rolled my eyes at her. Avery swore she had the best sex of her life with Justin after we danced together. We knew it was just a show, but apparently the guys liked the thought of our hands on each other.

"I have to keep it PG tonight. Benji's parents are here," I said, practically yelling.

Avery full-on pouted. "Just a little? Justin has been seriously distracted, and I need to be taken care of."

"Really?" Justin had always seemed so attentive to her.

The beat of the music continued while Avery danced behind me. Her arm slipped around my waist as I rubbed my butt against her. I snuck a peek at Layne. His mouth was slightly open.

I turned to face Avery, moving to the beat as my hand slid down her side, and we grew dangerously close to kissing. Her fingers traced down my hip, and her leg slid between mine. We rocked our hips to the rhythm, lowering toward the floor.

Avery snickered. "By the look on your man's face, his dick is so hard, he's in pain."

"Avery!" I laughed and tossed a look over my shoulder. My softly curled hair cascaded down my back as I winked at Layne. "Well, I hope it works for you. You'll have to let me know."

"Break it up, ladies. The parents are watching," Benji said, wheeling onto the dance floor and popping a wheelie.

I grabbed his hand, and he pulled me onto his lap. His laugh rumbled through his chest as he wheeled us around. Over the last several weeks, I'd forgotten what it felt like to just let loose and laugh. Thank God I had Avery and Benji to remind me.

I giggled while he spun us around again. "I love you, Benji Parker!"

He placed a kiss on my cheek when the music stopped. "Love you too." Beads of sweat glistened on his forehead, and I carefully hopped off his legs.

"Your poor boyfriend has had one hell of a show tonight. First, you're dancing with a hot chick, then you're on the gay guy's lap." Benji barked out a laugh.

"I have to make sure Layne can handle the real me, which includes you and Avery since you're my family. We're a package deal, and he needs to know what he's getting into." I laughed softly. "He said he loves me, so we'll see after tonight." I wiggled my eyebrows at my best friend.

Benji's eyes widened. "He told you he loved you?" He took my hand and squeezed, putting aside fun and games.

I nodded, realizing my slip. "I need another shot if I'm going to play soon."

Benji knew I would fill him in on the details when I was ready, but it wasn't the right time. I glanced at Layne and tilted my head in the direction of the bar. He grinned and nodded. It was funny how I'd struggled to articulate my thoughts all my life, but with Layne, all I had to do was nod toward Matthew, and he knew I was including him. There was no need to be jealous of the bartender.

Layne and I ordered some more shots and downed them. Loud cheers came from the doorway, and we turned to see who had joined us. Layne took my hand and led me back to the table. Some of Benji's friends from the swim team had filed in the front door, all talking over each other and slapping him on the shoulder. A wide smile broke out across Benji's face as he soaked up the love and support.

"He needs this," I said to Layne.

"We all do. When life sucks, you find out who your real friends are fast." A distant look clouded his features.

I realized Layne was talking about the tornado and Nicole, and I took his hand. Nothing I could say would ease his pain, but

I could show him I loved and supported him.

"Baptize Me" by X Ambassadors and Jacob Banks thumped through the speakers. I placed Layne's hand over my heart. "Dance with me."

He walked me to the center of the floor, and the lights dimmed as we closed the gap between us. Layne's arm slid protectively around me as his hips moved to the song. His head dipped down and his lips brushed mine. Before we knew it, several other couples had joined us, including Justin and Avery. I winked at her, then returned my focus to Layne.

I peeked up at him through my eyelashes while we swayed to the music. "I don't know what you're doing to me, Layne Garrison."

He replied with a slow and tender kiss.

"The night I saw you here at Barney's, I was terrified. I thought you were behind what Chloe had done to me." I shook my head at the memory. "I hated you. And now …"

Layne's thumb gently traced a circle on my cheek, and I leaned into his touch. His eyes filled with desire, but also with love.

"And now I can't imagine not being by your side." My heart hammered inside my chest as a flurry of excitement and fear grew in me. "Layne, I—"

Before I could say another word, the music changed, and Matthew's voice came over the speaker. "Let's have a big shout-out for Tensley Bennett!"

The small crowd cheered, and Layne and I released each other.

"Good luck," he said before walking back off the dance floor.

The thunderous applause sent shivers through me, and I hopped up on the stage. Matthew had everything set up for me, including my song choice to start off the performance with.

I tugged on the clear poncho over my clothes and pulled my hair up into a ponytail. The bar grew silent as the lights dimmed, and a spotlight lit up the stage. Blue, red, purple, and yellow paint filled the drum. I grabbed the drumsticks and held them above my head. "Champion" by Bishop Briggs began, and I immediately picked up the beat. Paint bounced in the air, taking on a life of its own as the tip of the sticks connected with the mylar.

Tap, tap, tap. The rhythm coursed through me, giving me a new life as I became one with the music. I jumped to the beat, splattering paint in every direction. The earlier fear and anxiety melted away, and the only thing that existed were the drums and me.

The song ended, and I traded out my sticks and alternated between the bass and snare drums. After tapping an intricate rhythm on the rim of the snare, I moved into the rest of the performance. My heart soared with every beat, and for the first time in my life, I had everything I'd ever dreamed of: an amazing boyfriend, a family, and my music.

2 0

I allowed myself to dream for just a moment as I finished the routine. The crowd came to life, clapping and cheering as I set my sticks down. My focus landed on Layne. His smile reached his eyes as he yelled my name and pumped his fist in the air. Benji added some catcalls, and I laughed while I removed my poncho. Avery was at my side in seconds, escorting me to the ladies' room to get cleaned up.

"How in the hell do you get better every time I hear you?" Avery asked, bumping the restroom door open with her hip.

"It's the emotions."

"You run a lot deeper than anyone thinks you do, then." She covered her mouth with her hand, a drunken giggle escaping her. "Hey." Avery turned the water on for me. "If Justin breaks up with me, do you think we could become lesbian lovers?"

My mouth opened and closed before I found the right word. "No. I like dick. Cock. Penis."

Avery doubled over with laughter. *Shit, how much has she drank tonight?*

She gasped, slapping her hand on the sink. "You should have seen your face."

I folded my paint-spattered arms over my chest. "I'm calling bullshit. What's going on?"

"Gah! That's my shirt you're getting paint on!" She grabbed my hands and pulled them to my sides.

"It's water-soluble. Relax. What's going on?" My voice was stern. Something had happened.

"Justin wants to see other people." Tears streamed down her face, and I pulled her in for a hug.

"I'm sorry," I whispered while she fell apart in my arms. "Did he leave, or is he still here?"

Avery shook her head while she full-on sobbed. "Gone."

My chin rested on top of her head. If I understood anything, it was how much it hurt when you wanted to belong to someone.

I brushed her hair out of her eyes. "Let's hang out tomorrow. Just you and me, okay? We can catch up and just be there for each other."

She released me and grabbed some tissue from the toilet paper roll in the stall. "I thought this relationship was special … that he was different." She blew her nose and sighed.

A sharp pang filled me. So many times, I had thought a particular foster home was where I belonged, only to find myself alone and empty.

An unfamiliar longing stirred deep inside me. I couldn't deny it any longer, but it was the worst fucking time for me to finally admit it to myself. For now, my feelings would have to wait.

"Ugh, I'm sorry. Tonight's about you and Benji. Tomorrow … tomorrow can be about me, right?" She dabbed at her smeared mascara then stood straight and plastered a smile on her face.

"One hundred percent." I placed my hands on her shoulders. "I don't know how, but it's going to be okay. Avery, you're beautiful, smart, and funny. I'm not sure what is wrong with Justin, but if he's not in this relationship with you, then girl, he's so stupid, you just don't want him in your life."

She stared me dead in the eyes. "Really?"

"Yeah. Really." I hated seeing my confident friend deflated. No guy was worth her feeling like less of a woman. I gave her a quick hug, then held my arms in the air. "I'm not sure how we managed, but you don't have any paint on you." I released a soft laugh.

"Let's get you cleaned up and grab another drink." She took a paper towel, got it wet, and began to dab my face.

Ten minutes later, we stepped out of the restroom, ready to join the rest of the group.

I grabbed Avery's hand and gave it a squeeze as I spotted Layne and Benji. Then I saw Franklin.

"Fuck." I stopped abruptly while butterflies ran amok in my chest. There was no other reason for Franklin to be there other than the test results.

"Hey, would you do me a favor?" I was a shit friend for asking while she was hurting so much. "Could you ask Layne to meet me back here?"

"Are you all right? You look a little pale." Avery touched my forehead with the back of her hand, making sure I wasn't running a fever.

"Yeah. I just need to talk to him. The crowd is a bit over-whelming." Well, Franklin was overwhelming, but Avery didn't know about him yet, and I didn't have the patience to explain it all right then.

"Sure. I'll send him back." She squeezed my shoulder, then made her way over to the group.

Leaning against the wall, I rubbed my arms and watched as Avery gave Layne the message.

His head popped up as he searched around the bar. In seconds, he was next to me. "Babe, are you okay?" He smoothed my hair as his eyes searched mine.

"Yes." I pulled on his hand. "I need to talk to you." I turned on my heel and shoved open the back exit door. The cold night air greeted us as we huddled against the outer wall of the building.

Layne pulled me to him, and the heat from his body warmed me. "Ten, what's wrong?"

"Nothing." I peered up at him. "I just needed a minute." I pushed up on my tiptoes and kissed him. "I love you." I was overwhelmed with so many emotions, my words caught in my throat. "I don't know what to do with it or how to ..." I shook my head, attempting to clear my thoughts. "All I know is that I love you."

Layne remained still. I wasn't sure if he was waiting for me to say something else or if he doubted my words.

"Babe," he whispered, "say it again." His mouth crashed down on mine.

"I love you," I answered between our heated kisses.

"Again. Tensley, I've waited so long. Please." His kisses became frantic, filled with need, as we whispered how much we loved each other in the darkness. That moment would be burned into my memory for the rest of my days.

A flicker of light caught my attention.

"Baby," I said softly, "I think our bodyguard is telling us to get back inside, where it's safe."

Layne glanced across the parking lot. "Let's get you warmed up. It's getting really cold." He gave me a gentle kiss, then opened the door, and we slipped back into the bar.

Before we entered the main area, I pulled on his arm. "Wait." My heart jumped into my throat. "Did I see Franklin?"

Layne turned toward me. "Yeah. But tonight is a celebration, so we don't have to talk about anything if you don't want to."

I struggled for words. "I'm scared. I need to know, but ..." My fingertips traced his chin. "Promise me, no matter what the results are, that you'll be next to me in the morning and that we'll be okay."

"I promise. And no matter what Franklin says tonight, I'm going to take you home and make slow love to you."

"I can't wait." I sucked in a deep breath, grabbed Layne's hand, and marched straight up to Franklin.

His bright-blue eyes landed on mine. "That was one hell of a performance, Tensley."

"Thank you, but I'm guessing that's not why you're really here." I clenched my jaw. My nerves were already frazzled.

A sad smile graced his handsome face as he slid a manila envelope across the table. "There's no hurry to open that. Finish your evening, drink, and have some fun."

My chin tilted up. From that, I already knew what the results were. "Can we talk? I don't want to wait. It will just mess with me for the rest of the night."

"If that's what you want, yes. I'll have my driver bring the car around so we can have some warmth and privacy."

"Layne? Are you okay if I talk to Franklin for a few minutes?" My eyes pleaded with him. I needed to know the answers and what the next steps looked like.

"Yeah." Layne kissed me on the forehead. "I'll wait for you here."

I grabbed the envelope from the table and followed Franklin to his car, which was a limo.

"I had client meetings tonight before coming here," he explained as he opened the door for me.

The moment my butt hit the plush leather, I could feel the heat from the seat warmer. Franklin joined me on the other side and turned toward me.

"What are the results?" I asked, my pulse spiking.

"Tensley, you're a fifty percent match to Jack Flannery. He's your father."

"Fuck. Fuck. Fuck. How? How can this man ..." I shook my head as the gravity of the situation hit me full force. "I'm sorry about my language. I'd just convinced myself that there was no way he was my biological fath— Ugh. I mean sperm donor. And what about the name? He wasn't Jack when he was with my mom."

"When the FBI began to trace his murders, they learned it all began before he and your mom were married. Bart Benton was an alias. I'm so sorry, Tensley."

"What does this mean now? What do we do about the FBI and cops thinking I'm helping him?" Disgust churned in my stomach, and I wrapped my arms around myself. "It makes me sick just thinking about what he's done. Those poor women." My stomach twisted into a million knots.

"We make sure you have an alibi. If you were at school, they have cameras."

I drummed my fingers on my leg anxiously. "I work at the library, so I'm either at college or at home."

"You have two roommates, so if you weren't at the library or classes, then hopefully you were with one of them. The picture of Jack on your property was taken six weeks ago, so we have a date to start with."

I pulled my phone out of my back pocket and opened the calendar. "What day was it?"

"October fourth at six thirty-two p.m." Franklin rubbed his chin, deep in thought.

"I worked until seven that night." I turned my screen toward him so he could see my schedule. "The library has cameras, so it should be easy to prove. In fact, I was gone from eight in the morning until almost seven thirty that night." A shiver traveled down my spine. "When I got home, neither Benji nor Avery was there. That never happened, so I bumped up some music." My eyes widened with fear. "Franklin, what if Jack was still there? What if he was watching me?" My hands began to tremble with the realization that I'd shared space with a dangerous serial killer, my father.

"I need you to listen to me for a minute. You're safe. Bodyguards are with you, and you and Layne are staying with Michael and Marilyn for as long as you need to. I think you should consider a stun gun, mace, or something for backup. I'm not positive why you're on Jack's radar, but I suspect it's because you're his daughter."

I nodded, grappling with the information.

Franklin's expression was full of kindness. "Let's get you back to your friends. It's almost midnight, and I suspect you're probably ready to go home."

"Yeah. I think I'm done partying for tonight."

"I'll watch you walk into Barney's, and we'll talk more tomorrow. My first order of business on Monday will be to access the library video to prove you weren't collaborating with Jack. It's going to be all right, Tensley. Hang in there. You're surrounded by people who love you, so when the days get tough, cling to that."

"Thank you. Have a good night," I whispered. I opened the door and hustled to the entrance. My attention immediately landed on Layne, Benji, and Avery as I entered the bar. I stopped abruptly when my gaze connected with Layne's. I nodded just enough for him to understand the results.

He nearly hopped over the table in order to get to me. His arms wrapped around me, pulling me tightly against him. "This changes nothing. I love you." His sweet breath grazed my ear and I sank into his embrace.

I gazed up at him. "I'm ready to go home, but I need to tell everyone goodbye first."

"Actually, this all worked out perfectly. Michael and Marilyn only rented Barney's until midnight, so they're closing down."

The moment the words were out of his mouth, some of Benji's friends waved to everyone, then exited through the front door.

"Okay, this works." I flashed Layne a big smile and proceeded to thank everyone for coming. Between the hugs and goodbyes, twenty minutes flew by, and before I realized it, we were the only ones left in the bar.

"Thank you so much," I said to Michael and Marilyn. "I think Benji and I both needed this."

Benji offered a lopsided grin then stifled a yawn. "It was great, but a lot of activity. I'm ready to crash for sure."

Michael held open the door as we all filed into the parking lot.

We watched Avery get in and start her car while Michael loaded Benji into the SUV. Marilyn sat in the front, and Layne and I joined Benji in the back.

"Everyone in?" Michael asked, ready to close the side door.

With everyone finally ready, I realized I really needed to go to pee. "Ugh. I'm sorry! I have to go to the bathroom really bad. I'll hurry—I promise." I hopped out and prayed Matthew hadn't locked the front door yet. I gave it a tug, and thankfully it flew open, so I hurried inside. Michael had parked right outside the entrance, so I wouldn't even have to walk a few steps in the parking lot.

I waved at Matthew as I flew by him. "Bathroom!" My bladder would have never held on until we got to Benji's house.

I finally reached the restroom and thanked the heavens as I relieved myself. I'd gotten so caught up in everything throughout the night, I hadn't realized how fast the alcohol had moved through my system.

I finished up and washed my hands.

But I didn't get a chance to leave the restroom because a large male hand clamped over my mouth before I had a chance to scream.

"Hello, Victoria."

21

"I'm not here to hurt you," the man whispered in my ear.

I detected a hint of barbecue on his breath, and a knife blade glimmered in the lights.

My head jerked up, and I met his eyes in the mirror—my eyes. Jack Flannery and I shared the same shape and color. I quickly assessed him, noting the similarities and differences between us, but it really didn't matter. I was nothing like the sick fuck.

"You have my word that as long as you don't fight me or scream, I won't slit your throat from ear to ear and watch my daughter bleed out in a public restroom. After everything you've overcome, it would be a shitty way to die." He wore his dark hair cropped close to his head, similar to a military cut, and his arm flexed as he held me tightly. There was no doubt in my mind that he was strong if he'd skinned women.

Flashes of the images that the detective had shown me assaulted my brain, and my body stiffened in fear. Foul bile burned the back of my throat. The only thing that might save me was the fact that I was this man's daughter, but I wasn't going to bank on that mattering. I wasn't sure how I was supposed to respond to him since his hand remained over my mouth, so I attempted a slight nod.

"Since we don't know each other—yet—I won't keep you long. I just wanted to meet my girl face-to-face. I have big plans for us." An evil sneer turned his lips up. "I'm going to drop my hand, but if you even let out a squeak, I'll go after your little stitched-together family. I'll start with the parents while you and Benji watch. Then I'll gut your boyfriend. Everything you've worked so hard to build, I will strip it away bit by bit. Am I clear? Do I have your word that no one will ever know I was here or that we had a conversation?" The dark stubble on his chin scraped my cheek as he spoke.

My knees trembled. He would hurt them all. He would kill them. I nodded, then he slowly dropped his hand. The knife was still inches away from me.

Jack stepped back slowly in the small women's restroom. "Turn around. I want to see you."

As if I were a young child, I obeyed my father without hesitation.

His eyes appraised me as if I were cattle for sale, then an almost normal smile eased across his face. "You definitely look like me. I bet that drove your bitch of a mother nuts."

"I don't know if it did or not. She was always high." My voice sounded small and insignificant.

"Huh. You know why, right? I mean, from what I've learned, you're smart, intuitive, calculating, and you trust very few people. You're definitely my girl. But your mother knew about my social activities."

My insides quivered. "What? She knew?" There was no longer any doubt in my mind that Jack had been checking into me and my past. I just didn't know for how long. But I was more concerned with why he was there if he didn't want to hurt me.

"What do you want?" I asked before I could stop myself.

"More importantly, why were you on my property?" Shit, why in the hell had I decided it was a good time to be bold and grow a pair of fucking balls?

Jack's low, dark chuckle echoed through the room. "Can't a dad meet his daughter? Have a little bit of quality family time together?"

"Someone will come looking for me any minute. Maybe we can wrap up our chat." I placed my hand on my hip, exhibiting way more bravery than I could actually pull together. I'd never faced a serial killer, but I'd met plenty of narcissists.

In two long strides, he backed me up against the wall, and his fingers wrapped tightly around my throat. "Make no mistake, little girl. I'll cut you into pieces if you give me any more shit. Don't you ever forget … *I* made you." With that, he let me go, turned, and strolled out the bathroom door.

Before I could lean over the sink, I puked all over my boots. My body shook violently as my brain processed what had just happened. I balanced on the white porcelain edge of the sink and turned on the faucet. The sharp squeak reminded me to move so I wouldn't have my back to the door. Quickly, I rinsed my face and mouth, then grabbed a handful of paper towels and dried off.

"Dammit," I half cried, unzipping my boots. At least my vomit had mostly splattered on the toes. I would have to let Matthew know to clean up the bathroom. *Poor guy.* Every time I was there, I dropped something or puked.

Minutes later, my boots were clean, and I attempted to pull myself together. There was no denying that my face was pale, though. Thank God it was dark and Layne wouldn't be able to see me well in the car. He couldn't ask me questions. Realizing it was up to me to keep him safe, I inhaled sharply and willed my heart to calm down.

I opened the door to the restroom and turned down the hall, nearly slamming into Vaughn.

"Are you all right?" he asked, nodding for me to walk in front of him. I searched the inside of the bar, but we're all clear."

"Yeah." I refused to look at him as he escorted me through the hall and toward the front door. Had he seen Jack leave?

Half the lights were off, and the hair on the back of my neck stood on end. The heels of my boots smacked the wood floor as I hurried toward the exit. In a quick burst, I flung the door open and stepped into the cold night.

Michael and one of the bodyguards were waiting outside the SUV. Michael's concerned gaze landed on me. "I was about to send Marilyn in for you. Are you all right?"

"Yeah, just a lot of information tonight. I'm fine." I gave him a little smile as Vaughn opened the back door for me. Layne hopped out, and I scooted in, situating myself in between Benji and Layne.

I assumed security was on all sides of the bar, so I had no idea how Jack had gotten in. Of course, only a few people were aware of what was going on. For all I knew, Avery had held the door open for him half an hour ago when I was talking with Franklin in his limo.

"Hey, sorry." I took Layne's hand and laid my head back on the leather seat. "Matthew caught me for a minute and just told me what a great job I did tonight." I inwardly cringed with how easy the lie came, but I had no choice. If Layne even suspected anything was wrong, I would lose him. Jack had made it clear that if I even muttered his name, he would kill everyone I loved.

"Hmm." Layne's jaw clenched. "You were amazing."

"Thanks. It was really good to get out." I leaned forward and again thanked Marilyn before turning to Benji. "How are you doing?" I took his hand in mine and wiggled my eyebrows at him. "This is a girl's fantasy, being sandwiched between two hot guys." I kept my voice low enough that his mom couldn't hear me.

Benji snickered and leaned over me. "Well, it's my fantasy

too." An ornery grin eased across his face. "Any chance your man is bi?"

I shook my head, giving Benji a sympathetic look. "We'll find you someone soon."

"Oh, Benji, was that Thomas I saw tonight?" Marilyn turned in her seat in order to see her son.

"What?" I smacked Benji on the arm. "He was here? Layne, did you meet him?" I was grateful for the small distraction.

Layne rubbed his chin and shrugged. "There were no introductions from Benji tonight."

"Yeah, Mom, it was him, but don't read anything into it. I made it clear that he wasn't welcome."

"Oh." Marilyn faced the front as Michael slid into the driver's seat. "I thought maybe he was there to beg for forgiveness."

"Maybe he was, but when you've messed around on me twice, you don't get an opportunity to do it again." Benji huffed then looked out the window.

I squeezed his arm, thankful he wasn't settling because of the wheelchair situation. He deserved better.

"Did everyone have a good time?" Michael asked, pulling onto Division.

"We did. Thank you so much for making it happen." I answered for everyone, but it seemed as though we were all incredibly grateful for the night out. *Until the end.*

"I had no idea you were so talented, Tensley," Michael continued. "Layne, had you seen her play before?"

A smile lit up his face as he looked at me. "The first night I saw her in Spokane, she performed at Barney's."

What would I do if I never saw his smile again or his blue eyes that melted me to the center of my being? Jack's sneer and threat loomed over my shoulder, and my grip tightened on Layne's hand.

A frown creased his brow. *Shit, he knows something's off.*

My tongue darted across my bottom lip, and I glanced down

at his crotch. Maybe that message would distract him enough not to ask questions, at least for the rest of the night.

He leaned down and kissed me gently. "I can't wait to be inside you," he whispered.

I couldn't wait either.

22

My fingernails raked down Layne's back as he slowly pushed deep inside me. His mouth teased my nipples, sucking on my breast while he pulled back out then thrust into me again.

A moan escaped me and I wrapped my legs around his waist. With every move, my body responded to him. Raw desire swirled low in my belly as he continued to claim me.

"I love you," he whispered. "Nothing feels more right than being here with you." He paused and gently brushed a stray hair from my face. His eyes penetrated my soul, and an overwhelming combination of love and fear consumed me. My heart belonged to him. I'd never loved anyone else like I did Layne, but it had been made clear to me that, as sure as the air I breathed, he could be taken away, and I didn't know what to do about it. *How can I protect him and everyone else I love?*

Layne's pace picked up, and I rolled him over on his back, taking control. I ground my hips against him and he sucked on his finger before massaging my clit.

His eyes darkened as he watched me. "Do you know what makes me come, Tensley?"

I shook my head, my orgasm building as he continued to touch me.

"You. The way your eyes close when you're about to come for me. The way your back arches with my touch. How you bite your bottom lip in order not to scream. Knowing it's for me, baby..." His fingers dug into my hips, and he panted, slamming upward and gaining a new angle I'd not experienced before.

"Layne." I leaned forward, my hands landing on the bed over his shoulders. "I love you," I whimpered as my body shuddered. Black dots floated behind my eyes. My slick walls tightened around him as his hips bucked up, and he released.

I collapsed on top of him, attempting to catch my breath. His arms wrapped around my back and he placed a kiss on my forehead.

"My baby." His voice was low and gentle, breaking through the walls I'd put in place to protect him. "There's nothing I wouldn't do for you. Nothing."

A whimper caught in my throat, and I moved off him.

Confusion twisted his expression. "Ten, what did I say?"

My feet landed on the soft carpet of the bedroom and I made a mad dash to the bathroom, closing the door behind me before I completely fell apart. Covering my mouth in order to silence my sob, I turned on the shower and stepped under the spray of water before it even had time to warm up. I sank onto the seat, curled into a ball, and wished I could go back in time and change the fact that Layne had shown up in my life again. Loving him would kill him. I would fuck something up and Jack would kill him. I couldn't live with that.

Sobs racked me under the lukewarm water as I searched every corner of my brain for a plan to keep the people I loved safe from an evil monster. But I wasn't sure how. Jack was smart, strong, and had already stepped into my life without me even realizing it. I didn't know how long he had been watching me and following my every move.

"Ten," Layne said softly before opening the shower door.

I shook my head, my wet hair clinging to my face. "Don't." I held up my hands in a feeble attempt to block him, but he scooped me up and held me anyway.

"I can't lose you," I said, sobbing. "I can't." I hiccupped as I placed my palm against his cheek. "You're the air I breathe. You gave me life when I didn't even think it was possible. And now ..." I curled up against him and buried my face in his neck.

"Babe, what do you mean? I'm not going anywhere."

I didn't know how long we sat there, but eventually my tears ran dry and a numbness sank deep into my bones.

Layne turned off the water and stood with me in his arms. "I've got you. I've always got you," he whispered. His soft words grazed my ear and pierced my heart.

I'd never had a guy dry me off before, but Layne took extra care with me. The soft plush towel dried every last tear and water droplet from my body.

"Let's get you tucked in." Layne wrapped me in the towel and guided me to bed. He turned the covers down then hurried to the dresser and grabbed some warm pajamas for me. I held up my arms like a small child while he dressed me, then he brushed and dried my hair with the dryer.

After he got me settled into bed, he placed a sweet kiss on my forehead and tucked the blankets under my chin. "I'll be right back."

Although the covers were warm, I shivered. How was I going to keep everyone safe without sharing my terrifying secret? *I* was Jack Flannery's daughter. But it went way deeper than that.

Minutes later, Layne strolled out of the bathroom in low-slung sweatpants.

"Are you warm enough?" he asked, joining me under the covers. He wrapped his arms around me and pulled me against him.

My teeth stopped chattering almost immediately, not because

I no longer felt cold, but because, at least at that moment, I felt safe.

Layne nuzzled my neck. "I know you talked to Franklin."

There was no reason to beat around the bush. "He's my father."

Layne's arms tightened around me. "This changes nothing, babe. I love you more today than I did yesterday. When I lost Nicole, I never dreamed I'd find tomorrow with someone."

I rolled over on my other side and faced him. "I'm the daughter of a serial killer. His blood runs through my veins. You should be afraid of me."

Layne propped up on his elbow, his expression growing intense. "Listen to me." He cupped my chin with his fingers and tilted my head up. "I know who you are. I fell in love with you before we ever learned who your father was. If you're scared, then hold on to that. I've loved you for a long time."

I placed my hand on his and leaned into his touch. "Earlier tonight …" My words caught in my throat. "When I was in the bathroom before we came home …" I pulled away from him and sat up in bed. If I confessed to Layne that I had seen my father, his life would be in danger. Pulling my knees to my chest, I looked at him. He was so trusting, so gorgeous. This man in my bed had proven over and over again that he loved me. Maybe it was time that I took another step and told him the truth. "Matthew didn't talk to me."

Layne's brows knitted together in confusion.

"I'm sorry. I lied to you." I hopped out of bed, paced back and forth, and waited for his anger.

An exasperated and confused expression settled over him. "Why? I don't understand. Did you want me to be jealous? Because I am. I'm man enough to admit it."

I shook my head. "I was trying to protect you. He said if I told anyone, he'd kill you all and make me watch." My heart rate skyrocketed. "Jack Flannery cornered me in the bathroom tonight."

"Jesus." Layne jumped out of bed and hurried over to me. "Did he hurt you? Are you all right?" He ran his hands over my face and shoulders, scanning me for any indication that the monster had hurt me.

"Oh God. What if I've done the wrong thing by telling you? Layne, I can't lose you. I'd never forgive myself if he found out and killed you. Or Benji or Avery." The pitch of my voice rose with each name. I wrung my hands together, my fear escalating. "I shouldn't have told you. I should have just lied to you and let it go."

His fingers tightened on my arms. "We'll go to the FBI."

I stumbled backward, horrified at the mere idea. "No. No, we can't. I've already taken a huge risk by telling you, but I don't know what to do. He's going to come back."

Layne sank down on the edge of the bed, staring at me. "What do you mean?"

"He said he doesn't want to hurt me, and although he didn't go into detail, I got the impression he wants to get to know me."

"Hell no!" Layne's shoulders slumped forward, realizing his voice was too loud.

"I have to leave." I dropped to my knees in front of him, my eyes never leaving his as the truth crashed down around me. "If I'm not around, he won't hurt you or anyone else I love." I shot up off the floor and hurried to my dresser. "I can't tell you where I'm going. Don't look for me and don't come after me." I tossed my clothes on the bed, then flung the closet door open and rifled around for something to put them in. I had some money saved up that would get me a few states away, but I would have to find a job soon, maybe even change my name again. I'd disappeared once—I could do it again. "That will work." I crawled into the closet on my hands and knees and dragged out a medium-sized duffel bag.

Layne watched me, wide-eyed, while I hurried to the bathroom and grabbed my toiletries. I quickly shoved my belongings in the bag, then realized I was still in my pajamas. "Shit." I shimmied out of them, added them to my other clothes, and pulled out a pair of jeans and a black sweatshirt.

"You can't tell anyone why I left." I slipped my tennis shoes on and hefted the bag on my shoulder. "This is it. We have to cut all communication." My chest tightened as reality slapped me in the face again, but it didn't matter. I would rather give Layne up and allow him to live a good life without me than attend his funeral.

Layne stood, and without a word, he slipped the duffel off my shoulder and kissed me. For a moment, everything disappeared around me, and we were the only people that existed. He deepened his kiss, his hands sliding up my back and pulling me against him. My knees turned to Jell-O. *How will I make it without him?* I'd finally let someone in. I'd fallen in love. And now …

"Tensley, we need to talk."

"I have to go," I replied between kisses. "The longer I stay, the more danger you're in."

Layne kissed the tip of my nose and hugged me tightly. "I think there's been a misunderstanding. When I told you I loved you, I meant it. When those words left my mouth, I committed to you on every level, not just when it was convenient or safe, but every moment we had together. I'm not letting you go, and you're not leaving me. *We*—did you hear that, Ten?—*We* will figure this out together. You've been on your own for way too long, but I'm here now."

I peeked up at him with tears clinging to my eyelashes. "I can't ask you to put yourself in harm's way."

"You're not. I'm telling you I'm not going anywhere. This is my choice, babe. You're what I want, and that's all. If that means we take down a sick son of a bitch together, so be it."

I shook my head in disbelief. No one had ever loved me

enough to stick around for long, much less put his life on the line in order to be with me.

Layne released me, grabbed the bag, and dumped the contents on the floor. "Now get the idea out of your head that you have to leave. Jack Flannery never has to know you told me."

I frowned. "How? He has eyes and ears everywhere. He knew more about my past than you did." I shuddered and rubbed my arms.

Layne bent over, grabbed my pajamas, and for the second time that night, put them on me.

"Bed." He pointed.

"Bossy, much?" I couldn't hide the small grin pulling at the corner of my mouth. "I might like bossy, Layne."

He cocked an eyebrow, then turned the covers down for us. Although it went against everything inside me, I agreed to stay. Layne and I would just have to keep our secret.

He gently stroked my hair while I laid my head on his chest. "I need some time to think."

Exhaustion tugged at me and I stifled a yawn.

His soft lips brushed my head. "No more secrets?"

"No more secrets."

I inhaled deeply, willing all the bad shit to disappear. I wasn't sure what would happen next, but there was one thing I'd learned about bouncing around foster care. Enjoying the good moments was important because they could be gone in a heartbeat.

JACK'S FINGERS wrapped around my throat and squeezed. I clawed at his hands, desperate to suck even a tiny amount of air into my deprived lungs. My feet lifted off the floor as I struggled.

"Babe." Layne shook me gently. "Babe, wake up, you're having a bad dream."

My eyes popped open. I gasped for air and sat up ramrod

straight. I reached for my neck, but no one had me pinned against the wall. Sweat trickled down the side of my face, and my heart pounded against my rib cage.

"Layne?" I reached out to touch him, and the warmth of his skin eased my terror.

"I'm right here. What happened?" The blankets had fallen to his waist, revealing his upper body. The muscles in his chest rippled as he took my hand in his. "You're safe."

I nodded and attempted to calm my out-of-control heart rate. "I thought you were Jack. He was strangling me in the bathroom at Barney's." It was a good thing I'd confessed what had happened to Layne because there was no way I would have been able to hide the nightmares. Plus, what if I talked in my sleep? I collapsed back on the bed and rubbed my bleary eyes. "What time is it? I feel like I just fell asleep."

"It's almost five thirty." Layne settled back into his pillow next to me. "Can I hold you?"

I turned to look at him. "Please."

He wrapped his arms around me, and I snuggled up against him.

Layne's fingers traced up and down my back. "Is there anything else I need to know? Did Jack say anything else, Ten?"

"No. I told you everything. I just have a really awful feeling, and not because he's here or because you're in danger. I'm not sure what it is. I just don't think we're going to get out of this without losing someone."

"You can't think like that, Ten. We have to stay ahead of him and figure out how to communicate with each other and the police."

That time, I didn't argue.

"I might have an idea, but you've got to trust me. I can't say anything yet until I'm sure," Layne said.

I stuck my lower lip out in a pout as I looked up at him. "I don't like this." I flattened my hand against his chest.

"Me either, but I'll tell you as soon as everything is ironed out. In the meantime, I'd prefer that you not go anywhere in public without Michael or me. I'm not trying to be a controlling ass, but if Jack got to you in Barney's and slipped past the bodyguards, this guy knows what the fuck he's doing. Plus he's eluded the FBI across eleven states. We have to be more careful."

I massaged my temples and blew out a big breath. "I know. I was just grateful Avery wasn't with me. She usually is, but she left since Justin broke up with her. Shit. I'm supposed to have girl time with her today. I can't not see her, babe. She needs me. And what excuse would I give her anyway? Oh, hey, so Jack Flannery held a knife to my neck last night, and I can't see you today because he might fillet us all." I cringed as the words left my mouth. The gruesome details of the women he'd already killed were front and center in my mind.

"Have her over. You girls can talk in here or in the family room. I'm sure Benji's parents would prefer that right now anyway. Benji and I will hang, maybe pick up some dinner for everyone."

"Are you and Benji getting closer?" My heart fluttered with hope. It would be beyond amazing if Layne and Benji became tight. I knew that sometimes friendships drifted apart when someone fell in love, but I refused to let that happen. Benji and I were a package deal. If Layne loved me, then he would have to love Benji too. Well, maybe not love him, but I couldn't have someone upset over me sitting in his lap or planting a juicy kiss on his mouth.

"He really loves you," Layne said, his voice full of respect. "He straight-up told me I'd better not break your heart, or there would be serious consequences."

"Did he?" I giggled. "And he would make sure you paid for hurting me too. I love him so much. He's the best friend I've ever had. There was just something with us that clicked. No judgment … just acceptance. It's been like that since day one."

"I can tell. I hope to have that with you as well."

I propped up on my elbows. "Layne Garrison, if I didn't have that kind of trust in you, I wouldn't have told you about Jack. I just hope like hell I didn't make a horrible mistake." I leaned over and kissed him. "I'm not sure what part of you is my favorite: your lips, your eyes, or your dick." I slid my hand beneath the covers and into his sweats. He was already hard and ready for me. "I need a distraction." I moved my leg over his and let him take control. Sometimes it was sweeter to surrender.

23

A very looked like hell. Her green eyes were swollen and red from crying. All I wanted to do was pop Justin in the nose for what he was doing to her. Instead, I hugged her and pulled her inside Benji's house. Other than the previous night at Barney's, it was the first time we were all together, but first, she needed girl time.

She slipped off her coat, and I attempted to mask my surprise. Avery never ever wore T-shirts, especially not wrinkled ones. Her eyes fell to the floor as a hint of pink crept up her cheeks. "Thanks for having me over." She tucked her dark-brown hair behind her ear.

Where was my confident friend? I wasn't sure what had happened yet, but it seemed as though Justin had done a number on her, and I didn't like it at all.

"Yeah, I think we will have more privacy here than if we went out for coffee. At least you can cry and yell if you need to without anyone staring." I took her hand then pulled her up the stairs and to my bedroom.

"Your ass looks great," she said, walking behind me. "Probably because it's getting tapped."

I giggled. "Thank you. I'm … really happy." I shut my mouth. She wasn't there to discuss Layne and me. This was about her and how I could make her feel better.

She flopped down in the middle of my king-size bed, and I closed the door before joining her.

I moved the cream and black decorative pillows, then crawled onto the bed and propped up on my side. "Spill, sweetie." Avery had my full attention.

She sniffled, then rifled through her jeans pocket for a tissue. "I don't know what happened, Ten. One week, I'm meeting his parents. Then the next, *bam!* Like, he wants to see other people? I don't know what I did wrong."

My heart cracked right down the middle. Why did women think that if a guy didn't like them, it was because something was wrong with them? Sometimes people weren't a good fit, and sometimes the guy was a straight-up asshole. I'd seen how well Avery treated Justin, so I didn't think it was anything she had done.

"There's nothing wrong with you. You're smart, seriously hot, fun, and you have an amazing heart."

"I caught him with another girl," Avery wailed.

Dammit. I would string him up by his dick. "What do you mean caught? As in they were in bed together? A kiss?" Not that it mattered. He was obviously a complete and total jack wad.

"Kissing while we were all at Barney's! They snuck off to the parking lot, and …" She trailed off, swiping away tears.

My stomach dipped. Jack had been out there. What if something had happened? Whatever plan Layne was figuring out, I hoped it was good.

"And then Ramsey caught us arguing," Avery continued. "I was so embarrassed." Her hands flew over her face as she broke down in sobs.

"I'm sure Ramsey didn't think anything about it. He seems pretty nice, right?" I had no idea if he was or not. I was just grasping at anything to say that would help her feel a little bit better.

"Yeah," she squeaked.

"He certainly was gorgeous. Did you say he's transferring to college up here?"

Avery wiped her cheeks and blew out a big breath. "In January. It's been a long time since we've seen each other, but our parents have been friends for years. We used to visit Ramsey and his family every summer. Well, sort of. We'd all meet in the Hamptons for the summer. I went until I turned seventeen, then I was too cool to hang out with them. It's been four years since I've seen them."

I cleared my throat and prepared to give the best speech I could. I wasn't sure if Avery would believe it, but I would.

"You know I love you, right?" I started.

Avery's eyes connected with mine, and she nodded.

"Although I pretended to be normal, bouncing around foster homes fucked me up. Men thought they had the right to screw me, and often times, the wife grew jealous even though I wasn't asking for it." I rubbed my forehead. Telling her about my past was harder than I'd anticipated. "I moved to Spokane to start over, and you and Benji became my family. There weren't expectations or sex involved, just me. You just loved me for me. It didn't matter what flaws I had, how difficult it was to get to know me, or how long it took me to warm up and trust you—you loved me anyway." I sat up and took her hand, hoping she understood what I was trying so hard to convey. "You loved me because you saw something inside me that was worth the risk. You showed up day after day until my walls crumbled, and I let you in. Avery, there's a guy for you that will do the same. He will show up for you over and over and know beyond a shadow of a doubt that you're worth every minute."

"Really?" she croaked. "You think so?"

I nodded. "I know so. Hon, Justin just isn't what you want. No girl wants to be cheated on or to feel unloved, unworthy." My heart skipped a beat as I realized how much Layne really gave to me, and all I wanted was for Avery and Benji to have the same.

"You're right. I definitely don't want to be cheated on."

"Hey, if I can fall in love, then anything is possible."

For the first time since she'd arrived, Avery laughed. "Tell me how it's going. I feel like I should be front and center with you on this new adventure, but between us temporarily moving out and my drama with Justin, I've not been a very good friend."

I rolled my eyes at her. "Please, girl. It's been a shit show lately with everything going on." She had no idea how much of one it had truly been, and I couldn't divulge the secrets either, not if I wanted to keep her safe.

"Ugh, you've gotta fill me in now that I'm done blubbering about Justin. So some criminal the FBI is tracking was on our property? Do they know why? And who is he?"

I cleared my throat. Lying to her wouldn't be easy. "They've been following him across several states, but I don't know other than he hid in our storage shed in the backyard. The police were concerned about our safety." There, I'd done it, and it was mostly the truth. Maybe it was enough for her to stop asking questions.

"Ugh. That's so stupid, but at the same time, I'd probably be scared to stay at our house, ya know? Mom and Dad have been super sweet while I've been back at home."

"Michael and Marilyn have too. It's been good to spend time with Benji as well, but I miss us all living together like we did before the assault." My gut twisted into knots as the memories flooded my mind.

"And to think the guy you hated so much saved you both." Avery's expression turned gentle and she took my hand. "I know you, Tensley Bennett. You're scared out of your wits about this relationship with Layne."

"Sort of. I'm doing a little bit better, but it's taking time. I'm afraid I'm going to wake up one morning and he'll be gone and I wasn't good enough to keep him."

"Hon, you've got a lot of years to undo of men hurting you. If Layne is a good one, like I believe he is, he will prove to you every day that he'll be there for you. Hopefully, one day, I'll find the same."

"You will. I know it. Until then, you have all of us. In fact, you should stay tonight. Let's shoot pool, watch movies, and drink. I know Benji would love to spend time with you, too. Say yes, then I'll have Benji make sure it's fine with Marilyn and Michael. I'm sure it is. Please." I stuck my lip out and turned on the puppy dog eyes.

"It would be a lot of fun. I miss you guys so much."

"Yes!" I hopped off the bed, grabbed my phone from my back pocket, and texted Benji. Seconds later, the parental approval came through.

"The guys are going to grab some pizza, so why don't we see what's on Redbox on Demand?" I reached my hand out to her, and she placed hers in mine. "Let's go to the family room." I smiled sweetly and led her down the hall.

"Thanks, Ten." Avery entered the room and immediately grabbed a pool stick. "Winner plays one of the guys. We can have our own tournament, but for alcohol instead of money."

"Ha ha! I know Benji's parents have plenty, but let's not clean out their cabinet. Maybe just some shots."

A mischievous grin eased across her face. "I'll replace it tomorrow."

"You got it. Game on, muthafucka." I barked out a laugh.

Forty minutes later, I'd kicked her ass in the pool game, and Layne and Benji had made it back with pizza. We joined everyone in the kitchen, and our laughter floated through the house. Benji joined his parents at the table while Avery, Layne, and I sat at the bar. Although I was terrified of Jack, this was what my heart needed: my family.

I licked the sauce off my fingers and caught Layne staring at me. "What? Do I have food on my face?" I grabbed a napkin and wiped my mouth.

"No." He leaned over until his breath was tickling my ear. "I love you. I was just thinking about how strong you are."

My eyes found his, and my fear subsided momentarily. He was calmer, and I suspected he had figured something out.

Marilyn stood, dabbed the corners of her lips with a paper towel, and collected our plates. "If you all want to watch movies and play video games until you fall asleep, we can help Benji get situated."

"I'm in," Benji replied. "The couch will be fine for me tonight. That just means everyone else will be on the floor."

We all agreed the sleeping arrangements would be fun, and within the next hour, everyone was settled. A mound of blankets, sleeping bags, and pillows were stacked to the side of the couch. Avery propped her feet up on the ottoman while Layne and I snuggled up in the opposite corner of the sectional.

"Did everyone get enough covers?" Marilyn asked, entering the room.

Avery gave Marilyn a sweet smile. "We did. Thank you so much for allowing me to stay. I really needed this."

"Anytime. We have plenty of space." Marilyn's focus bounced from Avery to me. "Tensley, can I have a word, please?"

My brows knitted together as I stood and made my way to her.

She took my hand and guided me into the hall. "Everything is fine, honey. I'm sorry. I just wanted to make sure you were doing okay and wondered if there was anything I could do to help. Tensley, I don't think you realize how special you are to this family. The circumstances are terrible, but Michael and I are elated that you're here. You've brought laughter back into my home. And although Benji is doing fine and committed to getting better, his spark has come back with you here. He needs you near. I've never seen two better friends." Kindness filled her eyes as she finished and squeezed my hand.

Overwhelmed with emotion, I threw my arms around her. "Thank you. I love you all so much."

Marilyn hugged me back, then pulled away. "I'll let you get back to your fun, but come get me if any of you need anything." She patted my cheek then turned to leave.

Tears pricked the backs of my eyes as I watched her gracefully descend the stairs. *How did I get so lucky?*

"What did I miss?" I asked, joining my friends again.

Benji wheeled around the couch, his intense stare never leaving me as he handed us all a beer. "Did you get the test results? Is that what Mom wanted to talk to you about?"

Dryness seized my throat, and I attempted to swallow. My eyes cut to Avery.

She sat up straight, and her mouth hung open. "If you got her pregnant, Layne Garrison, I will beat you senseless."

"Avery!" I choked out. "I know you're trying to take care of me, but that's not what Benji is referring to."

"Thank God." She smacked a hand over her face. "Sorry, Layne, but I hope you keep that in mind."

Benji quirked an eyebrow. "You didn't tell her?"

Avery's attention bounced between us. "Tell me what?"

A burning sensation filled my chest. "I … I took a DNA test to find out who my bio father is."

"What? Why didn't you tell me?" Avery slouched in her seat. Her feelings were obviously hurt.

"I'm sorry," Benji said, his eyes pleading for forgiveness. "I thought you'd talked to her about it."

Layne's arm tightened around me protectively.

"The reason I didn't say anything was because I just got the results last night while we were all at Barney's. Justin was being a douche canoe, and you needed me. Plus, I had to process the information." My gaze drifted to Benji as silence descended over the room. There was no need to say anything. I was sure Benji knew the results by the look on my face.

"Fuck." Benji shook his head. "Are you sure? Is Franklin sure? Can you retest?"

"Fifty percent, which means I'm his daughter." My voice hitched as fear and guilt gnawed at me. "Avery, I wasn't going to tell you because it could put you in danger."

"I don't understand. What are you talking about? Please, someone, fill me in," she said with a hint of exasperation.

"The guy the FBI is looking for ... His name is Jack Flannery, and he's a serial killer. And he's my father."

Avery's mouth gaped open. "You're fucking with me, right?"

"I wish I was. Franklin told me last night, but I've not even talked to Benji yet, so please don't feel like I shut you out." I pulled away from Layne and joined Avery on her end of the sectional. "I love you. You, Benji, and Layne are the people I love most in this world, and I'm terrified Jack will hurt one or all of you. He's evil. A murderer. I'm trying to protect everyone."

Avery leaned her head on my shoulder and peeked up at me. "I love you too. I get it. I don't like it, but I understand why you weren't forthcoming with the information, especially since you just found out less than twenty-four hours ago. But why was he at our house?" Fear flickered in her eyes.

"I think ..." My attention landed on Layne then Benji. "I think he wants me."

Benji's face drained of color. "Jesus Christ. You're never going back to that house, Tensley." He wheeled over to me and took my hand. "I'll talk to Mom and Dad, and we'll beef up security. I know Franklin will do everything he can to get the FBI off your back, but we have to keep you safe. If you think he's after you—"

"We can't," Layne interrupted. "If we increase security, it might tip Jack off, and he will know Tensley shared information, and it will put her at a greater risk."

"He's right, and the best way to get to me is through all of you." I inhaled deeply, attempting to rid my shoulders and neck of the stress I'd been carrying. After taking a long drink of my beer, I leaned my head back and closed my eyes. "From what I can tell, Jack wants to check in on his daughter. If he were going to hurt me, he would have already. He had complete access to me the night he was at our house. After I returned from working at the library, no one else was home except me. But listen, we can't discuss this with anyone. You both have to promise. I mean, Michael, Franklin, and Marilyn know the results. Franklin is going to pull camera footage of me working at the library the night Jack was photographed on our property. It should clear me of any involvement, but both of you swear to me that none of this leaves this room. Ever." I stared at Benji then Avery.

"Promise." Avery squeezed my knee. "But you'll talk to me about it if you need to, right? I don't want you to think you have to go through this alone because you're trying to take care of us."

"Ditto." Benji wheeled back to the front of the couch. His eyes were deeply troubled. He didn't even know the half of it.

I peeked over at Layne, but he had remained calm during the entire conversation. I had a sneaking suspicion that whatever he had figured out, he'd already put it into motion. If that was the case, I loved him even more for it.

"I'm so, so sorry," Avery whispered. Tears filled her eyes. "I can't imagine being a foster kid and living through the shit you've lived through, only having hope that maybe your dad would show up and remove you from that hell. Now to find out he's wanted for murder ..." Her voice trailed off. "You deserve so much better than that."

My chest tightened with her words. Avery had always protected me even when I hadn't needed it, but there was no question in my mind that she loved and cared about me. Some people were friends, but some friends were worth dying for. If it came down to it, I would gladly put my life on the line if it meant that Avery, Benji, and Layne were safe. My heart would never beat the same if anything happened to them.

"What about a movie to lighten the mood?" Benji grabbed the remote off the entertainment center and turned on the TV.

My phone buzzed in my back pocket. "Well, that's odd. It's after ten. No one calls me this late." I tapped the green button. "Hello?"

"Hey, Tensley, it's Matthew at Barney's. Someone just turned in your driver's license to me. You must have dropped it last night when you were here."

"Oh jeez! Thank you. I hadn't even realized it was missing. I'll be right over."

"I'll keep it in the office for safekeeping until you get here. I'll see you in a few." Matthew disconnected our call.

"It was Matthew at Barney's. I accidentally dropped my license when we were there, so I need to go grab it. You guys can start a movie without me, though."

Layne stood immediately. "I'll go with you."

"Thanks." I stood and stretched. "Does anyone want anything? A fifth of vodka? Cranberry juice?" I grinned.

"We have all that here," Benji replied, chuckling. "I'll make us all drinks after you get back."

"Sounds good." I kissed Avery and Benji on the cheek. "Thank you for being there for me tonight. I love you guys."

Benji winked at me. "Girl, please. I've always got your back."

"Ditto," Avery said, laughing. "Love you too. You two hurry back, and no side trips for a backseat quickie."

Layne chuckled and flashed me a seductive grin. "Now that you mention it …"

I playfully smacked him on the arm, grateful he was comfortable enough to joke around with my friends.

"Later." I waved and took Layne's hand.

"If you'll give me a minute, I'll warm up the car for us." Layne grabbed our coats from the hall closet and handed mine to me.

He opened the front door and disappeared into the frigid November air. Within a few minutes, he pulled up, and I hurried to the warmth of his vehicle.

"Thank you." I pulled my coat around me a little tighter. "It smells like snow."

"Do you like the snow?" Layne pulled out of the driveway and headed toward Barney's.

"I do." A black Mercedes followed a few car lengths behind us. "Do you?"

"I've not seen a lot of it, but I'm looking forward to it. You can snuggle up to me and we can watch it fall together. That sounds really nice, actually."

"Mmm. It sounds romantic. Maybe I can make my kick-ass hot chocolate too."

"I love hot chocolate. It's the best of both worlds, hot and chocolate." Layne chuckled at himself.

I giggled. "Oh my God. That was a horrible joke." We continued to make plans for the winter as he drove.

Ten minutes later, Layne parked in front of Barney's and turned off the car. "I'm going in with you." He wasn't asking.

"Thank you, but I don't think there's any concern that Jack will show up here twice. He knows the cops are looking for him. Plus it would be pretty stupid, and Jack is brilliant and calculating." I leaned over, gave Layne a kiss, then hopped out of the vehicle.

In a few quick strides, Layne opened the front door of Barney's. A rush of heat and music greeted us. I spotted Matthew through the crowd of people and tugged on Layne's hand. We walked together to the bar area.

"Hey," I said to Matthew. "Thank you so much for holding on to my license for me. I can't believe I dropped it. It must have fallen out of my pocket when I pulled out my phone."

"No problem. Glad I could help." He flashed me a sexy smile, then narrowed his gaze at Layne.

"Did you say it was in the office?" I needed to get things moving before those two went at it. Honestly, I could understand Layne being a little bit jealous, but they seemed to seriously dislike each other. Maybe they'd had words I wasn't aware of. I just didn't get it.

Matthew signaled for a waitress. "Hey, Lisa. Can you watch the bar for me? I'll be back in a minute."

A tall, curvy blonde I'd never seen before joined him. I didn't miss her heated gaze traveling over my boyfriend. *What is wrong with people? Can't she tell we're together?* We were holding hands, after all.

We followed Matthew down the hall and toward the back of the building. He turned right into a small office and closed the door behind us. "Man, I know music is necessary for a bar, but it's so loud, we can't hear each other talk. I hate yelling at people." He smiled. "I've got it right over here." He walked around the messy desk and opened the drawer. "Over there, Tensley."

It took me a minute to register what he'd just done.

"I don't have all fucking night. Move!" Matthew pointed the gun at us, his expression turning cold. "Layne, hands behind your head."

"Matthew, what are you doing?" The pitch of my voice climbed as reality sank in. "I don't understand."

Matthew ignored me as he approached Layne. "On your knees, asshole." Matthew delivered a quick kick to the back of Layne's legs and dropped him to the floor. "Say one fucking word and you can say goodbye to your girlfriend. Besides, even if you screamed for help, the music is too loud. No one will hear you."

My pulse pounded in my ears while my brain attempted to calculate how quickly I could reach the gun, but there was no way to sneak up on Matthew since he was facing me. He'd obviously had all this planned. I just didn't know why. *Does he even have my license?* I'd just trusted him and hadn't even checked my wallet.

"Layne," I whispered, my voice trembling. "I'm so sorry."

"I'm the one that's sorry, Ten. I should have trusted my gut about him."

Matthew rapped Layne on the back of the head and knocked him out. A scream ripped from my throat, but no one came running to help us. I watched helplessly while Matthew blind-folded and gagged Layne, then tied his hands and feet together.

"Why? Are you this jealous? I don't understand. Matthew, I never even realized you were interested in me until I started dating Layne."

Matthew's maniacal laugh filled the room, but his gun never left me. "Shut up. You have no idea what you're talking about."

"Then tell me. Please."

A back door to his office creaked open slightly, and terror shot through me as Jack Flannery walked in. "It's time to go, Tensley. I've got a wonderful father-daughter trip planned." Jack's gaze filled with hate as his attention landed on my crumpled-up boyfriend. "Good job, Matthew. Make sure he never sees the light of day again."

Overwhelmed with fear for Layne's life, I lunged toward Mathew and the gun. Before I reached him, muffled shots went off, and Matthew's body jerked backward. He slumped against the wall, his blood streaking the dirty white wallpaper.

"Oh my God! Oh my God!" I hurried to Layne and kneeled next to him.

Jack waved his gun at me. "We gotta go. Now. Tell your boyfriend goodbye."

"You killed Matthew," I hiccupped through my tears.

"He would have killed you. No one gets to do that except me." The corner of Jack's mouth twitched.

I kissed Layne's cheek and realized he was no longer uncon-scious. "Don't ever forget how much I love you."

Layne attempted to talk behind his gag, but it was useless.

"Where are we going?" I asked, attempting to give Layne some information in order to find me.

"You'll see." Jack grabbed my arm and jerked me forward. "Quit stalling. Let's go."

My heart hammered against my rib cage as he escorted us out the back door. *What does he want from me? Is Layne all right? Where is my bodyguard?* A cry nearly escaped me as I spotted several huge garbage containers blocking the view on three sides. Even if my bodyguard was patrolling the area for me, he wouldn't realize there was a door there.

Jack stopped at a black Honda Accord and opened the back door. Suddenly, I felt a sharp sting in my neck. Complete blackness filled my vision as I tumbled to the floor of the car.

24

My head pounded as I pried my eyes open. Sharp light blurred my focus and I blinked rapidly. When I attempted to move my arm, panic shot through me. I couldn't move my arms or legs. Jack had taken me. I was tied to a chair. My heart raced and my breathing became erratic and labored.

"Ah, Sleeping Beauty is finally waking up. Did you have a nice nap?" Jack asked.

The stench of vomit and urine burned my nose. I peered around at the small room, my nostrils flaring in fear. My throat burned from lack of water as the events of my evening fell into place. "Where am I?"

The last thing I remembered was being at Barney's, then nothing. *Layne. Oh God.* I hoped someone had found him. At least he wasn't dead when Jack had forced me to leave, but that didn't mean someone hadn't come in after we left and finished him off. I didn't have time to panic about him, though. I had to figure out how to get the hell out of there.

A soft, weak moan reached my ears, and my head snapped up, surveying the room. The space was set up similar to a medical facility. A table was covered in plastic, and a tray full of tools I couldn't make out from a distance was directly in front of me. A large drain was in the middle of the cement floor, which was cracked with years of wear.

"Fuck." Next to the door, a woman was curled into a fetal position, shivering. Her stringy black hair covered her face, but nothing else. She was naked, and her pale skin was completely exposed. She moved, peering at me with one horror-filled eye. It was then that I realized she was chained to the wall like an animal. Bile burned the back of my throat, threatening to spill over as I stared at her.

"Jack. What are you going to do to her?" Although the words escaped my lips, I didn't want to hear the answer.

The metal legs of the chair scraped against the floor as Jack positioned himself right in front of me and straddled his seat. "If you're good, I'll untie you. Don't even think about running. We're in the middle of fucking nowhere, and it's almost two in the afternoon. Even if you made it out the door, the sun would set in a few more hours, and you'll freeze to death." He folded his arms on the back of the seat and grinned.

My stomach dropped to my toes. "We traveled all night?"

"Yes. And it was a lovely first trip with my daughter if I do say so myself." Jack stood and widened his arms. "Welcome to training camp, Victoria."

"That's not my name ... Dad." Although I wanted to spit in his face, I would have to try another tactic to stay alive, and I checked my tone before I spoke to him.

His laugh echoed through the room. "Nice try. I told you we were a lot alike. Calculating." He tapped the side of his head. "Right now, I bet you're trying to analyze the situation to see if you'll get out alive. Don't bother. As long as you do what I say, you will. But her on the other hand ..."

"Let her go," I pleaded. "I'll do anything you want, but let her go."

Jack knelt in front of me. "You're not putting it together yet, are you? Maybe I drugged you with too much propofol."

No wonder I felt like shit.

"Let's give you some time first. You still look pretty groggy. If I untie your hands, do you promise to be the well-behaved daughter I've always dreamed you would be?"

"I promise. And do you have any fresh water? My throat is horribly dry."

Jack walked behind the chair, leaned down, and began to untie my hands. His breath grazed the back of my neck, sending chills down my spine.

"Thank you." I immediately began to massage my wrists, hoping the feeling would return. I must have been tied up for a long time.

Jack unzipped a backpack and removed an unopened bottle of water, then closed the bag again. "Make it last." He shoved it in my face.

I struggled to grasp it. My hands still weren't working. I glanced up at him. "Could … would you open it and help me? My fingers are really tingly, and I can't get it."

Jack sighed. "I suppose. If I'd been in your life all these years, I'm sure I'd have opened lots of things for you." He twisted the top off, placed the bottle to my parched lips, and tilted it back slightly.

I gulped greedily before he pulled it back.

"You'll puke if you don't slow down." He twisted the lid back on and sat the container next to me on the floor.

"Why did you leave?" My voice shook with my question. I'd dreamed of being able to confront him for years. Now he was right in front of me. "You left me with a drug addict. Do you know what happened to me as the years went by?" Anger swirled inside me.

"I don't, but I can guess. You were probably raped, beaten, or pimped out. Maybe all of it. Or maybe an amazing family adopted you, and you turned out to be a well-adjusted young woman."

I searched his face. There was no remorse, no sadness ... no feeling at all. His expression was completely void of any compassion for what his daughter might have gone through.

My mind scrambled for any way to reach him, any way to connect with a small part of his humanity. If he had any.

Swallowing hard, I massaged my hands. "Tell me about yourself. What did you do after you left Mom?" If I could keep him talking about his favorite subject—Jack Flannery—it might buy me some time to figure out how to get the hell out of there.

"I worked and traveled for the most part. I was in sales, so it was pretty easy to scope out my victims, especially at conferences."

I attempted to wiggle my toes in my tennis shoes. "What did you sell?"

"Anything they wanted, but most of the time, it was attention. Adoration. Wealthy women work a lot. They don't have time for a husband since they're married to their careers. First lesson, Vic ... Tensley. Everyone has a weak spot. It's my job to find it, then become exactly what they need to fill that hole inside themselves."

"Teach me how to read people like that." I swallowed hard, hoping he would think I was trying to work toward the loving father-daughter relationship most girls would long for.

The chain scraped the floor, and my eyes landed on the captive.

"Her." I pointed. "Tell me about her." I'd seen on some crime show that personalizing the victim might save her. It was worth a shot, although I wasn't sure Jack had a soul to be reached.

He rubbed his hands together, an evil smirk twisting his expression. "It's a shame she has to die. She was a lot of fun." His laughter filled the room.

"Fun?" I tried to hide my feelings of horror and focused on

maintaining a neutral expression. It had been a few years, but I was a master at hiding my emotions. It was time to tap into that skill again. It might save our lives. There was no way that Jack would allow me to walk out of there in one piece if I didn't agree to become his student. My stomach twisted in knots at the mere thought of harming someone.

"Lola. Such a beautiful woman. You should see her when she's going out for the night. We had amazing sex too. She loved it up the ass, and I was happy to oblige. Lola was even down with two guys at once. Who knew such a sophisticated, wealthy beauty would love being tied up and blindfolded while she was being fucked by one man and sucking off the other? She begged for it."

"It is fun." I leveled him with my gaze as it dawned on him what I'd said. "Two men touching you, fucking your tits, licking your pussy. I've done it all." My heart was screaming at me to stop and not meet him on his level, but it was the best opportunity I had to live.

"Are you a whore, or was it for survival?" He tilted his chin up in the air, assessing me. "Think carefully. One response I'll skin you alive for, and the other I'll congratulate you over."

"It's funny. I used to pray every night I'd die, but God just sent me to voice mail. Now I have the chance to end it right now, but I want to live. I want to know how much alike you and I really are. And to answer your question, I did anything for survival I had to. You can't rape the willing."

Jack grinned and grabbed his crotch through his jeans. "All this talk has my cock hard."

I winced. Fear ripped through me.

The sound of his zipper broke the silence. "Lola, let's have one last fuck, shall we?"

I slammed my eyes closed and begged a nonexistent God that Jack wouldn't touch me or make me watch.

Jack moaned. "That's it. Suck it harder."

Wet sucking noises filled the room, and I mentally tried to

block out the images my mind was producing. I tried to focus on Layne.

Lola grunted, and from the slapping sound of skin on skin, Jack was fucking her doggie style. The chain scraped the floor again, and I flinched. I'd seen a lot of shit in foster homes, including full-on sex parties, but this ... I couldn't even imagine how Lola felt now that she knew what a monster Jack was. Or maybe, if she were lucky, she was too far gone to comprehend or care anymore.

A slap echoed through the room followed by Jack's zipper. "Where were we?" he asked as if he hadn't just raped a woman chained to the wall in front of his daughter.

I didn't miss a beat. "You were telling me where you met her."

"A cancer fundraiser. She'd just lost a friend to that dreadful disease." He didn't even try to disguise the sarcasm in his tone.

"So she was lonely and vulnerable." I focused on not showing any emotion as I responded.

He snapped his fingers. "Exactly. Easiest job in the world to comfort a grieving woman and be a good friend. Just a friend. No touching, no kissing, no fucking. Before she realized what was happening, Lola asked me on a date ... to France. She'd fallen in love with me."

A quiet sob caught my ear, and I peered over at the trembling, crying woman. I wanted to throw a blanket around her and tell her it was going to be okay, but I couldn't. I wasn't even sure I could save myself.

My focus traveled back to my father. "Was France as spectacular as everyone says it is? I've never left the country."

"What? Well, that's just another trip we can take together. We can visit some of the most exquisite cafes and wineries while we scope out our next victim. I've found traveling often keeps me out of prison too." He grinned. "Are you tired of sitting yet?"

"Yeah. My ass is numb."

"All you had to do was ask." He strolled over to me as though it was the most natural thing in the world to have your daughter tied up. I willed myself not to kick him in the face as he bent down and untied me. My legs were too numb to run, and I would only make things worse for myself. I needed a calculated plan. I needed to see Layne again ... if he was still alive. My heart skipped a beat at the mere thought. There had to be a way back to him. There had to be a way to free Lola and take out this disgusting pig that called me his daughter.

"There." Jack stood and extended his hand. "You'll need some help. We can walk around outside for a few minutes, get your blood flowing again."

I nodded, welcoming the idea of fresh air. It would also allow me to see if he'd lied to me about where we were. I took his hand, and he easily pulled me out of the chair. I staggered forward, trying to find my balance.

"Easy does it. Good. Just stand there for a minute while the blood begins to flow again."

I wiggled my toes, willing my limbs to work correctly. Hopefully, if I behaved myself, he wouldn't tie me up again.

He patted my hand as though I were a little girl. "Are you ready?"

"I think so. Can we take it slow?" When I stepped forward, my body shook from hours of not moving.

Several agonizing steps later, we reached the door. Jack flung it open, and a burst of freezing, fresh air blew past me.

"Shit." I rubbed my arms. "It's cold."

"At least you had your coat on when we left Barney's. It will help a little bit. The temperatures at this level are much colder."

My hand clenched into a fist. He made it sound as though we were out for a Sunday drive instead of him killing Matthew and forcing me into a car.

Dried leaves crunched beneath my feet as we stepped outside. The early evening sun broke through the leafless trees, and I inhaled deeply. I had no idea when he would make us go back inside to Lola and the overwhelming stench.

"Isn't it lovely up here?" He searched around as though he were enjoying the great outdoors, but I suspected he was surveying his surroundings in case we'd been followed.

Apparently we hadn't. Whatever Layne had planned, it hadn't been fast enough.

I squeezed Jack's arm affectionately. "How did you and Matthew meet, and who was he to you?"

We stopped, and he dropped my arm. His cold gaze connected with mine. "I'd not kept tabs on you until you were eighteen. It was then I realized that you and I might have a lot in common. After your unfortunate events in high school ... well, I knew you were in Spokane. I made my way there a few times, and one night, I was at Barney's. This was before the FBI had identified me, so I could still be seen in public whenever I wanted. Matthew had a certain quality about him. You'll understand soon enough. As I said, I'll teach you what to look for. Anyway, it was late, and we were the last two people there. I explained I was trying to keep an eye on my daughter, told him who you were, and he offered to help. Over the last two years, he's given me updates if I had to be gone for a while. By the way, he hated that boyfriend of yours, but it made things easy for me when I told him I needed direct access to you. His feelings were easily played on."

"Matthew let you in the door in the office, didn't he?" It was all coming together: how he'd found me, how he'd gotten into the bathroom with me at Barney's, and the help he'd had to abduct me.

"He was good to work with. It was such a shame I had to put a bullet in his head. When you lunged at him, his finger was on the trigger. I couldn't take any chances. As I said before, if anyone is going to kill you, it's me." He tsked, then looked at the sunset.

I tilted my head up to the sky. My face warmed from the fading embers of the evening sun, and I wondered if it would be the last sunset I would ever see. My pulse spiked as I scrambled for a way out of this mess.

"Are you feeling better?" he asked, looking at me. "I know we have so much to catch up on, but we have plenty of time." He wrapped his arm around my shoulders and gave me a fatherly hug. "I'm looking forward to it."

I couldn't decide if he was so narcissistic that he assumed I was on board with his plans or if my acting ability was better than I'd suspected. I'd had years of practice, but I thought I'd found Jack's weak spot. More than anything, he wanted me to join forces with him.

I plastered an adoring smile on my face. "Me too."

"That's my girl."

We stood quietly for a few minutes as the sky darkened and the moon peeked between the trees.

The stench nearly doubled me over as we entered the small building again, and Jack closed the door behind us.

"Let's get to work. Torturing one-oh-one." He rubbed his hands together, excitement flickering in his eyes as he stared at Lola. "I know you're still a bit tired and weak, so I'll put Lola on the table and strap her down. Why don't you get into my bag and grab the gag for me? Although no one is around, her screams will become irritating. It will help muffle the sound a little bit."

I nodded, unable to find any words, unsure of what was about to happen. *Fuck. Is he going to kill her now? Training. Shit. Shit. Shit.* He was going to teach me how to skin a victim alive. Apparently, the drug he'd given me not only numbed my body, but it had muddled my brain. I clenched my jaw together tightly, forcing the bitter bile back down.

I located the backpack, unzipped it, and rifled through the contents. I spotted the gag but kept searching through his belongings. Maybe there was something that would help Lola and I escape. My eyes widened as I recognized my phone. I groaned inwardly. There was no way I could conceal it on my body. I attempted to power it on. "Come on, come on." I glanced over my shoulder to see where Jack was in the room. Hoping like hell there was battery left, I shoved it back where I'd found it. Cold metal touched my skin, and I sucked in my breath. Jack had left a scalpel tucked away in a pocket. Was this a test, or had he not remembered there was a surgical tool—a weapon in his bag? I slid it into my coat sleeve and hoped like hell he didn't catch me.

"Did you find it?" Jack asked, interrupting my progress. The chain hit the floor with a clank and he threw Lola over his shoulder as though she weighed nothing. Since she'd been curled up, I hadn't realized how petite she was.

I held it up. "Anything else?" I asked, stalling for time.

He tossed Lola on the table and strapped her ankles and wrists down. "No. That's all."

I made my way over to her slowly. It was then that I saw the cuts and bruises on her breasts and stomach. One of her eyes was swollen shut. He'd beaten her badly. No wonder she hadn't fought him. She had nothing left inside her, no strength and no will to live. She blinked at me as though she were trying to focus, then she closed her eye and groaned.

"Here." Jack held his hand out, and I handed him the gag.

I wondered if Lola understood what was about to happen. I didn't. Logically, I did, but I'd learned a long time ago that understanding a situation and living through it were often two completely different things.

Swallowing hard, I looked at my father. How had I ended up here next to a murderer? I wondered how many kids had a serial killer for a father. My fury rose to a boiling point, but I couldn't act on it. *Fuck you, universe!*

Jack whistled while he prepared his tray. "I don't bother cleaning the tools. It's not like she'll get an infection." He laughed at his own joke.

I held my breath, counting the minutes until …

"Well." He paused and stared at me. "This is our first of many father-daughter killings. I never imagined life could be so fun."

"It's strange how things turned out, isn't it?" I squared my shoulders and tightened the hatches on my emotions. It wasn't the time to feel anything. "Show me how it's done."

Jack paused, searching me for any sign that I wasn't ready. My heart hammered against my chest.

"Excellent. I was really shaky the first time I did this, so I'm going to teach you the proper technique. Just take a step back and watch. If you have to puke, there's the drain." He nodded toward the opening in the floor. "It's not uncommon to get sick during the first few skinnings, but it will get better."

Jesus. How am I going to remain conscious? The room spun around me and I pushed my fingernails into the palms of my hands. The sharp sting of bile cleared my hazy mind and I swallowed hard.

"First, you hold the knife just so." He gripped the handle tightly.

"Wait. The lighting sucks from this side, and I can't see." I leaned around the table to get a better angle.

Jack looked up at the overhead light. "I hadn't considered how it would look from the other side. Come over here next to me, then."

I joined him, now facing the entrance. Little beads of sweat dotted my brows. "That's better. Maybe the moonlight filtering through the window in the door is helping."

Jack bent over an unmoving Lola. "In order to remove the longest piece of skin, I always begin with the left side of the shoulder. Thinner pieces are easier to manage as well." He glanced at me. "Does that make sense? I start at the top and go all the way down her arm."

I nodded, staring at Lola.

He straightened up, his attention focusing on me. "I'm really glad you're here, Tensley. I've dreamed about having you in my life for years." He offered me a genuine smile, which sent shudders through my body.

"Me too, Dad." I conjured up tears like I had when I was a little kid. "I've always wondered where I came from, and now I know. Thank you."

He grinned, then made the first cut on Lola's skin. Her one good eye flew open and bulged grotesquely. I steadied myself as her muffled screams filled the room. The small space began to spin, and I bit my lip, tasting the metallic blood on my tongue. I couldn't pass out. I *wouldn't* pass out.

Jack ran the knife down her arm, grinning widely. "Just like this. Watch your shoes. Eventually, the blood drips to the floor and splatters." He continued to talk as he strategically selected the next place to cut. He leaned over Lola, focusing on his work.

One. Two. Three. I raised my arm up and plunged the scalpel into the side of his neck. A scream ripped from my throat as his blood spurted into my face.

Staggering backward, Jack knocked over the surgical tray as he tumbled to the ground, landing on his back with a thud. His terrified gaze connected with mine as he attempted to pull the scalpel from his neck.

"Goddammit, die!" I kicked him in the ribs. "Fucking die!"

Before I realized it, he grabbed my ankle and jerked me down with him. His words came out in a gurgle, but the flash of the knife he'd used on Lola caught my eye. I scrambled backward, but he wouldn't let go of my foot, and the floor was too slick. I wasn't able to make any traction.

The door flew open with a bang, and another scream ripped from my lips.

"FBI. Nobody move!"

In one final attempt, Jack plunged the blade down into my lower leg. White-hot pain seared through me. Then I blacked out.

25

White light blinded my vision and I bolted upright, releasing a gut-wrenching scream.

"Babe! Babe! It's me, Layne. You're in the hospital. You're safe. Jesus, babe, you're safe."

I scanned my surroundings. My pulse was racing so fast, I thought I would have a heart attack. Finally, I connected with the most beautiful eyes I'd ever seen. "Layne?" My hands immediately moved to his face. "You're alive? Did he hurt you?" I asked, the octave of my voice rising.

He gave me a sad smile. "I'm fine, Ten. I'm fine."

"I'm not hallucinating?" I kissed him tentatively. If this was a dream, I never wanted to wake up. I would rather spend an eternity in a coma, dreaming about the man I loved, than living a day without him in reality. Big tears streamed down my cheeks as he kissed me in return. "Layne. Oh my God. Layne." I threw my arms around his neck and held on to him for dear life while I finally broke down and sobbed.

"You're safe." He sat on the edge of the bed and rubbed my back while I cried. "He's gone."

I picked my head up off his shoulder. "What?"

"He bled out."

I frowned as my memory struggled to piece everything together. Dark circles shadowed Layne's eyes. I wasn't sure how long I'd been gone, but it was apparent he hadn't slept at all. He was still wearing the blue shirt he'd had on the night I was taken.

A chair scraped the tile floor and I nearly shot out of bed. I hadn't realized Marilyn and Franklin were also in the room.

"Oh, hon, I didn't mean to scare you," Marilyn said, approaching me. "We were so terrified." She grabbed me and hugged me tightly.

"Benji, Avery, Michael? Are they all okay?" I needed to know everyone was unharmed before I could settle down.

Compassion filled her eyes as she tucked my dirty blond hair behind my ear. "Everyone is safe and sound." Her hand shook slightly as she smoothed her burgundy top. She was exhausted. "They want to see you. Benji has been out of his head with worry. I just didn't think it would do him any good to be here until you woke up. He and Avery are at the house with Michael, waiting for me to let them know when you're coming home. But before I do, the FBI wants to talk to you."

Franklin cleared his throat and approached me. "I'll be right here with you, Tensley."

"Thank you." I leaned back against my pillow, refusing to let go of Layne or Marilyn's hand. A sharp pain shot up my shin, and I whimpered. "My leg. What happened?"

Concern clouded Marilyn's expression. "Do you remember anything, Tensley? It would be a blessing if you didn't."

I blew out a big breath. Flashes of Jack and Lola hammered my mind. "I stabbed him in the neck." My body trembled. "Are you positive he's dead?"

"Yes. He won't ever hurt you or anyone else again," Layne said gently. "You got him in the carotid artery. Your aim was exceptional."

I nodded, then burst into tears again. That sick son of a bitch was dead. He couldn't ever harm or kill anyone again.

"We'll be right here as you give the FBI and police details, honey," Marilyn said, reassuring me that I wouldn't be alone.

"Lola. Did she make it?" My brows knitted together as images of Lola's broken body bombarded my memory.

"You saved her life, Ten. She's in the hospital, recovering as well." Layne rubbed my arm as he updated me on the events.

"I wonder if she'll hate me or thank me. How will she live with the nightmares of what he did to her?" A dull thud filled my head at the thought.

"She'll have a lot of support and help, just like you." Marilyn leaned over and kissed my forehead. "The FBI and police are here. Are you ready to talk to them?"

I wiped the tears from my face and nodded. The faster I did, the faster I could move on. Or at least I hoped. I wasn't just worried about Lola moving on—I wasn't sure how I would either. My gaze landed on two men as they approached me.

"Miss Bennett, I'm Agent Tanner, and this is Detective Smith. We'd like to ask you a few questions. You're not in any trouble at all. We just want to know what happened. It will help us in other cases like this. It's not often a victim lives through this, much less two."

I flinched. I never wanted to be referred to as a victim again.

"Gentleman, I'm Tensley's attorney, Franklin Harrington." Franklin extended his hand to each of them.

"I wasn't a victim. I'm Jack Flannery's daughter." My voice sounded foreign as the words left my lips. "He wanted to train me to work alongside him. He took me to teach me."

Marilyn gasped, and her hand flew over her mouth. Layne blinked excessively, staring at me in shock, then his fists clenched and unclenched as his body grew rigid. The horror of what I was about to share overwhelmed me. Once I spoke it out loud, it would become even more real. My stomach churned. "I think I'm going to be sick."

Marilyn grabbed the blue plastic barf bag and I closed my eyes, but it didn't seem to help. All I wanted was to not relive the trauma.

After a minute, my nerves calmed down a little bit. "I'm okay. Thanks."

Detective Smith spoke gently. "I can't imagine how difficult this is for you. I'm sorry we need to dredge up the horrible experience, but if it helps us catch another killer—if it helps us understand how they think—then you'll be saving lives. You've already saved women across the United States just by ending Jack Flannery's life."

I nodded.

"We were informed that you were his daughter when you went missing. Can you tell us what happened?" Agent Tanner asked.

I released Marilyn's hand and rubbed my forehead. "Matthew Collier called from Barney's and said I'd dropped my driver's license when I was there the night before. Layne and I went to pick it up." Every nerve ending inside me stood on end while I attempted to grasp the racing thoughts of what had happened to Layne.

"When we got there, he pulled a gun on us and tied and blindfolded Layne. There was a back door to the office. I never even knew it existed. Jack came in that way. Then he shot Matthew because he was about to kill me." My focus drifted to my boyfriend as I recalled the last thing I'd said to him that night. I loved him. "If anything had happened …" I choked on my cries.

Layne stroked the back of my hand with his thumb. "I'm right here, babe."

"Take your time," Detective Smith said.

I didn't want to take my time. I wanted it over with. Shoving all feelings and fear away, I tilted my chin in the air and made eye contact with Agent Tanner. "After he took me from Barney's, I woke up where you found us. I tried to gain his trust and figure a way out. Eventually, he dropped his guard just a little bit because he asked me to get a gag out of his backpack. I guess he forgot he had a surgical scalpel in it. It was tucked away, so he probably didn't even know it was there." I shuddered. My attention traveled to Layne's reassuring expression, then back to the detective and agent. "He began ... cutting Lola. When he bent over her, I had access to his neck, and I stabbed him. He fell and took me with him. The last thing I remember is the FBI bursting through the door and a horrible pain in my lower leg. That's it." I blew out a breath.

"Did he talk about how he chose his victims?" Detective Smith asked.

"Yeah. He said that he identified their vulnerability, then became what they needed. Lola had just lost her best friend to cancer. She was lonely, grieving. He became the friend she needed and gained her trust. It wasn't long before he was able to worm his way into her life and heart."

"We've been tracking him across eleven states." Agent Tanner smiled softly. "If it weren't for you, we'd still be looking for him."

I sat up in bed. "How? How did you find us?" We'd been in the middle of God only knew where. I doubted there was even a phone signal out there.

Layne cleared his throat. "When you told me that Jack had caught you in the restroom at Barney's the night of the party—"

"What?" Marilyn's eyes widened in horror. "That son of a bitch was there?"

"He wasn't there to hurt me. Scare me, yes, but he said he wanted to meet his daughter. I couldn't tell you guys. He said he'd kill you all if I did." My voice cracked because I was so relieved that the nightmare was over.

"And the cute bartender let him in?" Marilyn shook her head in disbelief.

"He's not a problem anymore," Layne said in a low tone, the muscle in his jaw tightening as anger clouded his expression. "I knew he was trouble. I should have trusted my gut. I knew something was off about him, and it wasn't just that he was interested in Tensley."

I took his hand and kissed the back of it. "It's not your fault. But how did you find us?"

"Ten, for some reason, I felt I could trust Vaughn, the bodyguard with two different-colored eyes, would be able to keep my secret and help us. The same night Jack caught you in the bathroom and you confided in me, I located Vaughn while he was on duty at Michael and Marilyn's house. You were sound asleep when I snuck out and spoke to him. He did go to his boss, but they agreed to keep it under wraps. I guess Pierce works with the FBI sometimes and he was worried if there were additional bodyguards around, it would tip Jack off. Anyway, Sutton, Pierce's wife and tech genius, gave Vaughn what he needed. When Avery was over, I slipped downstairs, grabbed your coat, and made a small tear in the fabric. I slipped a locator device inside the filling of your jacket. But I didn't get to chip your shoes in time. Vaughn said the first place Jack would look was your phone, so we steered clear of it."

"You guys put a chip in my coat?" I sank back in the bed and hid my face in my hands. Forcing back the tears, I sat up and wrapped my arms around Layne's neck. "Thank you. You saved my life."

"I was terrified, babe." Layne gripped me tighter. "If you'd lost the coat, I would have never been able to forgive myself."

"No." I pulled away from him, and my thumb gently stroked his cheek. "You had the courage to do something. You not only saved my life but also Lola's. Even though I killed Jack, Lola and I would have died up there. It was freezing cold, and she didn't have any shoes or clothes. I couldn't carry her either."

"I love you." Layne gave me a gentle kiss.

"I love you too."

Marilyn let out a shaky breath. "Well, my goodness, that was a lot to take in. Agent Tanner, Detective Smith, do you have any additional questions for my daughter? If not, I think she needs some rest."

My eyebrow arched. She'd referred to me as her daughter. She and Michael had always said I was family, but this was different. She'd stated it in public to the authorities.

"No. We can follow up later if we need anything else. Thank you for your time, Miss Bennett. I hope you have a speedy recovery."

The room fell silent as we all watched them leave.

"I'm so sorry to just spring that on you. It just flew out of my mouth." Marilyn grabbed a chair, took my hand again, and sat down. "Michael and I realize that you're twenty-one, but we wanted to ... Well, honey, we want to adopt you."

"What?" I couldn't contain my surprise. "But I'm legal. I don't need parents." The moment it slipped out of my mouth, I knew it wasn't an accurate statement. I needed them. I needed a family.

"It's not about how old you are. You always need parents. If you agree, you'll be in our will with Benji. We've been thinking about this for a while. Benji has always wanted a sister, and we all love you dearly. We already consider you our daughter, and we would love to make it official. We understand that we could do all of this without adopting you, but this way, you'd legally be recognized as our daughter, and you'd have a family. Forever." Marilyn's eyes misted over, and she grabbed a tissue from the box on the table next to my bed.

I was so overwhelmed with emotion that tears streamed down my cheeks. "Yes. I'd love to officially be a part of the family."

"Oh." Marilyn fanned her face with her hand and laughed. "That's the best thing I've heard all day. Michael and Benji will be elated. Franklin already connected us with an attorney, so he'll draw up all the appropriate paperwork. We'll review everything and sign, and then it's legal."

I glanced at Layne, who dabbed his eyes.

"Will my last name be Parker?" I mentally sounded out Tensley Parker. I liked it a lot. Plus, it signified a new beginning.

Marilyn's focus cut to Layne then back to me. "It's up to you. You can take Parker, or you can hyphenate it, but I have a sneaking suspicion your name will change again soon."

My eyes widened, and I glanced at Layne. A huge smile eased across his gorgeous face. He remained silent but placed a sweet kiss on the back of my hand.

"Excellent. This will be done up in no time. Welcome to the family." Marilyn stood and wrapped me in a warm embrace. "We'll have a big celebration as soon as it's done and you're feeling better. Does that sound okay, daughter?" Marilyn's expression lit up with her smile.

"Thanks... Mom." I clung to her, reveling in the fact that I finally had a mother who loved me. I had parents who would protect me, teach me, and share my life with me every step of the way.

We released each other and I wiped my cheeks. "What's up with my leg, and when do I get to go home?"

Layne cleared his throat. "Unfortunately, the knife severed the muscle and tendons, but your bone was only scraped. They rushed you into surgery since you were bleeding. You'd lost a lot of blood by the time they got you to surgery, so we weren't sure you were going to make it." His eyes clouded with relief. "You'll be back on your feet in about six weeks, though. It might feel like a while, but it's not bad considering what you went through."

"I don't remember any of it. How long did it take them to get me to the hospital?"

"Forty minutes by helicopter," Layne explained.

My brows furrowed. "Where in the hell was I? I mean I know

I was in the woods somewhere, and I know he drove all night, if not longer, but—"

"Babe, we're in eastern Montana. The moment they contacted us, Franklin flew us over in his jet." Layne ran a hand over his hair and sighed softly. "It was the longest night of my life."

Layne's last sentence spoke volumes, since he'd also lost his daughter. My goal was to never put him through something like that again.

Marilyn patted my hand. "Michael and I thought it would be best if one of us stayed with Benji and Avery, but everyone has been beside themselves."

"They know I'm going to be okay, though?" I hated that they had all gone through hell.

"Yes. They're ready for you to come home. Let me talk to the doctor."

I turned to my lawyer, wincing as a sharp pain traveled through my leg. "Franklin, I can never thank you enough. You don't even know me, but you stepped right up and made sure I didn't die. You've been so good to me through all of this. I'm so grateful for everything."

"I'd do it again too. Michael and Marilyn have nothing but amazing things to say about you, but the first time I saw you, I knew in my gut you weren't guilty."

"You're a good man, Franklin." Marilyn stood and smoothed her dark hair. "Tensley, I'll see if I can locate your surgeon. You and Layne probably need a few minutes to yourselves." She smiled sweetly at Layne, then left the room.

Franklin nodded towards us. "I'll see you kids later." His dress shoes scuffed against the tile floor as he exited, leaving Layne and I alone.

I looked at my boyfriend and my heart began to beat rapidly.

He leaned over and kissed me. "All I want to do is crawl in this bed and hold you. I don't ever want to let you go again."

"I'm sorry. I'm sorry I put you through all of this. After losing Nicole, you—"

"None of this is your fault, Tensley. None of it. I told you the other night that I'd made a commitment. I don't get scared off easily."

"Promise?" Normally I didn't believe in promises, but a lot had changed in the last few months. I'd fallen in love, found my real family, and survived a serial killer.

Layne took my hand in both of his and smiled. "With all my heart."

26

The next afternoon, I used my new crutches and hobbled into Benji's house. Well, I guess it was my house now too. I wasn't sure if Avery or Benji's squeals were louder when they saw me. Layne stood behind me as Avery ran to the door and nearly knocked me over with a hug.

She trembled as she cried and clung to me. "Oh. My. God."

"I'm fine," I said, consoling her.

She pulled away and wiped her cheeks. "Are you sure?" She assessed my leg, then giggled nervously. "I'm sorry. What was I thinking? You probably need to sit down."

"I do. I'm a little tired. But first …" I turned to Michael, who was patiently waiting for me in the foyer.

He grinned and greeted me with a warm hug. "Welcome home."

"Thank you. You have no idea how happy I am to be here."

Michael stepped back and rested his hands on my shoulders. "Marilyn shared the fantastic news. Our attorney is already working on the documents."

Tears filled my eyes. "I'm ready." I took a deep breath, then kissed him on the cheek.

Benji wheeled over to us and laughed. "I guess this means we shouldn't share a bed anymore, sis."

"Um, no. People can think what they want. But who will know other than us anyway? The moment Layne pisses me off, I'm coming to you." I winked at Layne, then hobbled over to my soon-to-be brother.

Benji chuckled and gently pulled me onto his lap. "I love you." He leaned his forehead against mine. "While you were gone, I had a glimpse of what life would be like without you, and I'm not okay with it. At all."

"Me too. But I'm home, and now you're stuck with me." I laughed, lightly punching him on the shoulder. "Seriously, though, are you okay with the adoption? I need to hear it from you. If you're not, I completely understand, but your opinion matters to me." My heart galloped in my chest while I waited for his answer.

"I wouldn't have it any other way. But just because you're going to be a legal part of this family, promise me the dynamic of our relationship won't change." Worry lines creased his forehead.

"Benji." I placed my hand on his face. "No one and nothing can change what we have. Ever. No legal document, no name change, nothing. You're my best friend, regardless." I kissed his cheek and inhaled his familiar cologne. It was sweet and spicy, just like him.

I glanced at Layne, who was smiling like he'd just won the lottery. He didn't need to say anything for me to realize he was thrilled that Benji and I were both happy about the adoption. It was a weird situation. But there was nothing ordinary about us in the first place.

"Can you help me up?" I asked Layne. "If it's okay with every-one, I'd love to shower. I've not had one since before ..." Flashes of blood spurting all over me filled my mind. Marilyn had cleaned me up some while I was at the hospital, but I needed to sit under the hot spray and wash the stench of Jack Flannery off me.

Marilyn hurried over. "Of course. Take a nap too. I'll have something for dinner when you're ready." She placed a kiss on my forehead then on Benji's. "I love my kids."

Layne waited for Marilyn then lifted me off Benji's lap and into his arms. "I'll get your crutches later."

I leaned my head against his shoulder as he carried me up the stairs and into my bedroom. He gently kicked the door closed and placed me on the plush bed. I sank into it as he grabbed clean clothes for me out of the dresser.

"Hang on." He kissed me, then disappeared into the bathroom.

The sound of the shower being turned on was music to my ears.

Layne returned, and without a word, I tugged off the T-shirt he'd brought me in the hospital. Marilyn had also tossed in a pair of Nike sweats. The cops had once again confiscated my clothes from the hospital, but that was fine with me. I never wanted to see them again. I worked my sweats and panties over the cast and tossed them in the corner. Pain shot through my leg, and I winced.

"We have to keep the splint from getting wet, babe. Marilyn gave me this to tape around it."

I giggled while he knelt down on the floor and taped a kitchen trash bag around my lower leg.

"This is so romantic." I covered my mouth, suppressing my giggle. "I'm filthy dirty, naked, and my boyfriend is wrapping my leg in a garbage bag."

Layne chuckled. "I'm at your service, ma'am." He stood, bowed, then scooped me up in his strong arms again. "I'm going to put you in the shower, then I'll join you if that's okay."

"Yes, please. Just feeling your touch helps."

We approached the shower and Layne pulled on the handle with his fingers. He stepped under the spray, fully clothed, and set me on the bench. "I obviously didn't think this through very well, did I?" He grinned, stepped out on the rug, and shook his head as he began unbuttoning his shirt. "I probably should have undressed with you out there."

"Oh no. This is perfect. Please continue with the show." My smile grew wider as he removed his shirt. His chest and arm muscles rippled with every move. "What are we going to do?" My eyes traveled down his tight abs as he discarded his jeans. He stood in front of me, fully erect.

"Ignore that." He stepped into the shower. "We're not doing anything for the next week, so we'll just have to deal with it."

"Week?" I squeaked.

Layne laughed. "I know, but you have to heal. Once you're out of the splint, we can work around it."

I reached out and wrapped my fingers around his hard cock. "I can take care of you."

"Hey." He carefully removed my hand and sat next to me. The water streamed over us as he cupped my chin and tilted my head up. His eyes bored into mine, and silence descended over us. "I know in your past that sex was a bargaining and survival tool, but I love you. You don't have to take care of me in order to feel you deserve to be loved. Babe, you're my top priority. The sex is amazing, but I'm just as content to hold you. Tensley, you came back to me. I thought I'd lost you forever, but here you are. The best thing you can do for me is to relax and let me love you."

My heart pounded in my ears. I didn't know what I had done to deserve him, but maybe he was right. I shouldn't be alive. This was my chance to build the life I'd always dreamed of and know, in every fiber of my being, that Layne loved me for me.

"Okay." I leaned over and brushed my lips against his. I loved him so much. He was the reason I was still breathing and safe in his arms. But even before Jack had taken me, Layne had taken my brokenness and pieced me back together.

Finally, he broke our kiss. "Let's get you cleaned up and into bed. I'll be with you the entire time."

I nodded gratefully. Fear clenched my heart at the thought of being alone. "I'm afraid to close my eyes, Layne." I blinked the water from them. "I don't know how to deal with what I saw."

"I know. I'm here, though. If you wake up screaming, I'll be right by your side. If you have a flashback, I'll be here. I know how bad the PTSD can be, but you're surrounded by people who love you. You're safe."

"Thank you. Maybe when I'm feeling a little better, you can take me to see Vaughn. I'm guessing their assignment here is over."

"Yeah. But I know how to get in touch with him."

A SHARP PAIN shot up my leg and I bolted upright in the bed. Layne's soft snore filled the room, and I sucked in a deep breath. I was home on the softest mattress I'd ever slept on, and I was with my boyfriend. Lying back down, I fumbled around on the night-stand for one of the pain pills the doctor had given me. Layne had brought up some water in case I needed it in the middle of the night, but it was after six in the morning. I'd slept for almost nine hours without any nightmares.

I popped a pill, then lay back and tried to settle in again, but I couldn't sleep. This was the first time I'd had to think about everything. Even though Layne was next to me, no one was staring at me or searching for signs that I would lose my shit at any given moment. I didn't want to be the fragile girl who had to be handled with kid gloves, but I was. It had been only seventy-two hours since I'd been in the mountains of Montana with a serial killer, with my father. I had murdered my father so that I could save two lives. *I* was a murderer. Grief and anxiety drowned out any logic that attempted to fight its way through the harsh reality that stared at me. Fear wrapped its cold fingers around my heart, and I trembled beneath the covers. His blood flowed through my veins. I'd killed someone. I was just like my father.

"No, no, no," I whispered, my chest tightening as Jack's face flashed through my mind. I grabbed my head, willing the memories to go away, but they just kept coming.

"Babe. I'm right here." In one quick motion, Layne sat up and pulled me onto his lap. "You're safe. I've got you." He gently rocked me as I continued to shake.

A whimper escaped me, my body turning cold. "I killed him. I'm just like him. A murderer."

"Hang on a minute." Layne placed me on my side of the bed and hopped up. He pulled a shirt on and straightened his sweats. Then he approached me, picked me up, and carried me downstairs and into the kitchen.

"Oh no. Is she okay?" Marilyn hurried over to me. "We're right here, honey."

"I need to sit with her by the window and get her something warm to drink," Layne said. "She's having PTSD flashbacks."

"You sit with her and I'll make some hot chocolate." Marilyn gently stroked my hair. "I'd give her a nip of alcohol, but I know she's on the pain pills for her leg."

I stared blankly at Marilyn as she fluttered around the room in her silk bathrobe.

"The sun is coming up, Ten. I'm going to raise the blind so you can see it," Layne said softly.

I flinched as he pulled the shade up and the bright sunlight filtered into the kitchen.

"If you can focus on that, it will help. Look at the frost glow in the golden light and how the grass sparkles. There's not a cloud in the sky, and it's pure blue. Maybe we should try ice-skating after your leg is healed." He paused for a moment and my body began to relax. "It's going to be a cold and beautiful day. Thanksgiving is coming up fast, and I know how much my girl loves to eat." Layne rubbed my back and continued to talk in a soothing voice.

Before I knew it, I was lost in his warmth and the magnificent colors of the morning.

"Here, Tensley." Marilyn placed a steaming cup in front of me and sat down at the table with us. "I'm going to make your favorite pie on Thursday."

I sat up carefully, making sure I didn't bang my leg or kick Layne in the shin.

"Apple crumb?" I wrapped my cold fingers around the mug. The warmth broke through the last bit of fog in my brain, and I sighed. "Thank you. I couldn't pull my head out of—"

"Shh. Take a drink. We can talk about all of that later. Let's get some food in your stomach, and I'll tell you about the Thanksgiving menu." Marilyn patted my hand before she hopped up again. "Layne, do you like pancakes or French toast?" She began to pull skillets and bowls out of the cabinets.

"I love both, so whatever you decide to make, I'll eat." He kissed the side of my head.

"All right. I'll make French toast. It's Tensley's favorite."

My stomach growled in response and Layne's chuckle rumbled through his chest.

He nuzzled my hair. "I miss showing up at your door with food."

I giggled. "I loved it. It meant the world to me. It was about so much more than the food. It healed my heart from a lot of dark and hungry days."

He tightened his hold on me and rested his head against mine. "And we'll heal your heart again. We'll do it together."

27

The next six weeks passed slowly. Nightmares plagued my sleep, but each time, Layne talked me through it. He finally shared with me that after losing Nicole, he'd worked with a therapist to manage his PTSD. It was how he knew what to do for me when I was mentally trapped with Jack in Montana.

Michael and Marilyn had asked Layne to continue staying with them. They knew they wouldn't be able to keep him away from me even if they'd wanted to. But they seemed to love him almost as much as I did. After all, he'd saved their son ... and now their daughter.

We had signed my adoption papers, and I was officially a Parker. On the shitty days, I reminded myself it was proof I'd started a new life.

My leg was healed, but I still had some pain. It had taken me a while to walk again and rebuild my muscles, but at least physically, I was moving in the right direction. Benji was a massive support with my physical therapy. He busted my balls when I didn't want to do the exercises. He would make a great coach, and I loved him for being mine.

We celebrated the new year at home with movies and cocktails. I hadn't wanted to leave the house lately unless I had to. It didn't feel safe anymore. But that night, I didn't have a choice. Michael and Marilyn were throwing a party now that I was on my feet and the adoption was final. I had no idea who they had planned on inviting, but I hoped to make an appearance, then slip away with Layne. Since we were able to have sex again, that was all I wanted. If I could feel him inside me, it blocked out all the demons that were waiting to pull me into the darkness. My new therapist, whom I'd seen a few times, would have a heyday with that information.

Avery waltzed into my bedroom as though she lived there too. "Oh my God. You're stunning."

I turned toward her, smoothing my deep-blue A-line dress. Avery looked gorgeous in a burgundy dress with a plunging neckline. She'd opted for showing more cleavage than I had, but that was nothing new. Her dark hair was piled into a bun, and loose strands framed her face.

"Wow." I walked across the room and took her hands. "You look beautiful."

"Thanks. I'm actually done moping over Justin and ready to move on. There's an entire world for us to experience, right?" Her eyes twinkled with anticipation.

"And we'll do it together." I hugged her, then stepped back and sighed softly. "This is the first time I'm really going to be out in public again. I mean, other than physical therapy or doctor's appointments. My anxiety is through the roof."

"Girl, from what Benji said, there's so much security around the country club this evening, no one will get to you. They hired extra, and I'll go to the bathroom with you. And ..." Avery pushed her left boob up and reached into her dress. "I have this." She grinned as she produced some mace. "I've got your back, Tensley."

I returned her smile. "You're the best. I couldn't do this without you."

"Good thing you don't have to. Let's get going." She held her hand out to me, then we made our way downstairs.

Even though my leg was healed, I was treading carefully in my black high heels. A low whistle reached my ears and my head snapped up. My breath caught in my throat as I spotted Layne in a black tux with a blue cummerbund and bow tie that matched my dress. The blue brought out the color of his eyes, and I nearly stumbled over my own feet. Gorgeous didn't even begin to describe how he looked.

"I think I'm going to have to sneak off early tonight," I whispered to Avery.

"Damn straight. Wow. Maybe let him knock a ball into the eighth hole."

I giggled at Avery's golf pun. She released my hand, and I joined Layne in the foyer. I paused, greedily soaking him in.

He pulled me to him, and his warm breath grazed my ear as he spoke. "You're breathtaking, and you're mine."

His fingers stroked my bare shoulder, and goosebumps dotted my skin.

"I am yours. Forever." There was no way I would ever let him go if I had any say in it.

He bent down, brushing his full lips against mine. Heat pulsed through my body, but it would have to wait.

"Are you ready for a party in your honor?" Benji asked, wheeling into the foyer from the kitchen.

I turned to face him. "Good grief, how in the hell do you look better than everyone in this room? It's illegal to look that damned good."

Benji chuckled and Avery walked over to him.

"You two look so good together. Too bad you both like boys." I wiggled my eyebrows at my best friends and laughter filled the air.

"I tried, remember?" Avery squeezed his shoulder. "But we're together tonight, so I'll take it."

Benji grabbed Avery's hand and placed a kiss on the back of it. "I'm looking forward to it."

We continued some small talk while we waited for Marilyn and Michael.

"Kids, oh my." Marilyn's heels clicked against the marble floor. "I need pictures." She handed Michael her evening bag and directed us to the living room. "The light is better here." She smoothed her long, dark-red dress. Her smile reached her eyes as she spoke. "I'm so proud of all of you, but no more of that. I can't cry and mess up my makeup."

We laughed while she took pictures.

Marilyn waved at Michael to join us. "Dad, get in there."

Michael looked dashing in his tux. A broad grin eased across his handsome face as he hurried over. He stood behind us since he was the tallest, then he and Marilyn traded places. Avery snapped the last picture of Michael, Marilyn, Benji, and me. My heart fluttered inside my chest. Everyone was so happy, and so was I. I'd just had my first family photo taken.

"We'd better get going," Michael said, opening the door for us. "The limo is warm and ready. It's also fully loaded with champagne. After all, tonight is a celebration."

Twenty minutes later, we all strolled into the room Michael and Marilyn had rented for the evening. Large windows allowed visual access to the golf course and water feature the club turned on during the warmer months. A dance floor was situated in the front, and a bar with two bartenders was located to the right. Soft classical music flowed through the speakers, and I suddenly longed for my drums.

A few more people arrived that I didn't know. Although the party was to celebrate the adoption, Michael and Marilyn had invited most of their friends and some business acquaintances.

"Come on." I took Layne's hand and excused myself from the room, suddenly feeling stifled.

"Where are we going?" Layne asked, hustling to keep up with me.

"We'll be right back." I grabbed my wrap from the coat clerk and flung it around my shoulders. As I pushed the front door open, the cold air greeted me. My hold tightened on Layne's fingers and I made a mad dash around the building. "I needed air." I whirled around to face him and brought his mouth to mine, kissing him deeply.

He moaned as my hands slipped beneath his jacket and into the waistband of his tux pants. Before I had a chance to unzip them, someone shined a bright light in my face.

"You two need to make your way back to the party," a deep male voice said.

"Dammit. I forgot about the extra security tonight." I shivered, realizing that having a quickie in twenty-degree temps wasn't the smartest idea I'd ever had.

Layne laughed. "I love you, babe. Try to relax, though. Let's grab a drink or two."

I nodded. The security guard obviously wasn't kidding because he stood there, waiting for us to go back inside.

My boyfriend wrapped his arm around me, and we began to make our way back to the door. The flashlight moved to the ground, lighting our path for us.

"Thanks," I said, finally catching a glimpse of who the man was. I halted abruptly. "Vaughn."

"Good evening, Tensley. I'm happy to see you back on your feet and out in public again." His expression remained serious, but I'd never seen any of the bodyguards smile, much less laugh.

I peered up at Layne. "Babe, can I have a minute with Vaughn?"

"I'll make sure she gets in the building safely," Vaughn assured him.

261

Layne gave me a quick peck on the lips and left us alone.

My teeth chattered, and Vaughn slipped off his Westbrook Security coat and wrapped it around me.

I huddled beneath the heavy coat, grateful for the warmth. "Thank you. I won't keep you long—I know you're working."

"It's a little cold for you to be out here tonight anyway." He paused for a second then asked, "How can I help you?"

I rolled my eyes. "You sound so formal." I laughed nervously. "I wanted to thank you for helping me and for helping Layne. Please tell Sutton thank you as well. I wouldn't be alive if it weren't for both of you. But most of all, thank you for being someone Layne could trust."

His mismatched eyes held my gaze. "It's my job."

I shook my head. "No, you went beyond that. You kept a secret from the authorities in order to save me. I'll never be able to repay you, but I did want to thank you personally. Will you give Sutton my message?"

"You can thank her yourself. She and Pierce will be here any minute. Michael invited them to your party." The corner of his mouth twitched in an almost smile.

"Oh!" Apparently Michael and Marilyn had gone all out for the party. "I guess I'd better get inside, then." I slipped off his coat, and before I could stop myself, I flung my arms around him in a hug.

He wrapped one arm around me briefly then released me. "Take care of yourself, Tensley."

I didn't miss the compassion in his expression.

Vaughn escorted me to the door, and his brown eye caught the light as I turned to look at him one last time. "See ya." I gave him a little wave, then joined the crowd of people that had filed in while I'd been outside.

Layne exited the restroom. "How did it go?" Before I could answer, his gaze focused on my mouth. "Babe, your lips are blue. Come here." He guided me back into the main room and filled a cup with some coffee. "Hold this. I'm not sure it will do your anxiety any good if you drink it, but at least it will warm you up a bit."

He was right, but I took a sip anyway. The scalding liquid burned my throat and esophagus as it traveled into my stomach.

"It went well with Vaughn. I just thanked him for what he did for us. He said that Michael—I mean Dad—invited Pierce and Sutton, too, so we'll get to meet her."

Layne nodded, and I turned toward the doorway. Pierce Westbrook strolled into the room like he owned it. For all I knew, he did. Michael had mentioned he owned the highly successful security firm, and I assumed by the size of the rock on his wife's hand, he had money. A lot of it.

Sutton Westbrook was one of the most beautiful women I'd ever seen. Her long blond hair flowed down her back, and her emerald-green dress accentuated her blue eyes. She carried herself with confidence as she stood by her husband's side. Adoration was evident on her face as she glanced up at him. He gave her a sweet kiss, then began introductions around the room.

Layne squeezed my fingers gently. "Are you ready? We should start mingling. We can take a break any time you need one."

"I would like to thank Pierce and meet Sutton." We left the coffee station and made our way to Pierce. Franklin and a woman I assumed was his wife entered, looking gorgeous in her full-length gold colored dress that accentuated her big brown eyes and dark hair.

I approached the small group from the side. "Hi, Franklin."

"Tensley, it's so good to see you up and around." Franklin patted my arm. "How are you feeling?"

"Much better." A genuine smile spread across my face. "I wanted to meet your wife and thank you again for all of your help."

"Anytime. You've got an excellent young man by your side and a new family. There's no doubt in my mind that you're going to be all right. And this is my beautiful wife, Janice."

Janice didn't bother with a handshake. Instead, she released her husband's arm and hugged me. Her affection caught me off guard, and it took me a moment to return her embrace. She stepped back, compassion filling her big brown eyes. "You're just as beautiful as Marilyn said you were. I'm so happy that you're safe and sound. It will take some time to heal, but it gets better. I promise." She moved back, allowing Pierce to shake Layne's hand.

"Good to see you again," Layne said, grasping Pierce's outstretched hand.

"You take good care of her. You've got good instincts. Listen to them. And if you ever want a job ..." Pierce paused, assessing Layne's reaction.

Layne's brows shot up. "Really? I might have to see what that looks like."

Pierce handed him a business card. "Call me if you're interested."

I stared at them dumbly, butterflies fluttering in my stomach. Layne, a bodyguard? I didn't think I liked the sound of that, not at all.

"I'm looking to fill several positions inside the company. I've got a strong team of bodyguards but not enough good people behind the scenes, so let's do lunch soon." Pierce patted Layne on the back and returned to his wife's side.

I mentally sighed, relief flooding through me.

A soft laugh reached my ears, and my gaze landed on Sutton.

"It's all right, Tensley. We won't put him in too much danger if he comes on board." Her smile lit up the room.

"I think I've had enough danger to last a lifetime," I said. "But I wanted to thank you for delivering the chip so Vaughn and Layne could hide it in my coat. It saved my life. We were up in the mountains ..." I felt a sharp pang in my chest. I didn't want to discuss it. I was determined to stay focused on the future. A flush crept over my cheeks as my pulse spiked. I couldn't think about what had happened, not right then. "Anyway, thank you."

She gave me a brief hug. "You're very welcome. And congrats on the adoption."

"Can I have everyone's attention, please?" Michael's voice boomed through the speakers. "If everyone would take a seat for just a few minutes ..."

Layne guided me to a table toward the front. We joined Marilyn and Avery, and I looked around. I hadn't seen Benji in a while and wondered where he was. My pulse spiked as my mind fucked with me. My biggest unexpressed fear was that Jack had an acquaintance in his line of work that would come after me or the people I loved.

"Thank you all for coming tonight. As the invitation mentioned, Marilyn and I have officially adopted Tensley into our family."

Where is Benji? He should be present for this. My body began to tremble.

"Babe?" Layne whispered in my ear. "What's wrong?"

"Benji. Where's Benji? He should be here with us." I bit my lip, willing myself to not go into a full-on frenzy.

"Tensley, would you come up here, please?"

Fuck. Now? Dammit. My knees wobbled as I stood. I willed myself to take the twenty steps toward Michael without collapsing. Blood pounded in my ears, and I hoped like hell I wouldn't pass out.

Michael took my hand and lowered the microphone. "Are you okay?" he whispered.

I nodded, then smiled at him.

"Don't be nervous. I'm right here with you," he reassured me.

"I know, but where's your son?"

Michael squeezed my fingers and raised the mic again. "One of the things I've always loved and respected about Tensley is that she doesn't miss a thing. She's sharp and has a keen ability to read people and assess a situation."

Like my father.

"Benji, I don't think we can hide it any longer. She's about to pass out up here, she's so worried about you."

I turned to face Michael, confused as hell. "What?"

Michael nodded toward the door of the room, and my mouth dropped open. Tears immediately filled my eyes, and my hands flew over my face as I attempted to hold it together in front of everyone. Benji took a step toward me using crutches. Then he slowly took another, and another.

"Benji," I whispered through my tears. "You're walking."

The beautiful smile I loved so much spread across his face. "Just a little something I've been working on." He chuckled and took another step.

I bolted across the room and threw my arms around him while the entire audience stood and clapped.

"Careful. Don't knock me over." He leaned his head on my shoulder, unable to return my hug due to the crutches.

I laughed and stood back. "How? When?" I had so many questions.

"I wanted to be able to dance with you tonight. Ya know, not only as best friends, but as brother and sister."

"Shit." The tears kept coming. "You're messing up my makeup. I was terrified something bad had happened to you."

"Nope. I wouldn't miss tonight for anything. Now, would you be so kind as to allow me to escort you back to Dad?" Benji's eyes misted over, and I gave him a kiss on the cheek.

"Absolutely."

Michael continued to talk about what I'd overcome and how proud he was of both his kids. I got Benji settled at the table with us as relief flooded through me. I slipped into my chair next to Layne and discreetly dabbed my eyes, hoping my mascara wasn't running down my cheeks.

Layne planted a kiss on my temple and rubbed little circles on my back. My heartrate began to slow as I pulled myself back together. Gratitude washed over me because, not only was Benji okay, but he was walking again. After he'd been attacked, the doctors hadn't been able to determine if that were a possibility or not. Apparently it was. But I suspected Benji's raw determination had a lot to do with it as well.

"We've all grown to love Tensley so much, and we wanted to legally make her a part of our family. We couldn't be more honored to call her our daughter."

Everyone clapped and cheered. A flush crept up my neck. I wasn't used to being the center of attention, and it was a bit overwhelming.

Layne scooted his chair out and released my hand.

"Where are you going?" I asked, frowning.

He nodded then strolled up to the front and joined Michael. Michael hugged him then handed him the microphone.

What is he doing?

"I met Tensley in high school. In Arkansas, actually. It was fate that we both ended up in Spokane together. She's by far the best thing that's ever happened to me. Babe, will you come up here for a minute?"

What in the world is he up to? I shot a look at Marilyn, Benji, and Avery, but they just shrugged.

I stood, then made my way next to him.

"I've found over the years that all the crap that happens in life also steers us toward what we want, to who we want. The moment I laid eyes on you in high school, I knew. But then life happened, and it pulled us in opposite directions."

Layne knelt down on one knee and produced a small box from the inside of his tux. "There is no doubt in my heart that you're the one for me. You're strong, genuine, smart, and beautiful. I'd be a fool not to want you by my side for the rest of our lives. Tensley Parker, will you marry me?"

My knees gave out, and I sank to the floor with him. He lowered the microphone and held the engagement ring in his hand. "I can't live without you," he said quietly. "You're the beat of my heart, my entire world."

My gaze landed on the beautiful diamond ring, then shot up to his face. There was so much love in his eyes for me. He owned every part of me. He had touched my soul and given light to some of the darkest places inside me. There was no one else I wanted to be with.

"Yes." I nodded then laughed. "Yes."

He slipped the ring on my finger then stood, pulling me up with him. Thunderous clapping filled the room as Layne kissed me. "Tonight, we will celebrate when we're alone." He took my hand in his and guided us back to the table.

Marilyn jumped up and hugged us. "I know you'll need to take your time and graduate college first, but I can't wait to help you plan your wedding!" She kissed my cheek.

Michael, Benji, and Avery all congratulated us. My heart over-flowed with the love that surrounded me. I'd gone from nearly dying in a garbage dumpster to an amazing life. Love, safety, and family—everything I'd ever dreamed of—had finally materialized in front of me.

Michael grabbed the microphone once again. "Thank you all for joining us tonight. We obviously have a lot to celebrate, so let's get it underway."

Over the next hour, the alcohol flowed, and I danced with Layne, Michael, and Benji. Avery and I agreed we would save our dances for the bar. My feet were killing me in my heels, but for the first time since I could remember, I was happy—genuinely, truly happy.

The music slowed and Layne closed the gap between us as "I Wish I Was the Moon" began to play. I snuggled up to him and laid my head on his chest. In his arms was the best place to be.

He tilted his head to the side of us and grinned. "Ten, look."

"Holy shit." I clamped my mouth shut, thankful the music was too loud for anyone other than my fiancé to have heard me. My head whipped back around. "Are Gemma Thompson and Hendrix Harrington from August Clover really dancing next to us, or did you put something in my drink? And when did they get here?" I peeked back over at them, and Gemma gave me a friendly smile and a little wave.

"I'm not sure, but they snuck in. Let's go say hello." Layne released me, and we crossed the dance floor.

As we approached, Hendrix released Gemma, and they turned to face us.

"Hi," Gemma said. "It's so nice to meet you."

"I can't believe you're here!" Butterflies scattered in my chest, leaving me a bit light-headed.

"Franklin mentioned it and thought we'd like to stop by," Hendrix said. He ran his fingers through his shoulder-length hair, and I fangirled right in front of my own fiancé.

Layne extended his hand. "It's nice to meet you both."

"We won't keep you guys tonight," Hendrix said. "But Tensley, Franklin showed us a video of your drum performance, and you're amazing."

"Oh my God, I've never seen anything like it," Gemma added. "The real reason we're here is to see if you might be interested in opening for August Clover on the next tour."

My Southern manners flew right out the fucking door, and I stood there, gawking at them. I was speechless, shocked. *Mind blown.*

"I ... I ..."

Gemma giggled. "It's okay. It's a lot to think about, and you've had a really, really big night. Take some time to consider it."

"Better yet, why don't we all meet for dinner this weekend, and we can talk specifics?" Hendrix stared at me, hope flickering in his eyes. "I mean, if you're interested."

My gaze drifted from Hendrix to Gemma to Layne. He nodded, giving me his full support.

"I'd love to," I croaked, finally finding my voice.

"Oh, I'm so excited." Gemma hugged me. "If you do tour with us, we will have so much fun. You'll love the band. And you'll really love Mac."

"Mac, as in Franklin's daughter, Mackenzie?" I asked for clarification.

"The one and only." Hendrix chuckled. "Give us a call tomorrow. We've actually got to go but wanted to stop by and see if you were interested."

"Thank you," I gushed. "We'll talk tomorrow."

Hendrix and Gemma waved goodbye, and I stayed rooted in place, gawking at them as they spoke with Franklin, Pierce, and Sutton before they left.

Then I turned to stare at Layne. "Did that just fucking happen?"

"Congratulations, babe. I'm so proud of you." He wrapped his arms around me, picked me up, and spun me around. A delicious giggle filled my ears. *My* giggle.

He sat me back on the floor and tilted my chin up. "It's been a busy night. How are you doing, fiancée?" Layne grinned and leaned down to kiss me.

I sighed then gazed into the most beautiful blue eyes I'd ever seen. "Good. Happy. Delirious."

"If you want to tour, I say we make it work." His expression grew serious. "I mean it. You have my full support. You've got too much talent to say no, babe."

"But what about you? I mean, I'd be gone for a while. I don't know if I can ..."

"I can go with you. I can take online classes and be there to support you every step of the way. People do it all the time. Babe, we've got this."

"Really? You'd go with me?" I blinked back tears as I peered into my fiancé's eyes. My chest ached, but not from fear or pain. My heart was overwhelmed with love and the hope of new possibilities.

"I'd be honored too. I love you so much, Ten. And thank you for agreeing to be my wife." He slid his hand down my back and rested it above my butt. "I can't wait to start the next chapter of our lives together."

"I love you, too." I kissed him slowly, savoring the moment. "Did Benji, Marilyn, or Avery know about the proposal, or was it just Michael?"

Layne chuckled. "I asked your parents for permission to marry their daughter last week, and when they said yes, I talked to Benji. We have everyone's blessing."

"What?" I laughed. "I love it. Never in a million years did I think it would be possible that I'd have parents for you to even ask."

Layne rested his forehead against mine as we swayed to the music. "I think anything is possible as long as you're next to me."

My mouth brushed against his full lips, and I released a sigh of contentment. "Fairy tales aren't even this good."

"Just wait, babe. I have a feeling it's about to get even better." Then he twirled me around.

❦

Don't miss Fractured Intentions, book 2, in the Wicked Intentions series! Pre-order Today! Universal link https://readerlinks.com/l/1606876.

Enjoy giveaways, the inside scoop about J.A. Owenby, and never miss a new release again! Sign up today at https://www.authorjaowenby.com/newsletter

LET'S GET IN TOUCH!

Connect with me here:
    Author J.A. Owenby Website
    Join my Newsletter
    Follow me on Facebook
    Join my Facebook Group
    Follow me on Amazon
    Join me on Goodreads
    Follow me on BookBub
    Follow me on Twitter
    Follow me on Instagram
    Join me on Pinterest

ALSO BY J.A. OWENBY

OTHER BOOKS BY INTERNATIONAL BESTSELLING J.A. OWENBY

Romance

The Love & Ruin Series

Love & Ruin

Love & Deception

Love & Redemption

Love & Consequences, a standalone novel

Love & Corruption, a standalone novel

Love & Revelations, a novella

Love & Seduction, a standalone novel

Love & Vengeance, coming 2021

Love & Retaliation, coming 2021

Romantic Suspense

The Wicked Intentions Series

Dark Intentions, a romantic thriller standalone

Fractured Intentions, a romantic thriller standalone

Standalone Novels

Where I'll Find You

Coming of Age

The Torn Series, Inspired by True Events

Fading into Her, a prequel novella

Torn

Captured

Freed

For Jennifer Gibson, Susan Alexander, and Vicki Bennett. I can't thank you enough for all your love and support. I'm so blessed to have you along for this wild and amazing journey.

JOIN MY ARC TEAM

I appreciate your help in spreading the word online as well as telling a friend. Reviews help readers find books they love, so please leave a review on your favorite book site.

You can also join my Facebook group, J.A. Owenby's One Page At A Time, for exclusive giveaways and sneak peeks of future books.

Edited by: Adept Editing

Cover Art by: Iheartcoverdesigns

Photographer: Wander Aguiar

First Edition

ISBN-13: 978-1-949414-04-2

Gain access to previews of J.A. Owenby's novels before they're released and to take part in exclusive giveaways. www.authorjaowenby.com

A NOTE FROM THE AUTHOR:

Dear Readers,

If you have experienced sexual assault or physical abuse, there is free confidential help. Please visit:

Website: https://www.rainn.org/
Phone: 800-656-4673

ABOUT THE AUTHOR

J.A. Owenby lives in the beautiful Pacific Northwest with her husband and cat.

She also runs her own business as a professional resume writer and interview coach—she helps people find jobs they love.

J.A. is an avid reader of thrillers, romance, new adult, and young adult novels. She loves music, movies, and good wine. And call her crazy, but she loves the rainy Pacific Northwest; she gets her best story ideas while listening to the rain pattering against the windows in front of the fireplace.

You can follow the progress of her upcoming novel on Facebook at Author J.A. Owenby and on Twitter @jaowenby.

Sign up for J.A. Owenby's Newsletter:
BookHip.com/CTZMWZ

Like J.A. Owenby's Facebook:
https://www.facebook.com/JAOwenby

J.A. Owenby's One Page At A Time reader group:
https://www.facebook.com/groups/JAOwenby